A Great Country

ALSO BY SHILPI SOMAYA GOWDA

Secret Daughter

The Golden Son

The Shape of Family

Shilpi Somaya Gowda

A Great Country

A Novel

MARINER BOOKS

New York Boston

This is a work of fiction. Names, characters, places, and incidents are products of the author's imagination or are used fictitiously and are not to be construed as real. Any resemblance to actual events, locales, organizations, or persons, living or dead, is entirely coincidental.

HarperCollins books may be purchased for educational, business, or sales promotional use. For information, please email the Special Markets Department at SPsales@harpercollins.com.

FIRST EDITION

Designed by Renata DiBiase

Library of Congress Cataloging-in-Publication Data has been applied for.

ISBN 978-0-06-332434-3

24 25 26 27 28 LBC 5 4 3 2 1

For all my Archies—fierce, wise and loving friends

And for my mother, whose spirit and strength are behind every word

Out beyond
the ideas of wrongdoing and right doing,
there is a field.
I'll meet you there.

When the soul lies down in that grass,
the world is too full to talk about.
Ideas, language, even the phrase "each other"
doesn't make any sense.

—RUMI

PART I

Saturday

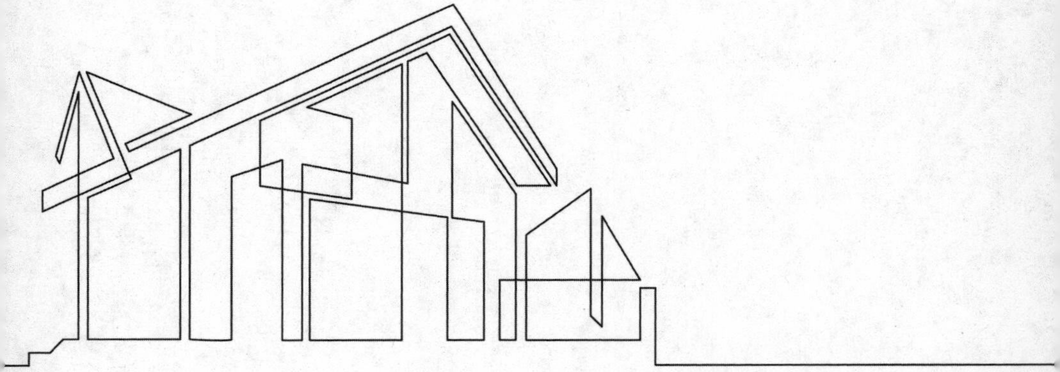

I

Saturday
5:00 p.m.–6:00 p.m.

WHILE TWELVE-YEAR-OLD AJAY sat trembling in a jail cell, his parents were enjoying themselves at a dinner party. The tony coastal enclave of Southern California was situated only hours, but worlds, away from the bustle of Los Angeles and the grit of Tijuana, and not far from the happiest place on earth. Rolling hills through the exclusive neighborhood showcased sprawling estates, bordered by expansive lawns and gated driveways. On one of these properties, perched high on a bluff overlooking the Pacific Ocean, cocktails were being served and all still seemed well.

"Congratulations, my friend. You have officially arrived," Vikram said, raising his tumbler of single malt toward Ashok. The thick crystal glasses made a satisfying baritone clink as they met. "Welcome to the jewel of Orange County."

Ashok couldn't keep the smile from edging onto his face, even as he shook his head modestly. "Ah, we still have a long way to go before reaching these heights," he said, gesturing around them at Vikram's lush backyard, the glimmer of the ocean in the distance illuminated by the setting sun. "But we have a start, thanks to you."

"Thanks, nothing." Vikram waved away Ashok's comment. "I have a vested interest in your moving into Pacific Hills. Now we just need to work on this guy." He nodded toward Ricky, whose scotch sat untouched on the thick teak armrest.

Ricky chuckled. "I don't think that's in the cards for us. Start-up life isn't really associated with excess cash flow. Besides, we're happy in Irvine. Our friends are all there."

Ashok feigned a mock expression of offense. "What?"

"Okay, not *all*," Ricky conceded. "But you know what I mean: Archie can get curry leaves from the neighbors next door, and Lalitaji down the street gives the kids dinner if we work late." He held his arms out wide to gesture to the expansiveness of Vikram's property, with its majestic palm trees soaring overhead. "I mean, this is beautiful, don't get me wrong. But we like our community."

"And how do you like your children going to that school?" Vikram asked, raising an eyebrow. "Packed forty to a classroom? One outdated computer for every three kids?"

Here, Ashok felt the need to speak up. "Oh, come on, Chavez isn't that bad."

"They're installing metal detectors at the entrance, Ashok." Vikram snickered. "*That* is not good. Just wait till your kids get used to Pacific Hills High. The place is like a country club—swimming pool, tennis courts . . ."

"No, of course," Ashok agreed. "I mean, that's why we moved here, for the schools, absolutely. I'm just saying, Chavez is a decent school too. Ricky's kids are doing well there." Ashok felt his body temperature rise, his armpits suddenly moist. Was he trying to convince Vikram or himself? The sting of earlier conversations with his daughter made an unwelcome intrusion on the enchanted evening.

"Yeah, I think the security measures are actually a good thing," Ricky said. "Some parents were uncomfortable sending their kids to school after that . . . incident."

"It's been happening all over." Ashok shook his head. "My friend in San Francisco saw some teenagers harassing an old Chinese man pushing his wife in a wheelchair on the Marina. Yelling and threatening, calling them names. The couple was over eighty. Can you imagine?"

"We could be next," Vikram said. "We're an easy target. Successful, educated . . ."

"Model minority," Ricky muttered.

Vikram pointed at him with his long index finger. "Exactly. When a community starts becoming successful, that is when the backlash starts. Nobody cared about opium in San Francisco until the Chinese started doing well. No one willingly gives up their place of privilege for someone new. You've got to scramble to get to the top, then fight to stay there. That's why you need to get ahead of it, to protect yourself."

"There's some truth to that," Ricky agreed. "Crime rates are soaring; gun sales are up. People are scared."

"You wouldn't . . . get a gun?" Ashok lowered his voice to a whisper on the last word. The illumined infinity pool began to glow as the sky grew dusky.

"Maybe." Vikram raised an eyebrow. His hair, more salt than pepper now, gave him the aura of someone wiser, though the men were all in their late forties. "Not a bad idea. But what I really mean is protect yourself like this, with assets. Have some space around you, a gate on your property. Send your kids to a country club school." He swirled the ice cube in his scotch before taking a long swig. "I'm buying up gold bullion, just in case."

"What?" Ashok laughed. "Gold? You can't be serious."

Vikram cocked his head. "What if it all goes to hell? What if they lock down your bank accounts for some invented reason and hoodlums are banging at your door for blood?"

"Okay, bhai, now you sound a little crazy," Ashok said, even as Vikram's suggestions formed hairline cracks of doubt in his own mind.

"Thank our president," Vikram said. "Nothing is inconceivable anymore. The best thing is to just try to blend in, be invisible. Personally, I don't like this term, *people of color*. I don't want to be categorized with Blacks and Mexicans. I don't even want to give white people the *idea* of targeting us."

"No one's going to target us," Ashok said. "We build their technology, we run their companies. They can't get rid of us. The internet would break." He laughed, trying to lighten the conversation.

"What about the Blacks?" Vikram said. "They're the best entertainers and athletes, and they're still targeted."

"That's different," Ashok said. "There's history there."

"It's different"—Ricky took a sip of his scotch—"until it's not."

Before their discussion could travel down that rocky path, it was interrupted by the timely appearance of Ashok's wife, heading toward them with a tray of samosas, which she placed on the table. The men busied themselves, spooning chutneys over their hot pastries as Priya swept back across the lawn to rejoin the other women.

INSIDE, PRIYA TOOK a stool at the vast marble island, watching uneasily as the diminutive housekeeper scrubbed away at the sink. Normally at these dinner gatherings, the wives helped one another. They all knew their way around one another's kitchens, how to warm the ovens, and where the plastic tubs were stored. Priya relished this familiarity with other Indian families, their shorthand interactions that approximated the feeling of family in this foreign land. Even after nearly two decades, she still thought of this country as her adopted home, a little uneasy with the remaining traces of her accent or habits in mixed crowds.

"Priya darling, more wine?" Veena asked, one perfectly manicured hand hovering a bottle over Priya's half-full glass before she poured.

"That poor woman," Archana said as the television in the adjacent family room showed silent footage of a middle-aged Black woman standing in front of a makeshift sidewalk memorial. "Just out for a walk, and her boy gets shot down."

"Well, not exactly," Veena said, reaching over to top off Archana's wineglass as well. "He was acting suspicious. Not that it justifies what the police did. I'm just saying, you have to keep your nose clean."

"Suspicious? He just had his hands in his pockets," Archana said.

"Yes, his very baggy pockets that could have held anything," Veena said. "At least that's what the police thought."

Archie sighed heavily. "Yeah, Mountain Dew and a box of Whoppers, as it turned out."

Priya watched the woman on the screen, her voice muted but her agony broadcast through her reddened eyes, the quivering of her mouth as she spoke into an assembly of microphones.

"My point is," Veena continued, "you can't give the police—or anyone—any reason to suspect you. When I go into a nice store, I dress up, make a big point of greeting the saleslady, making eye contact. And I take a very small purse. I don't give them anything to worry about. Right, Priya?"

Priya pulled her eyes away from the image on the TV. "Oh, yes, right." This was the code she and Ashok had lived by since coming to this country: work hard, don't make waves, keep placing one foot in front of the other on each new rung that appeared before them.

"Yeah, but you can't do anything about your skin color," Archie said pointedly.

Veena tilted her head slightly and a sly smile spread across her face. "Well, speaking of that, let me tell you what I learned from my dermatologist. There's a new procedure now that can eliminate all your dark spots, and even some wrinkles. Apparently, your skin looks so much lighter and fresher afterward." She lowered her voice to a whisper. "I have an appointment in two weeks."

"Okay, Miss Fair and Lovely." Archie laughed, pulling her mane of wavy hair around to rest on one shoulder, where it extended halfway down her toned arm. "Do I have to remind you we're not in India anymore? We don't have to stay out of the sun, per our mothers' instructions."

"No, really. Apparently, this can take a decade off your face," Veena said, though her delicate bone structure already gave her a youthful look, her smooth hair pulled into a graceful twist. Priya felt somewhat unremarkable next to her friends: not as elegant as Veena, nor as strong as Archie.

As Veena described her upcoming procedure, Priya reached for a samosa and found herself looking around. Veena and Vikram's house was spotless and impeccably decorated with a few homey touches—a pedestal bowl filled with oranges from their garden on the marble island, a luxurious faux fur throw draped casually over the modern sectional, a richly colored Indian painting prominent on the back wall. Every time Priya came to this home, she was filled with admiration for the way it looked and the way it made her feel. The Sharmas had wealth but managed it tastefully.

They had the kind of life Priya didn't even know existed when she and Ashok first came to America. Their first rental apartment here had been a delight simply because it didn't have to be shared with family members, as was always the case back in Mumbai, where the price of real estate was exorbitant and space was always at a premium. In that one-bedroom on Magnolia Lane, Ashok and Priya didn't even notice the chipped windowsills or the flimsy accordion closet doors. They kept an IKEA catalog on the kitchen counter and carefully deliberated over each piece, saving up for and assembling them one at a time. That apartment had lasted them many years, well after Deepa was born and her playpen and toys had taken over the family room.

"I can take this, Miss?" The housekeeper was now standing at Priya's elbow, gesturing at her chutney-soiled cocktail napkin.

"Oh, thank you." Priya smiled as the woman swept up her napkin. The kitchen sink and counter were now also pristine, with no sign of all the earlier cooking that had taken place.

"Virginia, could you please set up the buffet outside?" Veena asked, and the housekeeper responded with a small nod before heading off. Veena waited until she had gone before saying, "She is such a dream. I don't know what I'd do without her. The kids create so much mess everywhere, but she just manages to keep everything tidy."

"And she still stays here during the week?" Archie asked.

Veena nodded, biting delicately into a samosa. "It works out better that way. It's too far for her to drive every day. On Mondays, it can take three to four hours to get here, can you believe? She changes the days she comes and goes, so they won't notice any pattern at the border, which works out when I need her on the weekend, like today. Of course, she prefers to keep her home over there—her family's all there and Tijuana's so much cheaper. But she really appreciates having the free room and board here."

"But wouldn't it be better if she could afford to live where she works?" Archie asked, waving her glass in the air, and Priya wondered if she was a little bit drunk.

Veena shrugged. "What can you do? I pay her the going rate, a bit more in fact. Maybe if she had papers, she could get a job with an office cleaning crew or something, with benefits and security. But she has limited options. Do you remember what it was like for Ricky when you guys first came here?"

"Yeah, I don't miss that." Archie shook her head, her diamond nose stud glinting in the waning sunlight. "Tethered to that horrible company for that damn H-1B renewal every year. They worked him to the *bone*."

"Right?" Veena said. "But we all came here legally, followed the rules, paid our dues. Now we have the freedom to do what we want. When you sneak in the back door, you don't have that option."

As if on cue, Virginia slipped soundlessly back into the house through the folding glass wall. "Everything ready, Miss. I should put the food out there now?"

"Yes, thank you, Virginia." Veena moved to the other side of the island to allow her passage to the ovens, where large trays of rice pilau, parathas, spiced okra, and chickpea curry were warming. One by one, Virginia pulled them out with oven mitts and carried them to the chafing dishes lining the buffet outside. The Sharmas had an outdoor space designed for entertaining: a large covered patio with overhead heat lamps, a rustic chandelier centered over the impressive dining table, which had been cut vertically from a single gargantuan tree trunk.

Priya brought her shawl as the women moved outdoors. The men strolled across the lawn to join them.

"I see you got Ricky to dress up for the evening." Veena elbowed Archie.

"Mm," Archie murmured as she sipped her wine. "Pants instead of shorts with his flip-flops." She winked at them. Surrounded by young engineers all day long, Ricky still dressed like a student and wore his hair in a boyish mop.

As the group gathered on the patio, they all took a moment to appreciate the last vestiges of sun streaking across the sky, the beginning glimmer of stars overhead. After they filled their plates and took their seats around the table, the conversation turned to its usual topics.

"What are the kids doing tonight?" Veena asked. Their children all used to be part of these weekend dinner gatherings, but as they reached adolescence, each found excuses to peel away, busy with their increasing schoolwork, activities, or friends.

"The twins are home with Mom," Archie said. "I think they're doing some baking project. So I'll have to clean up the whole kitchen tomorrow, but at least we get to enjoy tonight." She smiled and took a sip of wine.

"Maya is off with her new friend," Priya said. "That girl is a social butterfly. She met Ashley after one week of field hockey camp, and they're already inseparable."

"Nice family too," Ashok added. "The Bakers, they live over on Piedmont—"

"That estate at the top of the hill?" Vikram interrupted. "I know that house. Everyone knows it. Baker Development." He let out a low whistle. "Good for Maya, picking her friends right."

"Ajay's at the robotics lab at school," Priya continued, "working with his team for their regional competition next month."

"You know, with his height, he should really play basketball or something," Vikram said. "Team sports are so important here, especially for boys." In the past year, Ajay had grown six inches and now towered above his classmates and his older sisters.

Ashok gave a mild shake of his head. "I wish, but he's not interested. I even installed a hoop in the driveway, but he has absolutely no desire."

Priya noticed the familiar note of regret in his voice, her husband's longing for the all-American boy. "Well, he's found something he loves. The robotics coach says he's really talented in programming. She thinks he can start taking college-level classes in a couple of years." Priya couldn't stop herself from boasting a bit. Despite his size, Ajay was still their shy little boy, and she was glad he was being recognized for his own gifts rather than compared to some American ideal.

A round of exclamations and praise pinballed around the table.

"And Deepa?" Archie prodded.

"Deepa will pick them both up and give them dinner," Priya said. "With any luck, everyone will be in bed by the time we get home." She held up crossed fingers.

"You're so lucky she can drive now," Veena said. "How nice, not having to cart everyone around. You can just enjoy your evening and still catch the sunset." She smiled and held up her wineglass.

Priya felt a small twinge in her chest, thinking of the secondhand car Deepa was driving at that very moment, and all that it represented in their family: not so much their independence as hers.

"Is that yours, darling?" Veena leaned toward her and touched her arm. Priya became aware of the muffled sound of a phone ringing from somewhere behind them, inside the house.

"Oh, one minute," she apologized, standing at the precise moment Ashok spoke.

"Just leave it."

"It could be one of the kids," Priya said over her shoulder.

"Exactly," Ashok muttered, shaking his head.

Everyone chuckled at the familiar pattern. By the time Priya dug her phone out of her clutch, it had stopped ringing, but there were two missed calls: one from an unknown number, the other from Maya. She rang Maya back and held the phone to her ear.

"Mom, when is Deepa coming?" Maya's voice was impatient.

"Well, I don't know. Have you tried asking her?" Priya glanced out to the patio. Ashok was right, she should have left it. Sometimes she wondered if her children were growing up without the basic functional skills they would need to navigate the world.

"I've texted her, like, a million times, and she hasn't even opened my messages. I can't stay here much longer, Mom. They're going out for dinner soon. It's getting awkward."

"If I can't track her down, Dad will come pick you up in ten minutes, okay?" Priya tried to catch Ashok's eye, but he was busy laughing, unusually relaxed for once. *Damn it, Deepa.*

Priya had just scrolled to Deepa's number when her phone rang again from an unknown caller. Maybe Deepa was using a friend's phone. Perhaps her phone had died. Perhaps the car had died. Priya's heart rate quickened as she answered the call.

"Mrs. Shah?" a man's serious voice asked. "Pry-yah Shah?"

"Uh, yes," Priya answered, accustomed to mispronunciations of her name and wondering if she could just hang up on this likely telemarketer.

"Are you Ay-Jay's mother?" The man pronounced it the American way, as if it were two initials.

Priya felt a hot flush travel up her chest and face. She instinctively turned to look at Ashok out on the patio. "I . . . uh . . . yes. Yes! I'm his mother. Who is this? What's wrong? Is he okay?"

"How old is your son, ma'am? He didn't have any identification on him."

"He's twelve. Why? Where is he?" Her hands began to tremble as she held the phone tighter.

"He's in police custody right now," the voice said.

"What?" Priya spun around and locked eyes with Ashok. His smile dissolved as he saw her face. "Why? Is he okay? He's only *twelve*, he's a child, for god's sake."

The clattering of silverware and conversation around the table came to an abrupt halt as everyone turned to watch her. Ashok rose from his chair.

"Where is he? The police station?" Priya cried, but she could only hear muffled, indistinct voices through the phone. Then the voice was back.

"No, ma'am." He cleared his throat. "County jail. Downtown."

Before Priya could process the words, Ashok was beside her, his arm around her shoulders. "What is it?" he whispered, absurdly still trying to maintain decorum.

"It's Ajay. We have to go." She grabbed her purse. "That was the . . . police." Her voice cracked in disbelief on the last word.

Ashok stared at her, his eyes wide. "Police? What happened?" he said, as the others drew near and began repeating the same question, mingled with looks of confusion.

But Priya was already headed toward the front door while Ashok hurried after her, leaving their friends to speculate what had happened.

2

Saturday
5:00 p.m.–6:00 p.m.

AS HER PARENTS sped down the highway toward the county jail, a hundred miles away at the US-Mexico border, Deepa could not hear the phone ring in her pocket. Her ears buzzed and her throat was raw from shouting. She took a drink from her water bottle and scanned the crowd. Only a dozen people had been there when she and Paco arrived, but now there were at least two hundred. Old, young, white, brown, people of all walks of life, holding signs, wearing T-shirts with homemade slogans. They stood at the southern tip of San Diego, only a couple hours from Irvine. Just across the bridge was Tijuana, where a small crowd of hopeful migrants was gathered, watching the protest in silent curiosity. Stern border guards manned the gatehouse between the two countries, checking cars and pedestrians as they crossed over into America. Media vans were parked on the side of the road, cameras and microphones pointed toward the crowds.

The San Ysidro Port of Entry was one of the busiest land border crossings in the world, with more than 100,000 people coming through every single day to go to school, work, shop, or see a doctor. These people were essential to the region, helping tend agricultural fields, build homes, prepare food, manicure lawns, raise children, clean homes and offices. The economy simply would not function without these workers, and yet they were being vilified and treated as criminals, denied their basic human rights. A country whose global advantage was its diversity born of immigration was turning its back on what had made it great.

When she watched news coverage of the issue, Deepa felt incensed—for herself, for Paco, for every child of immigrants who had seen and heard about the sacrifices made for their sake, for the opportunity for a better life. Standing here now, she poured her emotion into chanting, disregarding the sting in her throat. Police officers stood on the other side of barricades erected to keep the protesters away from the road.

Deepa hoisted her sign higher into the air. Made with markers on poster board left over from a science project, it read No Human Is Illegal with a rendition of the American flag. Paco's said Protect ALL Immigrants, a sentiment Deepa thought too mild for the situation. She had wanted them both to carry Abolish ICE signs, but Paco refused.

"We don't even *say* ICE in my hood, girl, don't even speak the word. It's like a superstition. I'm *sure as shit* not carrying a sign with those letters on it."

Deepa had this debate with Paco all the time. He accepted the cloak of fear that his mother wore, even though it didn't belong to him. He had been born in this country. As a citizen, there was nothing for him to worry about, from ICE or anyone else. But Lucia was another story.

She and Paco's father had come to California to visit her cousin two decades ago. They'd intended to stay only a few months, maybe a year, just long enough to earn some money and buy a little house back in Rosarito. But Francisco was a talented mason, and he found plenty of work applying stucco finishes to new homes. In the midst of the 2000s housing boom, the money was too good to walk away from, compared to what he would earn in Mexico. They shared a rental home in a working-class neighborhood of Irvine with Lucia's cousin and his wife, whom Lucia helped to clean houses. It was a good-enough life; they were getting by, and soon their son was born. They named him Francisco after his father but called him Paco.

After a few years in Irvine, Rosarito faded into more of a memory, an idea removed from their everyday life. It was easy enough to drive over the Tijuana/San Diego border on tourist visas when they wanted to visit family back home. Plenty of people did it every week, or every day, for work or school. Their earnings in Irvine, while not extravagant, enabled them to send some money home each month, and their families came to rely on this. After a while, Francisco was hired by a big development company that offered to sponsor him for a green card. Once it came through, he and Lucia planned to get legally married, and she could get her papers too. She would finally take classes to improve her English, maybe find work as a store clerk or a nanny.

For several years, as Paco attended kindergarten, then elementary school, after his two little sisters were born, their life seemed as if it was coming together and climbing a gradual but steady hill. They could stake out goals and achieve them slowly: a bicycle for Paco, a new refrigerator, a secondhand car, and their own rental house.

Until the moment things turned downhill. The development company let Francisco go after the housing crisis bust in 2009. He could still find work, but it wasn't as steady or reliable. Sometimes he camped outside the nearest Home Depot with other men, hoping to be picked up for day jobs. He had his green card by now, so he didn't have to worry about an immigration raid, but he could easily sit there all day and never get a job. A full day wasted, with no earnings, and still five mouths to feed when he came home. Those days, Paco said, put his father in a dark mood that was hard for any of them to penetrate.

Lucia began to work more, cleaning houses every day with Paco's two younger sisters in tow. She would sit them in the laundry room (or sometimes in the car, if her employer disapproved) with their blankets, coloring books, and snacks, and check on them between tasks. Lucia told herself it was better than leaving the girls home alone, but she worried they should really be in preschool. Paco taught them their numbers and letters when he came home from school, and this helped alleviate Lucia's guilt, but only a little. She and Francisco weighed going back to Rosarito in late-night whispered conversations after they thought the kids were asleep. Paco knelt next to his bed every night, in the room he shared with his sisters, praying to the Virgin Mary to stay in California, the only home he'd ever known.

By the time Paco was in middle school, the housing market had recovered somewhat, and his father was back to fairly regular work, but life still was not easy. With both of his parents working long hours, Paco picked up his little sisters from school, racing over on his bicycle to get there in time, then walked them home, made snacks, and started dinner before his parents came home, exhausted from work. He often stayed up late at night to finish his homework and went to school the next day bleary-eyed.

He and Deepa were sitting in study hall together one afternoon when the school counselor came to find Paco. Deepa felt her heart drop into her stomach. She watched Paco pack up his bag and follow the counselor, waited a few moments, then told the teacher she was going to the bathroom. She raced down the hall to the office area and looked around, spotting Paco's uncle through the narrow glass panel of the counselor's office.

Francisco and another laborer had been working in a six-foot-deep trench for a water line at his construction site. No one on the crew knew the trench had not been adequately shored. Regulators had not been on-site for the required inspections all week. When the trench began to cave in, the two men tried to scramble out. One was rescued, but Francisco was trapped under the avalanche of dirt and rubble. He was buried for five hours before his body was finally recovered. Deepa didn't find all this out until much later, when the evening news reports carried the story of an unnamed father of three who was tragically killed at a local construction site.

That day, she only saw a blank-faced Paco walk out of school with his uncle's arm wrapped protectively around him. It was a devastating loss for Lucia and her children, particularly the two young girls who worshipped him. At fourteen, Paco stepped into his father's role to become the man of the family, both his burdens and secrets growing heavier.

Without Francisco's income, Lucia could no longer afford the rent on their little bungalow, and the family was forced to move in with Lucia's cousin, where all four of them shared one bedroom. Lucia was expected to get a settlement payment from Francisco's construction company, which was culpable for the accident, but the process had been tied up with lawyers and negotiations for years now.

Lucia had never gotten her papers. They had inquired with an immigration lawyer after Francisco got his green card, but they couldn't afford the thousands of dollars in legal fees, nor could they navigate the forms themselves. There would always be time, they thought. Francisco was only thirty-eight years old when he was killed. Now, Lucia would have to wait until Paco turned twenty-one and could sponsor her to be a legal resident of the country where she had lived, worked, paid rent and taxes for two decades—the country where her three citizen children had been born and her husband had died.

When her parents announced they were moving neighborhoods, and therefore schools, Deepa could not fathom leaving Paco or Cesar Chavez, certainly not to go to that whitewashed Pacific Hills High her parents coveted. Increasingly, it seemed, their dreams felt foreign to her.

Now, resting her sign on the ground, Deepa linked her arm through Paco's and leaned against his shoulder. In front of them, two police officers moved toward each other to exchange words. Deepa could only make out *disperse* and *dark*. It seemed like the protest was starting to wind down, and the reporters were loading back into their vans. Deepa glanced at her watch, uneasy to see she was already late.

3

Saturday
5:00 p.m.–6:00 p.m.

BACK IN THE comfortable confines of Pacific Hills, Maya glanced at her phone again. Still no response from Deepa. Her sister had become even more distant since their move over the summer. She was the only one in the family not excited about the new house or their new neighborhood and seemed determined to ruin it for the rest of them. Deepa was often off with her school friends on weekends, but this was now becoming really annoying.

Maya had been at the Bakers' house all afternoon. She and Ashley had practiced their field hockey drills on the wide expanse of back lawn, furnished with a full-size net. They later changed into their swimsuits and alternated between the pool and hot tub until their skin was puckered. Maya had worn her new bikini, in case Chase happened to be around, which he was. Draped in bright striped towels, they all ended up playing foosball together in the pool house, which had its own TV and kitchen stocked with drinks and snacks. When Ashley and Chase had left to get showered and dressed, Maya stayed in the pool house to change back into her clothes, and now felt conspicuous in her shorts and tee, with her straggly wet hair.

At first she didn't mind that Deepa was late. Sometimes when Maya lingered at Ashley's house in the afternoons, Mrs. Baker invited her to stay for dinner. Their home always felt warm, and the dinner conversation was bright and friendly. But tonight, they had reservations at a restaurant for Mr. Baker's birthday, and Maya was starting to feel uncomfortable enough to interrupt her parents at their dinner party. At least everyone *else* in her family was off having a fun Saturday night, Maya thought wryly.

"I'm so sorry," Maya said to Mrs. Baker. "My sister must be running late. My parents won't let her use the phone while she's driving, so I'm sure she's on her way. She'll probably be here any minute. I can just wait outside." She stood up. "I don't want to make you guys late for your dinner."

Mrs. Baker glanced out the window at the darkening sky. "Oh no, I can't let you do that, Maya."

Just then, Chase came down the stairs, his dirty blond hair combed and damp, his dress shirt tucked into khakis. Maya caught a whiff of his freshly showered scent. She felt her knees waver a little as she steadied herself on the banister.

"Oh, Chase can run you home!" Mrs. Baker said, smiling at him. "Okay, honey? Ash is still going to be a little while; she's drying her hair. Just meet us at the restaurant? You know where it is."

"Uh, yeah. Sure," Chase said, grabbing his keys from the foyer table. "No problem. You ready?" He flashed his perfect smile at Maya.

She was still holding on to the banister, thank god, as she felt her chest pound in response. "You sure it's no trouble? I'll grab my stuff." Maya followed Chase through the mudroom to the garage, which held four cars in parallel. She felt her toes tingle with the realization that she was going to be alone—*alone!*—with Chase Baker for the first time, and *in his car*. Chase was a junior, captain of the varsity soccer team, and had dimples that lit up his whole face when he smiled. She dashed off a quick message to her parents: *On the way home now. Sorry to bother you. Have fun!* She was still vacillating between feeling angry at Deepa and grateful that her tardiness had forced this situation.

Chase chirped open the BMW's doors with his fob, and Maya climbed into the passenger seat, squeezing her backpack, sports duffel, and field hockey stick into her seat.

He smiled over at her as he turned on the ignition. "You can put that stuff in the back seat, you know," he said.

Not wanting to appear rude, Maya stowed her things in the back and sat next to him, hands awkwardly positioned in her lap over her gym shorts. For the millionth time, she appreciated how much good fortune had come into her life to bring her to this moment. The new house, where she no longer had to share a room with her sister. Starting high school at Pacific Hills, with its campus resembling a page out of a college catalog. Lucking into that field hockey camp this summer, where she happened to meet Ashley on the first day and fall into a close and easy friendship.

Ashley had lived in this neighborhood since kindergarten; she knew practically everyone in their incoming freshman class and was able to smooth Maya's path into her new school. Of course, the new environment took some getting used to, but Maya quickly learned what she needed to do to fit in. She began shopping at thrift stores to find affordable versions of the right branded clothes. She convinced her mother to buy her an expensive pair of popular sneakers with the promise that it was the only pair of shoes she would ask for all year. And she took meticulous care of those sneakers: scrubbing them with a toothbrush every weekend and air-drying them so they would continue to look new.

Finding the right backpack had taken a little more effort. Everyone at school had a certain kind of bag, and while it wasn't terribly expensive, Maya knew her mother would balk at buying something new when she already had a bag with some wear left. So, she worked the frayed spots of that old backpack until they became obvious, tore at the mesh pocket that held her water bottle, and jammed the zipper over some loose threads. When she presented the newly dysfunctional bag to her mother, Maya also explained how the new backpack she wanted came with a lifetime warranty, so would not cost any more in the long run.

Maya enjoyed this game, or rather she enjoyed the fruits of her resourcefulness—that feeling of ease in her new peer group, being comfortable with how she presented herself. That was the real challenge at her new school. Academics were easy for her. She had always been a good student and followed all her parents' rules. Maya knew that everything she wanted came much more smoothly when she greased the wheels of her parents' expectations. Sometimes she wished Deepa understood this a little better; it wouldn't take much for her sister to reduce her friction with their parents. At the same time, Maya knew she benefited from the contrast her parents saw between the two of them.

As she directed Chase through the winding hills to their house, they discussed her classes and teachers, the field hockey coach she and Ashley loved, and the school musical coming up in a few weeks. Maya was nervous but thought she managed to appear cool, even causing Chase to laugh and look over at her a few times.

When they arrived, Maya could see her house was completely dark inside. "Well," she said, "I guess my sister really did just forget about me."

Chase smiled. "This is your house? It's nice. I like the porch swing."

"Yeah, thanks." After chatting easily all the way here, Maya suddenly found herself stuck for words. She reluctantly opened the car door and retrieved her gear, searching through her backpack for the house key her mother insisted she carry for emergencies, fumbling through lip gloss, pencils, charging cords, and gum wrappers.

"Something wrong?" Chase turned on the car's interior light and looked back.

"Um, I can't find my key. Sorry, I'll just do this outside." Maya stuffed everything back in the pocket and zipped it up, her face growing flush. *God, what an idiot!*

"Here," Chase said. "Let me help you." He turned off the car and walked around to help carry her field hockey stick and duffel up the driveway.

Under the porch light, Maya easily found the key in her backpack. "Thanks for the ride," she said. And then, impulsively, because she was rarely home alone; because she felt something crackling in the air between them, though it might have been just her; because his smile now revealed his dimples, she added, "Do you . . . want to come in for a minute?"

4

Saturday
6:00 p.m.–7:00 p.m.

AT BISTRO MICHEL, the rest of the Baker family was seated at their usual table with the ocean view. As they waited for Chase, Miranda ordered a glass of Pinot Gris, and Spence began with an old-fashioned, a nod to the cocktail his late father had favored. Spence was fifty-five years old today, his age revealing itself in the gray hair sprinkled through his sideburns and the lines etched at the corner of his eyes. But he didn't mind getting older. Birthdays always presented Spence with an opportunity for reflection, an evaluation of his life to date. And on that score, he felt quite content. He was a fortunate man, celebrating at a favorite restaurant with his beautiful wife of twenty-five years and their two younger children.

Miller, their oldest, was a freshman at the University of Southern California, where he'd been recruited for their Division 1 water polo team. He hadn't played yet this season, and perhaps he wouldn't next year either, but it was enough that he had gained admission to such a prestigious school and earned a spot playing the sport to which he'd dedicated himself. Years of evening practice, summer training camps, and traveling for meets had paid off. Miller had joined a fraternity and was making great friends at USC. He hadn't been able to make it home from Los Angeles for the weekend, but Spence didn't mind. His son was enjoying the quintessential collegiate experience, and he was proud of him.

Ashley, wearing a floral dress instead of her usual athletic garb, had been transformed. It seemed to Spence as if she had crossed the threshold to being a young woman without his quite noticing. At times like this, when she looked so grown-up, he had to search her face for the little girl who used to curl up in his lap. He and Ashley had always been close, perhaps because she held a tender spot as his only daughter, or perhaps—as Miranda liked to joke—because they were both Libras, with birthdays only a week apart.

"Ah, there he is!" Miranda interrupted his ruminations, and Spence looked up to see Chase striding across the restaurant toward them, twenty minutes late. He was struck, as he often was, when he saw his son at a distance. Chase was broad-shouldered and tall, a finely built young man who exuded confidence and masculine energy. Sometimes Spence envied his son the years of youthful adventure that still lay ahead of him.

"Sorry," Chase said, pulling out a chair. "It was way out there, on the other side of the Hills. I got turned around coming over here from a different direction." He picked up a menu and exhaled. "Did you guys order? I'm starving."

"Thank you for doing that, honey." Miranda reached out a hand to Chase's forearm. "Did you see they have the filet today?"

"Yeah, thanks for driving Maya home." Ashley closed her menu. "I'm getting the truffle risotto."

After they placed their dinner orders, Miranda chose a special bottle of Cabernet with the sommelier's guidance and made a toast. "Happy birthday to a wonderful father, husband, and man. Even if your tennis game still needs some work before you can beat me." She beamed as she teased him.

"Ah, yes, so true," Spence said. "I'm sticking to doubles. My partner's an ace." He winked at Miranda before turning to Chase. "Son, any more thoughts about college?"

Chase was a nationally ranked forward and had received interest from several college soccer programs, but many of the offers were from the East Coast or the Midwest. Spence was encouraging him to sign with a West Coast university, ideally in Southern California. He knew that the network of friends his son built in college would form the basis for his professional life, just as it had for Spence himself.

The Bakers had deep roots in the Orange County area, going back three generations. Spence had started his real estate development firm with the modest financial backing of his own father, who had started out as a carpenter and eventually built a small construction company. From those working-class beginnings, Spence had worked hard to grow his business, finding his father's connections with tradesmen, city planners, and building inspectors invaluable. Eventually, when his father was ready to retire, Spence had merged the businesses into one vertically integrated company that could reap greater profits. It could only happen in America, where innovation and growth could flourish relatively unrestrained by regulation or corruption.

Spence had found great reward in building his own business—not only financially, but also the deeper satisfaction that came with charting his own path, taking care of his people. Most of his employees had been with him for a decade or more: he'd attended their housewarmings and children's graduations knowing that his company had helped fund those milestones. Anita, his longtime assistant, had cried in his office when he gifted her the down payment for her house rather than the loan she'd requested after the bank had denied her.

Sure, there were headaches and costs, notably the cadre of lawyers and accountants he now paid to handle the complexity of taxes, compliance, and perennial litigation that seemed to be the price of doing business these days. But it was a good living and made for a good life.

His hope was that Miller and Chase would do something similar—find success in an adjacent business, perhaps real estate brokerage or financing, and expand the reach of their family enterprise. There was so much opportunity to be had in the ever-growing building sector in Southern California—it seemed a shame to not capture it within their fold. Spence wanted to preserve and protect what he'd worked so hard for, but he wouldn't simply hand it to his sons. He would make them work for it, and for this they needed the right kind of connections.

But how to explain all this—the things that would truly matter to his son's quality of life one day—to a kid with starry eyes and big dreams?

Chase sighed. "I just want to go somewhere I belong, Dad. Don't you think I'd get lost at UCLA or Cal? They're just so . . . huge."

"You'd have your teammates," Spence said. "They'd be your family, your circle."

"Frankly, you're lucky to even have the option at those top schools," Miranda said. "They're nearly overrun now with perfect Asian students. Between that and the extra boost some other groups get . . ." She shook her head. "I don't know how regular smart kids are expected to get in anymore. Whatever happened to good old-fashioned merit?"

"And you want me to compete with all those perfect kids in college?" Chase chuckled, sipping from his father's cocktail, now abandoned for the wine. "They set every curve. It's practically impossible to get an A."

"You don't need As," Spence said. "You just need to do well enough. You'll do what Miller does. His brothers pool their collective knowledge and help each other out." He was referring, of course, to the file cabinet in Miller's fraternity house filled with previous years' tests and exams.

Miranda nodded. "It's the only way to level the playing field with these kids who have no life, no personality. Studying in the library till midnight every day. I feel sorry for them, actually. College is supposed to be *fun*." She took a long sip of wine. "Well, all I can say is *thank god* for your talent on the field, Chase. Sports seem to be the last remaining way to get an edge these days."

"You'll have lots of good choices, son. You'll be just fine," Spence said, and he knew it to be true.

Chase then excused himself on the pretense of going to the restroom, but really went to ask the waiter to bring a birthday dessert for his father, as his mother had asked.

AS MIRANDA WATCHED Chase walk away, she registered his athletic stride that reminded her so much of her younger brother. In just a few years, Chase would be older than the uncle he never had a chance to meet. Jack's life was cut short by an overdose at twenty-four, just as his promising college lacrosse career had been devastated by an injury three years earlier. Miranda had seen her parents watch helplessly as Jack's grades dropped, then when he took a leave from college before dropping out entirely. Alcohol and marijuana, combined with pain meds, eventually led to street drugs. Her brother's descent was rapid, and her parents were caught unawares, always one step behind in their efforts to help him. By the time he died, Jack had depleted their parents' savings with three bouts in rehab and was living in a flophouse.

In the end, her brother squandered any head start in life their parents had handed him. Every day since, Miranda's heart ached with the wasted promise of his life, more so now that she had her own boys. When she and Spence had children, Miranda was determined to be present and vigilant in their lives, to spare her family that kind of pain. Kids who were happy, healthy, and social, that's all she wished for.

"Oh, that reminds me." Miranda turned to Ashley. "We have to make sure to get your reel together for Elite field hockey camp in December. I'll book the videographer for your next game." She pulled out her phone to make a note. "Do you want to see if Maya wants to apply too? It would be fun for you two to do it together. Maybe I'll give her mother a call this week." Miranda would invite Maya to come as Ashley's guest. She knew the cost of the camp was exorbitant, not to mention the private coaching, gear, and travel that would be involved. It was one of the benefits of their fortunate position, to be able to take care of these things for others. Money couldn't solve all problems, Miranda had learned, but it could certainly ease some. She was glad to use it to that end when she could, particularly for new friends.

5

Saturday
6:00 p.m.–7:00 p.m.

AS ASHOK DROVE, Priya closed her eyes and tried to focus on drawing deep breaths in through her nose, against the tightening of her chest. She idly worked at the elastic hair band on her wrist, snapping it against her skin, rolling it between her fingers, twisting it into a figure eight. She was never without one of these black bands, even if she wore it, as she did tonight, under a cluster of gold bangles. Not exactly stylish, but pragmatic.

"What did he say, exactly?" Ashok asked.

Priya opened her eyes and tied her shoulder-length hair into a low ponytail, as she usually wore it at the office or in the kitchen. She couldn't concentrate with hair falling into her eyes or brushing her shoulders. "He didn't say *anything*, just told me Ajay was in police custody. Maybe he got lost or something, and they took him there to keep him safe?" Her mind began to wander into dangerous territory—all the terrible things that could befall her sweet little boy.

Ashok nodded. "Yes, must be something like that. Don't worry." He put his hand on top of hers, and Priya held tightly to it against the feeling of disintegration, a crumbling of the pillars they had built together. Eighteen years in this country, twenty years of marriage, filled with hard work and careful choices. Everything they'd ever done was to create opportunity for their children, long before they had even come into existence.

Priya had been in her final year of college when she asked her parents to begin seeking a match for her. She hadn't known what to make of Ashok when she had first met him in Mumbai, at a meeting arranged by her father's aunt. Her parents didn't think he was terribly impressive on paper, with a degree from a second-rate university and lacking the accolades that would signal future success in Indian society. His parents were of modest means; his father worked as a clerk at a sari emporium, rolling and folding swaths of fabric. They lived on the far outskirts of town in a small one-bedroom flat, where Ashok and his older brother slept on bedrolls in the common room. Their family employed no servants, and though Ashok's mother explained with pride that she liked to do her own cooking, it was also understood they couldn't afford to hire help. His family was of a lower, yet still acceptable, caste than her family. All this was to say that Priya didn't have high expectations before meeting Ashok.

Right away, Priya noticed how well-groomed Ashok was. He wore pressed pants and a Western-style button-front shirt in a nice thick fabric not usually found in India's climate. His hair was trim and neatly combed. But it was when he opened his mouth that she was really impressed. Ashok spoke with a vocabulary that exceeded what she might have expected. Despite his modest background, Ashok presented himself as well-educated and spoke about applying to graduate programs in the United States. He had already identified thirty such institutions admitting qualified candidates from India on student visas, which included a provision for spouses. Ashok spoke with a glint in his eye about campuses in Pittsburgh, Pennsylvania; College Station, Texas; West Lafayette, Indiana; and though Priya knew nothing about any of these places, his enthusiasm and ambition were infectious. Despite his humble beginnings, Ashok Shah was definitely going places, and Priya wanted to go with him.

She met a few more boys after Ashok, but he was the one who gleamed brightest in her mind. He was the one with whom she pictured walking around the sacred fire on her wedding day, boarding a plane to America, making a home together in that foreign land, full of possibility and far away from her home and family.

Her parents suggested she might wait a year or two, perhaps complete a master's degree before marrying, which would raise the quality of her potential candidates. But Priya was eager to get married and begin her life. It was not uncommon for young women in India to marry in their early twenties. Bollywood films had bred into them dreams of love stories and the expectation of romance. Though young women in urban centers like Mumbai increasingly held higher degrees and jobs, all of this was still deemed secondary to a good marriage and family. Priya had her own reasons, which had less to do with finding a husband, and more with finding an escape hatch from her home. And Ashok seemed the most likely candidate to whisk her away from all that, quickly and reliably.

Their engagement ceremony took place two months after they first met, and their wedding date was set for a month after Priya's college graduation. In the intervening weeks, they began a courtship blessed by their parents: evenings at the movies, strolls down Marine Drive, picnics at Hanging Gardens. Ashok kept a small book of Tagore's poetry in his pocket, which he read from as they sat by the waterfront with ice cream cones. His voice was so lyrical that she could almost believe the words were his own.

"I do write," Ashok admitted shyly, "but my poems aren't very good. I just enjoy it. It's a nice way to . . . to let go, in my mind."

"Will you show them to me after we're married?" Priya teased, as she felt herself falling for her future husband. They discussed their dreams: making a home, raising children, and building an exciting new life together.

It was a long way from their current reality. Ashok was still sleeping on the floor of his family's flat, working full-time at a multinational IT company while scrambling to amass enough credits through night classes to qualify for American graduate programs. Given the requisite paring back of foreign credentials, he would have to earn the equivalent of a master's degree in India for it to qualify as a bachelor's degree to American schools.

Priya was trying to finish her last term at college while helping her mother plan the wedding. She often stayed up late with her books in the sitting room, complaining the light in her bedroom was inadequate. Sometime well after midnight, once the whole house was asleep, she finally dropped into bed, exhausted. Priya became accustomed to the particular feeling of being the only one awake in the quiet house. In their traditional joint family household, her father and Babu uncle lived, now with their wives and children, in the same flat in which they had grown up with their own parents. Not only was this customary, but with the skyrocketing cost of living in Mumbai, it also made economic sense to share living quarters.

Priya was an only child, as was her cousin Manu. Both brothers had chosen to have a single child so they could afford the investment to properly raise a child in the city: school fees, uniforms, courses, and extra tutors to keep up. The flat had been subdivided into more rooms as the household grew from four people to six, then eight, after both children had been born. Each new bedroom was smaller, holding only a bed and cupboard, but the building, at the center of Churchgate, had appreciated in value considerably over the years. The flat was now the family's most valuable asset, and its ownership made them seem more affluent than their liquid net worth. Still, the home had come to feel oppressive to Priya, and as she progressed through her college years, spending more time on the nearby campus and away from the flat, the more she wished to leave it completely. After all those late hours of study, Priya graduated at the top of her bachelor of commerce class, and while she could have had her pick of accounting jobs at one of Mumbai's large companies, she did not apply for a single one.

ASHOK SHARED PRIYA'S desire to leave India. Even before the wedding, he began applying to graduate programs abroad. His father had always spoken of America with starry eyes, his reverence based entirely on the foreign customers he'd served at the sari emporium. *Must be a great country, where even a humble farmer can rise to become president or a billionaire,* he would say. Ashok's family came from a rural area of Maharashtra, six hundred kilometers from Mumbai. For generations, his relatives had toiled as manual laborers, constricted by the caste into which they'd been born. When Ashok's older brother began to show great aptitude for mathematics, he was sent to Mumbai to live with an uncle and attend a better school. Soon afterward, the rest of the family followed, but his father's prospects were limited by his education. If Ashok stayed in Mumbai after marriage, he would have to live in a joint household with his family; there was no question of being able to afford their own apartment. America represented his passport out of their native country, where it felt impossible to break free of the life into which he'd been born. In a country of over one billion people, every single step in life was fraught with competition, with someone who wanted to elbow you aside or step on you to get ahead.

The vastness of the Indian population made everything feel unachievable, like trying to scale the sheer wall of one of its urban skyscrapers with bare hands. Think of it—1.4 billion people—even if you only took the urban educated share, you were still talking about *hundreds of millions* of people. The upper strata of society—high-caste Brahmins, wealthy traders, the military and political elite—had dominated society for so long that their descendants had generations of wealth and privilege to draw upon. They owned the best homes, attended the best schools, won the best jobs, helped one another out, and the cycle repeated itself for their children.

At the other end was the vast underclass population below the caste system, oppressed for centuries and renamed according to changing political tastes through the years as Untouchables, Dalits, and now Scheduled Castes. The government had taken steps to improve economic mobility with its reservation system, in which Scheduled Castes were entitled to a certain number of seats in universities and coveted government positions.

A quarter of spots reserved for the lowest castes, the rest dominated by the highest class, but what about someone like Ashok: one of the vast, forgotten middle? In that qualified population of hundreds of millions, you had to set yourself apart with excellence *and* have good luck, and only one of these was in your sphere of control. And for Ashok, no matter how hard he worked, the level of excellence that would set him apart from everyone else seemed out of reach. Ashok was unsure of himself around Priya when they were introduced, conscious of his family's modest background and lower caste. But after they came to know each other better, Priya told him this was precisely what she liked about him: his scrappiness (his word, not hers), which represented a kind of dynamism.

"Change," she'd said. "The potential to *change* your path and your fate. That is more important than anything. If you can progress from where you are, you will always be fine."

Ashok watched his older brother graduate at the top of his class and go on to the Indian Institute of Technology, that brass ring of all academic achievement and a golden ticket in India or anywhere in the world. He had never seen his parents so proud as the day his brother left home for university. His father always reminded his sons to bear their family name with honor, even though it had never opened a single door for him in India. Ashok didn't have the same marks as his brother, but he was determined to make up for it with drive, hard work, and ingenuity.

It was ingenuity that led him to identify certain graduate programs in America: less popular programs at mid-ranked universities, where he was more likely to gain admittance and funding. And it worked. Within a year of his marriage to Priya, he had a student visa and sponsorship to attend a graduate program in Southern California, their own golden ticket.

6

Saturday
6:00 p.m.–7:00 p.m.

THE ORANGE COUNTY Jail was downtown, in a seedy part of the city the Shahs had never had occasion to visit. Just a few blocks away from the hip restaurants, nightclubs, and fun-seeking pedestrians, the streets transformed to graffiti-sprayed walls and flashing neon signs for liquor stores and motels. The block adjacent to the jail was populated by four different storefronts advertising bail bondsmen and no other type of business.

As Ashok tightly gripped the steering wheel, Priya navigated using her phone's GPS. When at last they reached the address she'd found for the county jail, Ashok slowed down. They stared at the one-story-tall metal gate with an oversize insignia of a sheriff's badge and a sign declaring No Public Entry.

"We'll have to park somewhere and find the entrance on foot," Ashok said. He slowly drove away, past a man sitting up against the next building with a brown-paper-wrapped bottle in his lap. Ashok swallowed and scanned the area. Garbage littered the sidewalks, and the street parking was filled with beaten-up cars. He occasionally felt self-conscious of his Camry in Pacific Hills, populated with its Teslas and German iron, but here his modest sedan stood out for its full paint coat and intact hubcaps.

Ashok circled the area for a parking lot that appeared safe, as Priya grew more anxious with passing time. He found an outdoor lot two blocks away, unmanned but requiring patrons to stuff cash into the small metal slot of a central box. Ashok double-checked that the car was locked, and Priya clutched her purse across her body as they left the lot. They traversed a darkened highway overpass, where a tent was lodged on the sidewalk. As they approached, the tent flaps rustled, and a man with a ruddy face and a nest of hair lunged out. Ashok grabbed Priya's hand and pulled her into the middle of the road. The risk of getting hit by a car on these abandoned streets seemed preferable to a violent encounter. But the man didn't look up as they passed by, apparently talking only to himself. Back on the sidewalk, garbage was strewn everywhere. They passed what appeared to be an abandoned meal: a bottle of ketchup, Fritos dip, french fries, and a banana carefully placed atop a sheet of newspaper.

They finally identified the jail entrance after seeing a woman in uniform out front, speaking on the phone in an urgent tone of voice. A nondescript metal barrier in front of the building displayed a sign that read: No Parking. Jail Entrance. As two overhead cameras trained angry red lights directly on them, Ashok tried to picture his son inside this place. It required both hands to pull open the heavy metal door.

On the other side of that door, it was a busy Saturday night. The jail lobby was filled with people who were rough from living on the streets, from the vagaries of addiction, stained by previous crimes and accustomed to being forgotten. The collective stench of body odor and stale liquor wafted through the area. When the Shahs passed through those doors, still dressed from their dinner party—Ashok in a crisp shirt and Priya in her silk embroidered salwar top—it was clear they didn't belong.

Inside, they tried to make sense of the mass of people waiting in the lobby lines. Each chained-off line led to a window with a clear full enclosure, behind which sat a person. Some windows were labeled Professional Visitors, but most were not, and after some discussion, Priya and Ashok decided to stand in one of these. Seven or eight people were ahead of them, and the line was unbearably slow.

As they waited, Ashok took in the unfamiliar surroundings. The windowless room had gray cinder-block walls. Weak fluorescent lighting overhead cast a dingy pallor over the whole space. There was no place to sit, no vending machine, no water fountain, and a sign announcing that there were no restrooms. Oddly, it seemed to him, one of the only things in the lobby was a pair of ATM machines, right next to each other.

Every wall was plastered with bold-lettered signs prohibiting smoking, food, drink, photos, drugs, cell phones. Notices to bail bond agents stated it was unlawful to solicit any person for bail in any prison or jail. One sign advised visitors going to the fourth floor to check out a gun locker key at window #6. Another displayed a reference to California Penal Code section 4571: "It is a felony for anyone who has been previously sentenced to prison for a felony conviction to enter the grounds of a state prison without the warden's consent."

To counter his discomfort, Ashok tried to smile at a woman in the next line, resting her weight on a walker with tennis ball feet. Her smile back revealed several missing teeth.

As they drew closer to the front of the line, a poster tacked up on the wall behind the shielded desks came into view. It was the same one that hung over the copy machine in Ashok's office: the image portrayed a single drop of water and the ripples emanating from it. The word *Attitude* was printed in large letters across the image, with an inspirational quote below: "A positive attitude has a ripple effect. Change your attitude and you change your world." The poster had been left behind by the last company that had rented Ashok's office space. He decided to keep it up, taping over a small tear, even though it was faded from the sun. Ashok had thought this was the kind of thing he should be doing as a manager. He made a mental note now to take it down when he returned to the office.

When it was finally their turn to approach the window, Priya spoke before Ashok could open his mouth. "We're here to pick up our son. Ajay Shah? I received a call that he's here."

The woman sitting behind the clear shield was Black and middle-aged with tight-cropped hair. She wore a name badge that read Shirley. She glanced down at some papers on her desk, then up at her computer screen, and typed something. Her voice was crackly through the small round metal speaker. "Spell the last name?"

Ashok did so, in sharp punctuated letters, leaning forward to direct his words through the small speaker in the shield. "He's only twelve years old."

Without taking her eyes off the screen, Shirley said, "I don't see him here. If he's a minor, he's probably over at the juvenile facility. You might want to check there." Again, her words came through the speaker crackled up and difficult to discern, as theirs must have sounded to her. How could they make this woman understand the truth and urgency of their situation?

"No, I . . ." Priya was flustered, now scrolling through her phone. "He told me he was here. The officer who called me. He specifically said, 'County jail. Downtown.'"

The phone rang and Shirley moved to answer it. "You'll have to wait." She nodded toward the back of the room where people were standing. "I'll take a look." She answered the phone and began a conversation Ashok could not make out, in the same disinterested tone. It might be the worst day of his family's life, but it was just another day at work for her, he realized.

"Come on." Ashok led Priya away by the elbow as he tried to think. It was important to stay calm, to show respect to those in power. Ashok knew his fate always rested with the authority figure opposite him. Once, in his first year of graduate school, Ashok had to make a quick unexpected trip home after the death of Priya's uncle. Someone from their family had to be there, and Priya suggested that he go. Though it was her Babu uncle who had died, she and Ashok were considered a family unit now, and it was more customary for men to be present at death rituals.

Ashok was returning to the US when border officials at LAX detained him for several hours. His student visa was expiring at the end of the school term, after which it would be renewed for the following year. September 11 had been six months earlier, and the national wounds were still raw. All the immigration officer saw in Ashok was a brown face entering his country with the potential to overstay his visa. Ashok quickly tamped down his sense of indignation and adopted a compliant manner, while frantically trying to track down someone from the university's foreign student office on a Sunday. The officer rummaged carelessly through Ashok's suitcase and pulled out a vintage book of Sanskrit poetry Ashok had found at a secondhand bookshop. "What's this—Arabic?" the officer asked, thumbing through the book before confiscating it.

Ashok was kept waiting for hours in a glass-enclosed room. He sat upright in the hard plastic chair the entire time, unwilling to nod off or try to get comfortable. Fortunately, he'd just had his monthly haircut and cleaned his fingernails before the cremation ceremony, so he looked presentable. When he tried to inquire how long he would be held, Ashok was told he'd have to wait until they could get confirmation of his immigration status, even if that was overnight. Ashok was too nervous to ask for food or water, or even to use the bathroom. This was before cell phones, and he had no way to communicate with Priya, who was waiting at the airport for him and would be frantic.

After six long hours—exhausted, famished, and parched after enduring thirty hours of travel—the officer tossed Ashok's passport and visa down on the table. "Make sure you book your return flight before that expires," he'd said in a menacing tone.

Ashok was still shaking when he emerged from the innards of the airport to meet an anxious Priya, waiting for him on the other side of the divide. He had spent eight months in this country, feeling fortunate to be here, but also deserving. He had earned a spot in his program, alongside Americans and other foreigners. He was doing well in his classes, earning good grades, adhering to all the rules, and fulfilling all his responsibilities. And yet, with that single encounter, the precariousness of his situation and the fragility of his future were clear.

This feeling of vulnerability had never entirely gone away, even after nearly two decades in America, even after taking his oath of citizenship. The first time he'd proudly shown his American passport at the border, Ashok was advised by the immigration officer to take more

English classes to lose his accent, now that he was a citizen. No matter what his papers said, he was a visitor here, at the mercy of whoever guarded his path with a badge and gun.

Standing in the lobby of the Orange County Jail, Ashok had hoped things would be different for his son in this country, born and raised as an American.

7

Saturday
6:00 p.m.–7:00 p.m.

IN THE ADJACENT county sheriff's building, Officer Mateo Diaz peered at a computer screen as his partner approached.

"You find the parents?" O'Reilly asked.

Diaz nodded without taking his eyes off the screen.

"What's the problem?"

Diaz rubbed his eyes. "Turns out he's *twelve*, Jim. Just a kid. I thought he looked young in the face."

"Did *you* see a government-issued ID?" O'Reilly said. "Anyway, kids commit crimes too. Better safe than sorry—you hesitate, might be the last mistake you ever get to make." He hiked his pants up by the belt loops. "Coming to dinner? We're going to Cappelli's."

"Nah, you go ahead." Diaz turned back to the screen. "I'm going stay here and finish up the report."

"Suit yourself," O'Reilly said. "Chicken and ribs special tonight, if you change your mind."

Diaz's smile dissolved as O'Reilly walked away. He was troubled by what might have happened earlier if he hadn't pulled his partner aside when he'd been questioning the boy at the scene.

"What the hell, Diaz?" O'Reilly had snapped at him. "He's just about to talk. I feel it."

"He asked for his parents, Jim."

"*No*, he asked where his mother was," O'Reilly had said. "He did not ask *for* her or for a lawyer. There's a difference. Anyway, does this guy look like a minor to you? He's taller than both of us."

They arrested the young man and took him into custody.

After twenty years on the job, I trust my judgment, O'Reilly often said, and Diaz understood the importance of this. If you showed up to a call for an erratic person in a crowded area and didn't anticipate how to react if he had a gun or knife, or was just so tweaked on drugs that he was a weapon himself, you'd be dead. Worse yet, civilians could be dead. Cops had to exercise their judgment, rely on instinct. Sometimes, he worried that O'Reilly's strong convictions created blind spots. Still, raised in a military family, Mateo Diaz had been taught respect for authority, and that included his senior partner.

Mateo was thirteen years old when his father returned from his second tour of duty in Afghanistan. Before his father had been deployed, Mateo had known a man who got excited about balancing three scoops of ice cream on a single cone and trying to eat it all before it melted. But his father had come back from war a different man—not as bad as some of the other men on base, who drank too much or picked fights. Mateo's father just grew very quiet and turned inward. A year after he returned, he left the army and found a job in private security at a small sports arena. But he found it too stressful to handle all those interactions with people, and finally asked to become a janitor in the same arena, where he still worked to this day.

Mateo's older brother could remember those earlier good years too, the father who'd carried them on his shoulders at the Fourth of July parade, who painstakingly filled water balloons for the kids to throw at the barbecue afterward. But their younger brother, five years old when their father deployed, only knew the sullen man who came back.

War brings out the worst in people, Mateo's father had said to him when he was a little older. *No—actually, war shows us the worst that was already there. They taught us our enemy was evil, but we did exactly the same things to their people when we had the chance. They radicalize their kids, and then our job was to kill those kids. Kids younger than you.* He tousled Mateo's hair with a vacant, faraway look in his eyes. *Do some good at home instead, mijo.*

There was plenty that needed cleaning up right at home. When their family moved off base, it was into a rough multiethnic neighborhood. Mateo's high school was populated by gangs, drugs, and crime. His friends were a ragtag crew of Black, Vietnamese, and Mexican kids whose parents were either gone, strung out, or working around the clock. They hung out in one another's garages and basements, listening to music and smoking joints that Mateo always passed on. He learned the nuances of West Coast vs. East Coast rap, and that "Just a Friendly Game of Baseball" wasn't really about America's favorite pastime.

When Mateo looked around his neighborhood, he saw needs everywhere: roads to be fixed, grocery stores too far away, schools using worn-out books. But the first line of defense, he saw, was the streets. The streets had to be safe before anything else could get better. When he graduated from high school, Mateo was the first in his family to break ranks and join the civilian force. By then, his older brother had already bought into the family business, having grown up on the base among other military kids. He enlisted the day he turned eighteen and was now serving in the same unrelenting war that had transformed their father.

By the time Mateo finished the last section of the report, signed it, and submitted the file, his stomach was grumbling. He pulled a few bills from his wallet and smoothed them out for the vending machine. He would pick up an extra candy bar for the kid; he wanted to check on him before the parents arrived. Diaz stood up from the desk, with the desperation of that mother's voice still echoing in his ears.

8

Saturday
6:00 p.m.–7:00 p.m.

IN TIJUANA, POLICE officers were walking the length of the barricades. "Okay, folks. Time to pack it in," one of them said, a hand on the baton at his hip. "Move on out and go home."

What happened next would be rumored and debated for some time. Since the TV cameras had left, there was no official footage, but there were shaky cell phone video clips and personal reports. There was hearsay and anger and confusion.

What was clear was the shout that came from somewhere back in the crowd, "*You* go home, PIGS!" and the glass bottle sailing through the air until, with uncanny precision, it collided with the police officer's forehead.

Deepa saw the slow-motion unfolding of confusion on the cop's face as he looked down at the glass shards and touched his temple, his fingers coming away covered with blood. In that suspended moment, she felt Paco grab her by the arm and pull them back from the barricades.

The scene erupted like a lit match. Suddenly, there were two . . . six . . . *twelve* cops in front of them, weapons drawn, batons and yellow Tasers pointed at the crowd.

Even as Paco was trying to pull Deepa away, the throng of people pressed them forward. Protesters lunged past them and leaped over the barricades. Deepa looked back over her shoulder and saw a cop slam his baton onto the shoulder of a young man, who crumpled to the ground. She cried out as she felt Paco's hand slip out of hers.

ONE HOUR LATER, Deepa was sitting amidst other protesters on the ground, their hands zip-tied behind their backs. She and Paco had been separated in the crowd, and while they could glimpse each other, they were too far away to speak. She could tell from Paco's face that he was worried. He tried not to make trouble for his mother; to be helpful with his younger sisters, do well in school, earn money on weekends with lawn work and odd jobs.

Deepa was worried too. Her parents had a tendency to overreact to everything, to believe the worst about her. When she was thirteen, they had sent her to India for the summer as a punishment. She had been nearing the end of middle school, and her two best friends from eighth grade were scattering to different high schools: one moving away because her father was in the military; the other, a talented drummer going to an arts magnet school. The three girls had decided, in a move of friendship solidarity, to get piercings at a tattoo parlor near school.

Deepa forged her mother's signature on the consent form. It was her body, Deepa reasoned, and she should be able to do what she wanted with it. The whole idea of parental consent was outdated. And a piercing was less permanent than a tattoo, at least. If she changed her mind, she could just let the hole close up. One of the girls was piercing her ear cartilage, the other her nose. Deepa chose her belly button solely because it would be easier to hide from her parents, rather than from any real desire to have it pierced. And she may have gotten away with it too, if she hadn't developed an infection at the site. When the wound grew painfully red and swollen, she was forced to tell her mother.

Before Deepa was finished with the ten-day course of antibiotics, her parents had booked her on a flight to Mumbai. They told her she was going for six weeks to stay with her mother's family. She had two cousins, her uncle Manu's daughters, whom she recalled only vaguely from previous visits as bespectacled bookworms. They were serious students who received extra tutoring during the summer. Deepa would join them for their lessons every day and get a jump start on her high school math and science curriculum. In a single blow, all her summer plans were swept away: the theater arts camp and surfing lessons with friends.

It was the second time they'd sent Deepa off to India by herself, though she had no memory of the first. That time, when she had been only one year old, hadn't ever really been explained to Deepa's satisfaction. Each time Deepa didn't fit neatly with her parents' life plans, it seemed, they sent her away. She couldn't help feeling that whatever success her parents had found in America was divorced from her—they could make the progress they desired only when she was out of the picture. By the time she returned from India, the piercing had closed up. Her parents never mentioned the transgression again, but Deepa knew she'd been marked by it; they considered her a lost cause and instead began investing their hopes in her younger siblings.

So, Deepa hadn't dared to tell her parents about the border protest. This one, like the others she'd attended without incident, *had* been peaceful. They just should have left before the chaos broke out, before some strung-out activist from LA decided to throw his damn kombucha bottle. Now she had to get home before her parents knew where she'd been. Deepa couldn't see her watch, but she knew she should have left long ago to pick up Maya and Ajay.

She felt her phone vibrating in her pocket but was powerless to check it. It would probably be Maya with some snarky comment, asking her to wait at the end of the Bakers' block so no one would see her beat-up Corolla. But rather than her usual irritation toward her sister, Deepa now felt only remorse, and her eyes began to well up. As she sat on the ground, gravel digging into her ankles below the hem of her jeans, the air growing cooler on her bare arms, the calls and messages on her phone grew more persistent.

9

Saturday
7:00 p.m.–8:00 p.m.

PRIYA WAS STANDING in a corner of the jail lobby when the door banged open and a drunken, rambling man entered. She stumbled backward and met the wall, then felt Ashok moving her away from the commotion. Uniformed corrections officers appeared quickly to restrain the man and escort him out. Priya took a couple of deep breaths to calm herself, then turned back to her phone.

"Did you find the name?" Ashok whispered, leaning over her shoulder.

"No!" Priya said, flustered. "I have the call right here on my phone, but he didn't say his name. I didn't . . . He just said . . . I *told* you what he said." Her voice rose with emotion as she leaned against a prescription drug drop box.

"I'll get in line again," Ashok said. "Maybe someone else will know something."

"Wait," Priya called after him. "Don't leave me here."

As they stood in front of a different window, Priya could see into the office behind the clear shield. In the distance, a counter held two pizza boxes. Next to the industrial-style wall clock was a placard proclaiming the mission statement: "We provide the highest quality detention processing and customer service to the community."

"Mr. Shaw?" Shirley called out a common mispronunciation of their name.

"Yes." Ashok strode over to her window and Priya followed, feeling a flutter of anticipation that all of this could be cleared up.

"I found your son in the system," Shirley said, looking at her screen. "A.J.?"

"Yes, Ajay. Oh, good," Ashok said.

"We'll take him home, then." Priya tucked her phone back into her purse.

"He's here," Shirley said. "But you'll have to wait until he's processed."

"Processed? For what?" Priya asked. Ashok shot her a warning look, which she disregarded. This was their *son*—she was going to say and do whatever was necessary.

Shirley finally looked away from her screen and made eye contact with them.

"After an arrest, the sheriff's office has to file its report, complete the paperwork, determine bail—"

"Arrest?" Priya cried. "What could he have been arrested for? There must be a misunderstanding. He's tall for his age, but he's just a boy." Her voice cracked.

"Where is he right now?" Ashok said, pointing at the doors behind Shirley. "Is he in there? Can we just see him? This must be a mistake. I'm sure we can clear it up quickly."

"He's being processed, and you'll have to wait until that's done," Shirley said, her tone cold now.

"You have to let us see him. He's a minor! It's the law."

Priya wondered how her husband could be so certain about this—from watching television shows? What did they know about American laws? In India, corruption was rampant, bribery was commonplace, and everyone looked the other way at both. A country of over a billion people, all striving to get ahead or just survive, simply could not be all that regulated.

"Mr. and Mrs. Shaw, you'll have to sit down and wait. There's nothing else I can tell you right now. He's been arrested, he's being processed, then he'll be arraigned within forty-eight hours."

Priya felt her chest heavy with weight. "*Forty-eight . . .* that's how long he'll be in that jail? Before we can *see* him?"

"At the outside, not including weekend days. And since it's Saturday—"

"How can we get him out before then? There must be a way. Someone I can talk to?" Ashok asked.

"After booking, they might offer bail. That's not up to me, Mr. Shaw." Shirley looked past them, at the rest of the line.

"Who decides that? Can I talk to them?" Ashok said.

Shirley just shook her head, picked up a pen, and began writing in the notebook on her desk. "Mr. Shaw, we'll call you. You'll have to wait."

Priya closed her eyes for a long moment before turning away. Ashok placed a hand on her back as they left the window, but she took no comfort in this. "This is a nightmare," she said. "Why won't they let us see him?"

"It's a misunderstanding. We'll sort it out," Ashok said, projecting a confidence she knew he couldn't possibly feel. "You know how he is—"

"I know—*that's* what I'm worried about," Priya interrupted. "They don't know how to talk to him. He's probably completely shut down. He must be terrified." Her phone sounded with a notification from within her purse. "Ajay," she said, searching for it frantically. Her shoulders fell, and she showed Ashok the screen—a message from Maya.

Everything good! Home now.

Ashok rubbed the bridge of his nose. They agreed not to call the girls just yet. They didn't want to worry them about Ajay, at least not until they knew something more. No use upsetting them and creating more questions they couldn't answer. For now, at least, they could take solace that their two other children were safe at home.

Ashok stood up. "I'm going to call Vikram, see if he knows a lawyer who can help us figure out what's going on."

10

Saturday
7:00 p.m.–8:00 p.m.

ASHOK PUSHED OPEN the jail door as he dialed. He knew he was testing the bounds of a relatively young friendship with Vikram, but he was desperate and didn't know where else to turn. He had met Vikram Sharma for the first time six years earlier at a networking event for Indian entrepreneurs in Orange County, though it was a stretch to consider their businesses in the same category. Vikram had founded a medical technology company and sold his products to hospitals across the country. Hundreds of employees worked in a building that brandished the BioFlex name. There was a manufacturing facility in India, as well as a laboratory that tested new products in Portland.

In contrast, Ashok's small business had grown organically out of his first job in America. At the advertising agency, his main responsibilities had been ensuring the main network backbone was functioning, periodically updating software systems and upgrading equipment. It was fairly simple work from a technical standpoint, but the agency's staff always seemed to think he performed miracles. "Ashok the Great" they nicknamed him.

After five years at that job, he could do it in his sleep. The networking industry was booming in the early 2000s, as every office space needed a steady supply of computers, printers, routers, and modems to do their work. Companies in adjacent offices asked him for help, so Ashok started moonlighting on weekends and evenings. Soon, he began to realize, there would be a widespread need for his services on an outsourced basis. He could build his own company and charge his own fees, rather than drawing a flat salary as an employee.

Perhaps being around advertising executives and overhearing their pitches for so long had seeped into his consciousness, building his confidence to start something of his own. So much of what he saw around him seemed like pure invention. If you portrayed a certain lifestyle in an advertisement alongside a particular product, you were declaring the two to be associated, whether they were or not. One day, early in his tenure at the agency, he was called to fix the projection system in the large conference room for a big client pitch and stayed to ensure it continued working.

The client was a beverage company, and the pitch was for one of their juice brands. The images on the screen showed active children—playing soccer, running through sprinklers, eating apples at a picnic. And in every image was the foil-pouched beverage, part of this fun and healthy lifestyle. It was a product Ashok had once brought home from the grocery store because it was on sale, much less expensive than the regular juice boxes Priya bought for Deepa. He'd been quite proud of himself until Priya showed him the label, which revealed that the product was not really fruit juice, but artificially flavored and colored sugar water.

Yet, here the agency was declaring that this product, with no nutritional value, should be happily consumed by young children as part of a healthy, active lifestyle. All the kids portrayed in the pitch were slender, physically fit, and had good teeth. And so, the principle of assertion in American capitalism began its appeal to him. Ashok, too, could broadcast what he wanted people to believe about him, and it would be so. He began to build his business on the side, developing a website, printing business cards, and signing a couple of his weekend jobs as his first clients. When he resigned from the ad agency, they threw him a party to wish him well.

Ten years later, he had a handful of employees, a small office/warehouse in a strip mall, and a client roster that had grown to include several local and county government agencies, who gave preference to minority-owned businesses in the bidding process. For the past few years, as the business grew rapidly, Priya began working with him part time: keeping the books, sending out invoices, and paying bills.

ASHOK WATCHED THE other Indian entrepreneurs at the event mingle amiably in the hotel courtyard and wondered how to approach Vikram Sharma, who had just been given an award by the local Chamber of Commerce. By good fortune, Vikram walked over to him and held up his Kingfisher, which matched the sweating bottle in Ashok's hand. "Can you believe we can get this over here now?" he said, and Ashok had to glance around to make sure Vikram was speaking to him. "I'm pretty sure it tasted better back home. Or maybe my palate has improved." Vikram chuckled and held out his hand to Ashok. "Vikram Sharma."

"Oh, yes," Ashok replied, shaking his hand. "I think the memories might have been better than the real thing." He took a sip. "Yes, definitely."

"Are you new to Orange County?" Vikram asked. They discussed where they lived, their wives, and their children's ages. "Ah, we were in Irvine too, when we first moved here. It's like the new immigrant ghetto—starter homes, decent schools. But we've been in Pacific Hills for a few years now and, let me tell you, it's another world." A few other men drifted into the conversation, drawn to Vikram's animated gestures.

"Here's what I mean," Vikram said. "Right after we moved in, our SUV was parked on the street since our garage was still full of moving boxes. At seven o'clock in the morning, a neighbor knocks on our door. She'd been out walking her dog and saw a pickup truck hit the back of our SUV. I look out to the street and, sure enough, the back corner of our bumper is all crumpled. So, this woman hands me a slip of paper with a license plate number on it. She tells me she already called the police to report it. Then she *apologizes* to me because we're new to the neighborhood and says we'll really love it there."

One of the other men laughed and shook his head.

"I go out to see the car and it's pretty bad," Vikram said. "The whole bumper's going to have to be replaced, like a couple thousand dollars of damage. So"—he held up an index finger—"within an hour, the doorbell rings again, and it's two police officers. They ask me what happened, take photos of the car, the license plate. I was a bit panicked, even though I did nothing wrong. I've never been questioned by the police before and it's nerve-racking, you know?"

The other men nodded and murmured agreement. Ashok had been pulled over only once for a broken taillight; he sat nervously as the cop wrote out his ticket, and the feeling didn't subside until after he'd safely gotten home.

Vikram placed his empty bottle on a nearby table. "They ask me to get a repair estimate and send it over to them, which I do. Then I kind of forget all about it because we're still unpacking and we barely leave the house for a while. But a couple of days later, the cops come back and hand me a cashier's check. For the full amount of the repair!" Vikram looked around the circle. "They tracked the guy down—some laborer on a construction site a couple of blocks over—and strong-armed him into coming up with the money. Probably cost more than his old pickup truck. I felt kind of bad, but can you believe that? I didn't have to lift a finger, call insurance, anything! It's like having your own private security force in Pacific Hills."

"Yeah, but what did you have to slip them?" one of the men asked, rubbing the tips of his thumb and fingers together to imply a bribe.

"Nothing!" Vikram bellowed. "The cops here are honest, not like India."

There was universal disbelief in the group as the men chuckled and shook their heads. Everything from the vigilant neighbor to the bloodhound cops was unfathomable in the neighborhood where Ashok and many of the other Indian families lived. The homes were older bungalows, and the residents were split between retirees living out their days protected from property tax increases, and younger families attracted to the good, yet still affordable, school district. The way people showed off in their neighborhood was with a well-groomed lawn and seasonal flowers, perhaps a new car in the driveway. But mostly, if they could afford to, families like Ashok's wanted to move out to something better as soon as they could.

After many years, Priya and Ashok had finally managed to do just that. The Sharmas had shown them around Pacific Hills and helped them find a good realtor. They'd been generous and welcoming after the Shahs moved to the new house, bringing over biryani the first night and some potted plants for their doorstep.

Ashok envied the confidence with which Vikram carried himself and the success that seemed to accompany him. As they came to know each other better, he learned that Vikram had been raised in privileged circles of Indian society; his grandfather was an important government minister, and Sharma was an esteemed Brahmin surname. It was unlikely their paths would have crossed in India—as equals, as friends. Yet here they were. On the level playing field of American society, Ashok was relieved to find caste irrelevant, and it was a constraint he was only too eager to leave behind. He had managed to not only rise above the limitations he faced back home, but to climb the ladder rungs of this great country to a perch that would make his father proud. Moving into Pacific Hills represented the culmination of all his and Priya's hard work since coming to America, at least until Deepa had thrown a wrench into their dreams.

Now, shivering on the sidewalk outside the jail, Ashok willed Vikram to answer the phone, hoping his friend could produce another miracle.

11

Saturday
7:00 p.m.–8:00 p.m.

AS PRIYA WAITED anxiously for Ashok to return from his phone call, she chided herself for believing that life would be easier after the move. In actuality, there had been challenges from the beginning. Two months earlier, still surrounded by unopened boxes in their new house—the one they had, through persistence and good fortune, been able to purchase just weeks before the school registration deadline—Deepa had made a pronouncement. "I shouldn't have to switch schools," she said. "It's not fair."

"Not fair?" Priya snapped, wiping perspiration from her forehead with a sleeve. They hadn't yet turned on the air conditioning, and the afternoon heat was gathering inside the house like a swell. "It's not fair for you to go to the top high school in the county? One of the best in California?" She returned to the cartons that held their carefully packed kitchen goods. A few minutes earlier, she had been full of energy for the task of unwrapping every dish and glass, washing and stowing them in the cupboards. The excitement of their new home had kept her buoyant through the tedious weeks of packing and moving, but Deepa had now managed to slash through all that.

"Mom, I'm happy at Chavez, and this is my junior year. It doesn't make sense for me to switch now. I've picked my classes; I know my teachers. I don't want to start over at a new school. It's not fair," Deepa repeated.

Fair! As if her children knew anything about fairness or justice. They had lived their entire lives without seeing the oppression she and Ashok had grown up with, where the wrong surname or lineage could doom you to a certain path in life. Where how your grandfather made a living or the village your people once came from could render it difficult to escape your destiny. In a country riddled with illiteracy and poverty, crippled by dysfunctional government and poor infrastructure, the only honest way to get ahead was through education, a gift her daughter was now disparaging.

Priya turned to Deepa, trying a softer approach. "You'll learn to be comfortable at Pacific Hills. You'll make new friends there." She placed her hands on her daughter's shoulders.

Deepa shrugged off her touch. "I don't want new friends. I have friends. No one makes new friends junior year. No one has to switch schools this late. It's stupid."

Priya hated that word—she thought it was disrespectful, and perhaps this was why her daughter used it so casually. She turned back to the cartons and began slicing through the sealing tape with swift, violent movements. "Have you unpacked the cartons in your room, Deepa? Unless you want to sleep on the floor tonight." With her next swipe, the blade ran into her left thumb, and a bright line of blood appeared in its path. The utility knife clattered to the floor. "Damn!" She reached over to put her bleeding hand under the kitchen faucet and glanced around until she spotted the paper towels. Wordlessly, Deepa retrieved the roll and tore off a sheet for Priya, who tightly wrapped up her thumb.

ANOTHER FULL WEEK of relentless lobbying from Deepa ensued. Both Priya and Ashok believed unequivocally it was best for Deepa to attend Pacific Hills, but she was wearing them down with her obstinacy. In their minds, parents always chose what was right for their children, and children obediently accepted this. But Deepa was nearly seventeen and had spent much of her life in this country, where children were raised to have their own opinions. Despite their efforts to instill *their* values, American influences had clearly seeped into their eldest daughter's personality, and how much could they do about that now?

Finally, Ashok decided to visit both high schools to discuss the matter, hoping for more ammunition to convince their daughter. The counselor at Cesar Chavez confirmed that Deepa was doing well there and was slated to take all the advanced classes offered by the school. She acknowledged there were only two college counselors for the school's graduating class of over six hundred, and, yes, this meant each student would get less attention. But Deepa had a high class rank; her teachers knew her and would be able to provide good recommendations.

The discussion with the Pacific Hills counselor was more sobering. By transferring in her junior year, Deepa would be at a disadvantage compared to students who had been maxing out their weighted classes for two years already. Though all her credits would transfer from Chavez, her relative GPA would put her somewhere in the middle of her new class. Her peers had established track records in their clubs and athletic teams, and most leadership positions had already been determined.

"The truth is, Mr. Shah," the counselor said, "it could hurt your daughter's college prospects to switch schools at this point. It might make more sense for her to graduate from Chavez High."

Ashok wondered if the counselor just said those things to keep Deepa out of this country club school—he couldn't quite rid himself of the idea that he was being judged for some intrinsic, unchangeable quality. He'd been kept out of places all his life, first in India because he didn't have the right caste or connections, then in the US because of his immigration status or skin color or accent. The idea of walking away from a privileged place by choice was inconceivable to him.

12

Saturday
7:00 p.m.–9:00 p.m.

BEING WITH PACO at the border now, Deepa knew it had been the right move for her to stay at Chavez High. Though her parents had relented in the end, they made it clear they wouldn't go out of their way to help her. Deepa got a job at an artisanal ice cream shop, where customers tipped generously and she could clear over a hundred dollars a day. By summer's end, she'd saved enough to buy a secondhand Toyota Corolla so she could drive herself to school in their old neighborhood, twenty minutes away. She couldn't imagine being happy at Pacific Hills, where Maya now dressed and did her hair exactly like everyone else, like those Instagram influencers she followed. Her sister spent hours flat-ironing her naturally wavy hair until she didn't even resemble herself.

As the sky grew dark, the police began questioning the protesters one at a time. Deepa was taken to a small gray room with a single open window, where an officer patted her down, then took her identification and phone before leaving her alone, wrists still tied.

When he returned, he tossed her driver's license and phone onto the table. "You're a long way from Pacific Hills," he said with derision, snipping the zip-ties with blunt scissors. "I'm giving you a warning this time, but stay out of trouble. You still have a provisional permit and a driving curfew."

Deepa rushed back to her car, parked in the dirt lot adjacent to the border crossing. She prayed Paco would be released soon as well and they could get out of there. Once she was safely locked inside the Corolla, she let herself cry, fear and anxiety flooding through her. Her phone screen was filled with messages and missed calls from Maya. The last message said that she had found a ride home, so Deepa should feel free to enjoy herself, the words seeping with sarcasm.

She had a single missed call from her mother, who would be furious. Deepa dreaded facing her. No one had mentioned Ajay, but her parents must have gotten him from school, as robotics had ended over an hour ago. Deepa placed her hands on the steering wheel and pressed her body back into the seat, trying not to imagine what awaited her at home.

Not only did Deepa's parents not know about the protest, but they also didn't know about the extent or depth of her friendship with Paco. Deepa had met Paco in their ninth grade advanced English class, in which they reenacted Shakespearean plays and learned poetry composition. In that poetry workshop, they had been paired up by the teacher to provide feedback on each other's work. Paco was broad-shouldered and athletic, exuding Latin machismo like many guys at their school. So, she was surprised by his tender poem—about the beauty of someone's smile, how it could melt him inside and make him feel weak, using the metaphor of a bird flying away when the person's smile faded.

Deepa gave him a few suggestions for line breaks and word choices, then boldly asked, "So, who is she?" The way his face flushed involuntarily, and the brief flicker of fear that passed over it, somehow helped her understand the truth in an instant. "Or *he*?" she said softly. Paco wouldn't meet her eyes, shuffling his papers back into the binder until the bell rang, and they dispersed from class without another word.

But slowly, as they spent more time together over the rest of that school year and the next, Paco came to trust her with his secret—the one he was only just beginning to admit to himself, the one he kept from his Catholic parents to spare them any more anguish. Deepa was struck by how he didn't seem to hold any resentment over this. They both came to rely on their friendship, sharing secret crushes, worries about their future, frustrations with their parents, indignation over current events.

Deepa's parents were reticent about all boys. Of course, there was nothing to be worried about on that front; not only was Paco safe, but he also served as her informal protector. But Deepa didn't share this with her parents. It wasn't hers to share, and she didn't want to give them more reason to think less of Paco. He was already from a poor Mexican family, raised by an undocumented mother. She didn't tell her parents this last fact, either.

Finally, she spotted Paco in the distance. He was shivering as he hurried across the dirt lot, his hands jammed tightly into his pockets, his eyes trained on the ground. As he drew close, Deepa jumped out and walked toward him, holding her arms open. But Paco only moved briskly toward the passenger side of the car and opened the door.

"Let's go. It's late," he muttered.

"What . . . happened?" Deepa started tentatively, climbing back into the car. "Did . . . ?"

Paco stared straight ahead through the windshield. "Can we please just go?" His voice was small.

Deepa watched him for a few long moments, then started the ignition and began to drive. As the distance from the border grew, Paco began to breathe deeply. Once they pulled onto the highway, she tried again. "Can you tell me what happened?"

Paco gazed out the window for a few beats before exhaling. "Well, first they patted me down pretty, uh, *aggressively*. And took every single item out of my pockets and wallet.

"Then they gave me their taco orders in a fake accent. Followed by the standard drug-running jokes about me crossing back and forth to Tijuana. Then they left me in the room alone forever without letting me use the bathroom. Finally, they came back, tossed all my stuff onto the table, and told me to stay out of trouble and off the streets." He closed his eyes and leaned his head back against the seat.

Deepa looked over at him. "Off the streets?" She laughed. "Well, obviously, they had no idea who they were talking to. I can barely get you out of the library." She meant it lightheartedly, but she saw Paco flinch.

"Hey," she said, putting a hand on his knee. "They did the same thing to me, gave me a warning. They're just trying to scare us. Don't let them get in your head. You have every right to express your political opinion."

"Don't you understand?" Paco snapped. "It's not the same for me, Deepa. What if they arrested me and called my mom because I'm a minor? And they asked her about her status? What if they come to my home to check up on me next week, and she answers the door? Even though I'm safe, she's not. And what would happen if they find her because of some"—he waved his hand futilely—"some stupid *protest* I went to. Do you think that's worth her getting deported and my sisters and I being left here alone?" His voice trembled with anger, and he turned his head to look out the window.

"I'm sorry, Paco," Deepa said. "I'm sorry. I know, it sucks."

"That's just it, Deepa," he said quietly. "You *don't* know. You can't possibly."

They drove mostly in silence the rest of the way home, Deepa switching between the radio stations occasionally to fill the quiet. When they passed the neighborhood where Paco's family used to live before his father died, she saw his gaze drift out the window. Deepa pulled into the parking lot of his apartment building and turned to him with a hopeful look, which he disregarded.

"See you Monday." Paco slung his bag over his shoulder as he headed toward his family's shared apartment, without glancing back.

13

Saturday
9:00 p.m.

A TALL WHITE man entered the jail lobby and glanced around. He was smartly dressed in a sport coat, having been out to dinner with his wife and two other couples when he'd received the call from Vikram, asking for a favor. Once he spotted Ashok and Priya, he strode over to them and extended his hand. "Mr. Shah?"

"Yes," Ashok said. "And this is my wife, Priya."

"Jonathan Stern. I'm not a criminal attorney, but Mr. Sharma is a good friend and client, so I'll do what I can to help you out tonight, hopefully get your son home."

"Thank you for coming," Ashok said.

"Please, we *have* to get him out," Priya said. "He's already been here for hours."

Stern nodded. "I know you must be worried. As you can see, county jail can get pretty busy on weekends, so unfortunately things can take a while," Stern explained. "Once someone's brought here to the station, they go through all the steps in the booking process before we can get much information. That means photographs, fingerprints, body search." He saw Priya's stricken eyes and put a hand on her elbow. "I know it can be hard to wait, but the police have to write up the arrest report, determine charges and bail, see if there's a lawyer—all that can take several hours. That's what's been happening here this evening. Saturday night, people are out drinking, things get backed up . . . And you have no idea why he was arrested?"

Priya shook her head.

"Did you tell them you're here for Ajay, as our lawyer?" Ashok asked.

"I'll do that now," Stern said, nodding toward the Professional Visitors line. "Once he's booked, I can see the arrest report. For most misdemeanors—trespassing, drug possession, petty theft—they won't keep him in custody. They'll let him go with nominal or no bail. So that's most likely what we're looking at."

"He would never do any of that," Priya muttered.

"We can pay, whatever the amount," Ashok added.

Jonathan Stern nodded. "If the prosecutor moves forward, they'll tell us when the arraignment is, and that's when we'll hear the specific charges. But for a misdemeanor, for a juvenile, let's hope it won't come to that."

"How can they keep him like this, as a minor?" Ashok rubbed at his forehead. "Isn't that a violation of his rights?"

"They do have to call if a juvenile asks for his parents, but they may not have known when they picked him up. You said he's quite tall for his age? Would he have had any identification on him?"

"Why would he have ID?" Priya snapped. "He's a child! He's not walking around with a passport in his pocket."

"Right," Stern continued, "so he was probably brought here as a matter of course. Adult cops, adult jail. Usually, they'd transfer him to a juvenile hall, but it sounds like they'd already called you to pick him up here. Juveniles have a different process, a different court, and sometimes those records are sealed. We can always request a transfer to the juvenile system, if it comes to that."

"They can't question him alone, can they?" Priya asked.

"Well, they might have, before they took him into custody and read him his rights," Stern said. "And they can use anything he said. They can also use any physical evidence they found to charge him."

Priya covered her face with her hands, and Ashok pulled her toward him.

Stern looked at his watch. "Okay, let me go see what I can find out."

14

Saturday
9:00 p.m.

DEEPA DROVE SLOWLY toward home, even though she was already late, already in trouble. As her car climbed into Pacific Hills, the gulf between Paco's home and her own grew more pronounced. Was she growing away from him, from her friends and her old life, just by living here? Deepa missed their neighborhood: the gritty strip malls populated by halal shops, taco stands, Korean convenience stores, Chinese dry cleaners, and Vietnamese nail salons. She missed hearing all those languages as she walked around, feeling part of a mosaic of cultures.

When she reached home, Deepa was surprised to see the garage empty. Perhaps she'd been lucky, and her parents had just dropped off her siblings and returned to their party. A small wave of relief passed over her. She would make dinner for Maya and Ajay, maybe even put on a movie and let them eat on the couch as they watched.

The house was unexpectedly quiet when she let herself in, with only one light on in the foyer. "Hello?" Deepa called out. She began to climb the stairs and saw light coming from under Maya's bedroom door. Since they'd moved into the new house, it seemed as if Maya kept her door closed all the time, reveling in her newfound privacy. From outside, she could hear the shower running in Maya's bathroom. Deepa continued down the hallway to Ajay's room and flipped on the lights. Empty. Their parents must have taken him back to their dinner party. The Sharmas had a home theater equipped with a Wii system Ajay loved. He would be in heaven.

Deepa pushed off her sneakers and tossed her backpack toward the closet before falling onto her bed. She reached down under her bed to find Panda, where she always tucked him out of sight. Clutching the stuffed animal to her chest, his matted fur pressed to her nose, she gazed at the ceiling. It could have gone terribly wrong today. Not just for Paco, but for her. Her parents would certainly give her a stern lecture when they got home later, but for this moment, right now, everything was okay. She reflected on all that had transpired today and how she'd arrived here.

EARLIER THAT WEEK, Deepa had stopped at the kitchen sink to fill her water bottle before school.

"What is this?" her mother had asked, pointing to a bold black sticker on Deepa's water bottle imprinted with the words Defund the Police. She raised an eyebrow in judgment.

"What does it look like?" Deepa said, sarcastically.

"I'm asking, what do you mean by this slogan? You want to do away with the police?"

"I think we could direct a lot of those resources to better uses, yes." Deepa nodded. "That would be a start."

"A start to what?" Her mother chuckled. "Anarchy?"

"To a better society," Deepa said. "One where the police don't gun down innocent people because of their skin color."

"Well," her mother said, "let's not be extreme. This isn't apartheid South Africa. People aren't gunned down just because of their skin color. It's a complicating factor—"

Deepa laughed. "A complicating factor? That's a nice euphemism."

"Yes, race complicates things," her mother said. "But if you're driving around with drugs in your car or stealing cigarettes from a convenience store—"

"Then you deserve to be shot by the police?" Deepa said. "Instead of just arrested or given a ticket, or let go with a warning, like most white people would be?"

"Look, most of these things happen in bad neighborhoods, where there's a lot of crime. That's why the police are there in the first place. If you just get rid of them—"

"Bad neighborhoods, because Black people live there?"

"No, bad neighborhoods because of crime and poverty—"

"So, now it's people's fault if they're poor? *That's* a crime?"

Her mother let out a dramatic sigh. "That's not what I said. But people also have to take some responsibility to make a better life. If you work hard and have the right values, you can do it."

"Ah, yes, everyone can aspire to live in a place like Pacific Hills. And since you and Dad did it, it's possible for anyone."

"Deepa, the police are there to protect us, like they did at your school last year when that riot broke out."

"It wasn't a riot, Mom. It was just a few kids getting into a fight, like kids have been doing at high school throughout time."

"And using racist Asian slurs! Who do you think is going to protect us, Deepa, if you abolish the police? Who's going to protect our home? Who's going to prevent thieves from breaking into the office or our warehouse?"

Deepa threw her hands into the air and grabbed her water bottle from the kitchen counter. "Well, I guess we're pretty lucky we're just brown and not Black then, huh? And that we get to live in Pacific Hills!" She spun around to leave.

"Not just luck, Deepa," her mother called after her. "Hard work!"

Once Deepa was out of her mother's sight, she shot her middle finger up into the air. Her mother was so *ignorant* about everything. No, it was more than that. Her mother's willful ignorance was an act of racism. Her parents didn't bother trying to see what life was like for Black people in this country, to understand the legacy of slavery and how it had reverberated through centuries of life in America: Jim Crow, voter suppression, redlined districts, underfunded public schools. Entire communities had been neglected when it came to infrastructure, from safe drinking water to access to fresh food and health care. You barely had a chance, if you were unfortunate enough to be born in one of those neighborhoods.

Their old neighborhood in Irvine was a kind of a bridge to that world, spanning between the truly forgotten neighborhoods and the gated communities like Pacific Hills. At Chavez, Deepa saw kids with single parents, like Paco, who had to help out at home with chores and younger siblings, who worked part-time after school and on weekends when Deepa was free to do schoolwork or socialize. Her parents had never gotten to know those families or even understand what it was like for them. They had their sights focused on making the most they could out of the neighborhood and trying to graduate out of there as soon as possible.

Her parents, she realized, were part of the problem. They believed they were just working their way up the socioeconomic ladder, as they were expected to as immigrants. But they never bothered to look back at who was left behind. They felt no kinship with other minorities like African Americans or Hispanic immigrants like Paco's family, no responsibility to help. Her parents thought they were better because they started in this country with a work visa and an education—but also with none of the biases Paco's family faced, getting a mortgage or buying a house, or even being hired for a job. Her parents didn't just look the other way when it came to systemic racism—they helped perpetuate it.

Blood had coursed through Deepa's body as she climbed into the Corolla. She had to do something to help set things right, to show solidarity with people who needed it, even if her parents wouldn't. She reached for her phone to text Paco, feeling her anger morph into exhilaration. *Let's do it. Tijuana Saturday.*

DEEPA'S ALARM CLOCK now glowed from her nightstand: it was after nine o'clock. She should get up and make dinner. As she walked back down the hallway, she knocked on her sister's door, behind which she now heard music, and yelled, "Maya, come down for dinner when you're done." In the kitchen, Deepa rummaged through the pantry before deciding to make a double batch of macaroni and cheese, comfort food for them both. She would ask Maya for Ajay's favorite cookie recipe, a surprise for when he got home. She would even clean the whole kitchen afterward, an unspoken apology to her parents.

Just as she was ladling the macaroni into bowls, Maya came into the kitchen, her hair damp. "I'm starving," she said, sitting down at the counter.

Deepa pushed a bowl across the counter to her sister and tried to gauge her sister's anger. "Hey, I'm sorry I wasn't there to pick you up. I was just . . ." She stopped for a moment to consider how much to share with Maya before deciding to just tell her everything. It would come out eventually. "I went down to Tijuana today, to join a protest at the border. It was mostly peaceful, but there was a bit of . . . There was some stuff that happened with the police." Was it really appropriate to lay all this on her sister, who never did anything to cross their parents?

Deepa carried her own bowl over to sit across the island from Maya. "The police made everyone stay and answer questions, so that's why I was late. I'm really sorry, M." When they had shared a room for so many years, the sisters labeled their belongings with Post-its marked with their first initial and had since called each other by those personal nicknames, M and D.

Maya seemed disinterested as she shoveled macaroni into her mouth, or at least not as angry as Deepa had expected.

"Where's Ajay?" Maya asked. "I thought you were bringing him home."

"You . . . didn't see him?" Deepa said. "I . . . I thought Mom got you both and just took him back to the Sharmas."

Maya slowly shook her head. "I haven't seen anyone. The Bakers drove me home."

Deepa felt her heart plummet. She reached for her phone and put it back down. *"Shit."* Were her parents still at their dinner party? Where was Ajay? Their little brother didn't have a phone. He had no need for one, since he only went to school and back and was driven everywhere by their parents most of the time. Deepa stood up, grabbed her car keys and wallet, and jammed her feet back into her shoes. "He might still be waiting at school."

"Wait for me!" Maya jumped up and followed her out the door.

DEEPA GRASPED THE steering wheel as she sped toward the school, rolling quickly through the stop signs at each intersection. She willed herself not to let her mind go to the worst place, to instead imagine Ajay sitting on the front steps of the middle school, reading his graphic novel or poring over a robotics drawing in his notebook.

But as Deepa's headlights swept through the parking lot and schoolyard, she saw nothing. She drove around the entire perimeter of the school, calling Ajay's name through open windows.

When they circled back to the front steps, their designated pickup spot, both sisters got out of the car. Deepa ran up the steps and looked around, while Maya searched behind the bushes and trash cans for any clue as to their brother's whereabouts. The doors to the school were locked, but something near the base of the flagpole caught Deepa's eye. She drew closer. "Look!" she called out to Maya, holding up Ajay's canary yellow water bottle. With renewed vigor, they continued searching, calling out his name, honking the car horn.

When they found nothing else, the sisters sat together on the steps of the school, the water bottle a beacon resting between them. "Okay, let's just think for a minute," Deepa said, fighting against the pressure building in her chest for the second time today. "Where would he go?"

"Maybe he decided to walk home?" Maya's normally placid face was creased with worry. "You know how he always takes the exact same route everywhere. Maybe we should check the path Mom drives home from here, past that one house with the flat roof he likes?"

Deepa blinked rapidly to hold back the tears. She was struck by how Maya, despite her seeming self-absorption, knew their little brother so well, all his quirks and eccentricities, how their mother amused him by driving out of her way to pass the modern concrete house that Ajay found so fascinating for its stark symmetry.

They got back into the car and drove slowly up and down the surrounding streets, high beams on, craning their necks to see out the window. Deepa kept glancing at her phone, willing it to ring or buzz with any news of her brother. Dread seeped into every cavity inside her body. They traced the entire path between the school and their home three times, taking the likely route, then alternates Ajay might have followed. Back in front of their own house, Deepa put the car into park and closed her eyes, trying to think.

"Should we go down the street, ringing doorbells? Or call his friends?" Maya offered.

Deepa shook her head. "He doesn't know anyone here yet. And no one knows him." Ajay didn't make friends the usual way, and he was new to this school and robotics team. Maybe one of the other parents had taken him home and told their parents? She exhaled loudly. "Okay, we have to call them." She dialed their mother's number and hit the speaker button so Maya could hear. No answer. She tried again and got voicemail. She tried their father, and his line went straight to voicemail. "Shit!" Deepa said, her throat tightening.

"Let's just go over there," Maya said, tapping at her phone. "I can find their location here, on that app. Here, I've got it."

Deepa leaned over to look at her screen. "That can't be right. The Sharmas live up in Pacific Hills, and that's all the way downtown."

Maya zoomed in on the map and names began to appear on the screen . . . Home Depot, Albertsons, El Paso Taqueria. A blue icon appeared near the dot that represented their mother's location, and Maya spoke the words slowly, looking up at Deepa. "Orange County Jail?"

15

Saturday
10:00 p.m.

SATURDAY NIGHTS WERE busy at the county jail. Many of the arrests were for drunk and disorderlies, domestic violence calls, and the occasional roadside drug bust. By that measure, this could be considered an ordinary night. But by the standards of the Shah family, none of whom had ever had any kind of real encounter with law enforcement—not so much as a speeding ticket—the night was extraordinary, indeed.

Below ground level, young Ajay sat alone on the corner of the bench in a holding cell. Once his true age had been ascertained, someone wisely decided to separate him from the other men in custody. The sounds of those other men shouting and swearing still reached him, though, and felt like daggers in his brain. Ajay tried to focus on the speckles in the concrete blocks lining the walls—first counting them, then trying to envision images that might be hidden in them, like constellations in the sky. This helped to calm him slightly, though he was still disturbed by everything that had happened tonight.

For one, the way his fingertips had been pressed into that ink pad, he knew some of the ink remained in the ridges of his skin. The average fingerprint had as many as 150 individual ridges, with a depth between 40 and 60 microns. The way that man had pushed his fingers with such pressure, Ajay was certain that some black ink had been left behind, though it might be invisible to the human eye.

Before that, they had taken him to see the nurse. His jaw was scraped and sore where he had slammed into the pavement. Blood was crusted under and inside his nose. The nurse was gentler, but the antiseptic pads she applied to his face stung as if he were being attacked by bees. He squirmed, but she held his chin firm while she applied bandages. At random moments now, he still felt twinges of that stinging sensation and tried to brush them away.

They had taken his backpack, and he was worried about Drummond. They took his belt, and now his jeans were falling down. They took his shoelaces, and his sneakers were loose on his feet.

After a long time, they took him into a room with a table and chairs, where a stern old man asked him so many questions that Ajay had to turn off his brain. Finally, the nicer young man in the blue uniform, the one who had helped pick up his bike, came into the room and replaced the mean one. This man brought him a can of root beer and sat next to him. He didn't stare straight at Ajay like everyone else had. Because the man seemed nice, Ajay told him that he wanted his mom and told him her phone number, which was easy to remember because the digits added up to fifty, the same as two quarters, which is what gumballs cost at the car wash he went to with his dad.

The nice man told him he would have to finish his root beer in that room. Since then, Ajay had been sitting in this cell alone, with people always watching him, people walking by. He was hungry and scared.

It was too much, so now he was just trying to focus on the speckles.

OUTSIDE, AJAY'S OLDER sisters were running up to the front door of the building, disregarding the grittiness of their surroundings, hoping only to find their parents and to see their little brother safe. On the way over, there was a tense silence in the car, as both girls tried not to voice their worst fears. They had each cried at different points, but neither acknowledged it to the other. Now, when they pulled open the weighty metal door to the jail and maneuvered around the snaking line of waiting people, they spotted their parents standing together with a tall white man against the side wall. The girls rushed over to their parents.

"I'm so sorry," Deepa said, in a rush.

"What are you doing here?" Priya startled at their sudden appearance.

"Is it Ajay?" Maya blurted out. "Is he okay? What happened?"

"We don't know yet." Priya shook her head, pulling Maya close to her in a hug. "We're just trying to find out."

Ashok put his arm around Deepa's shoulders. "These are our daughters," he said to Jonathan Stern, who introduced himself to the girls.

Jonathan held a paper in his hands. "Okay, so here's what we know." He scanned the page. "Your son was picked up between four-thirty and five p.m. outside the gates of John Wayne Airport. Do you know what he might have been doing there?"

Priya and Ashok looked at each other with mirrored expressions of confoundment.

"The airport?" Priya said. She turned to Deepa. "Weren't you supposed to pick him up at school at six?"

"He wasn't there," Maya spoke up quickly. "We looked all over. We even found his water bottle."

Deepa looked at her sister, wondering when she had become so skillful at deception. This account was true but omitted the salient fact that it had all transpired hours later than it should have. Deepa did not know what to say: she was no longer concerned with protecting herself, but how could she explain everything that had happened tonight without creating more distress for her parents right now?

"Wait, he left school *before* six o'clock?" Deepa asked, trying to piece together the timeline, recalculating how much of the blame belonged to her.

"Why would he go to the airport?" Ashok said. "How did he get there?"

Jonathan Stern flipped to another page. "A bicycle, a backpack, and its contents were checked in as evidence."

The Shah family was quiet, searching one another's eyes for some explanation as these details unfolded, forcing them deeper into a reality they had all been trying to avoid.

16

Saturday
10:00 p.m.

NEXT DOOR, THE County Sheriff's building had been bustling with the hum of a Saturday night. The weekend and nice weather had brought out revelers seeking a good time, and patrolling units had been back and forth all day with new bookings. With the high number of arrests, it was going to take all night to clear the people in custody.

Three men stood together in the corridor, each representing a different layer of police hierarchy. The lieutenant had been in a supervisory role so long he could barely remember what it was like to work on the streets. His main concerns were keeping the chief happy, staying on the right side of the district attorney, and avoiding negative headlines. Sergeant James O'Reilly was a twenty-year veteran of the force, more comfortable on the streets than many other places. And there was O'Reilly's young partner, whom he liked to call Greenie with some affection. Mateo Diaz was earnest and seemed to want to learn everything for himself, unwilling to take O'Reilly's (or anyone else's) wisdom, no matter how hard-earned.

The lieutenant hooked his thumbs into his belt. "The kid's parents are over there now, and they've got a lawyer asking questions. We going to charge him or cut him loose?"

"I say book him on the lesser charges now," O'Reilly said. "And give the detectives a chance to check him out, some time to get a warrant. We've gotta check him out, especially with everything that's been going on. Heck, I wouldn't mind talking to those parents myself." O'Reilly prided himself on his inquisition skills. With enough time, he could usually get someone to talk. This kid had gotten under his skin, the way he couldn't get through to him at all.

"He's just a kid," Diaz said. "What if he was just goofing around, didn't know what he was doing? He seems a little clueless to me, honestly. And he didn't say anything that seemed suspicious."

"That's the point, Diaz. He didn't give us anything because he's trained. He knows how to answer. Al-Qaeda's full of kids that age."

"How old?" the lieutenant asked.

Diaz cleared his throat. "Twelve."

The lieutenant's eyebrows rose. "And explain to me why we didn't send him to juvie?"

"Because we didn't know when we picked him up. He looks eighteen *at least*," O'Reilly said. "Didn't have ID on him. Wouldn't answer any questions. They were already processing him by the time we found out. Diaz called the parents, and they were on their way down."

"His mother confirmed his age on the phone," Diaz said. "Actually, she *yelled* it at me multiple times. She seemed pretty worried."

"Oh?" O'Reilly adopted a mock-sympathetic tone. "Well, if his mommy vouches for him, I guess we should just let him go." He exhaled loudly and shook his head. "Sorry, long night," he muttered. "Listen, what's the harm in investigating, just to make sure? He destroyed the evidence and tried to run. Made furtive gestures. Resisted arrest. That's plenty guilty behavior for me. Wouldn't look me in the eye. Wouldn't give me a straight answer. Just kept looking at the ground."

"See?" Diaz said. "Lieutenant, I actually think there's something wrong with the kid—"

"You agree!" O'Reilly leaped on this, pointing at him.

"No." Diaz shook his head. "I mean, I think something's not right with him. Like, he's one of those kids that doesn't know how to deal with people."

"Hm," the lieutenant said. "On the spectrum, you mean? My sister's kid is that way. I set him off once when I brought him a baseball cap for his birthday. Tried to put it on his head, he almost took my hand off."

Diaz wobbled his head a bit. "Maybe. I don't know exactly. But something's off."

"Something *is* off with him," O'Reilly said. "As I've been saying."

"Well, you did rough him up pretty good, O'Reilly. That probably helped shut him down." Diaz's tone was clipped.

"He was trying to run! What, would you prefer I shoot him?" O'Reilly held his arms out wide. "Look, most of the time, I'm right. My instincts are right. You know it's true. You want to take that chance, Greenie, with all your vast experience?"

His nickname for his partner was playful but accurate. The kid had less than two years on the job and a head full of dreams. Diaz believed the force and community harmonized all the time. He thought the training and handbook were always right.

O'Reilly knew better: what the training and handbook left out was judgment and instinct. What they left out was *experience*. That's why the force paired rookies with older cops. O'Reilly had learned much of what he knew from his first partner. Ronnie had a lot of pride in his community as a Black man. He believed in keeping neighborhoods safe for people like his elderly parents, living in the same North Long Beach house where he'd grown up. And for his sister's kids, so they could walk to school without seeing used needles at the park. Ronnie believed crime was a scourge that kept his people down. *Broken windows,* he always used to say. *Gotta fix those broken windows if you want people to have dignity where they live.*

Eight years ago, he and Ronnie had been called to a convenience store robbery. The store owner had hit the silent alarm when a couple of teenagers tried to steal some beer. Ronnie went in the front door and told O'Reilly to cover the back. Fresh out of sensitivity training, O'Reilly told himself not to react the way his body wanted to. Hand on the gun, but not out of the holster. He found Ronnie trying to talk down a strung-out looking redhead, who must have felt cornered with not much to lose. The kid pulled a gun, and the store owner pulled hers from under the counter. O'Reilly reacted quickly enough to wound the kid in the shoulder, but not before sloppy shots were fired by the civilians. Ronnie was hit: the bullet tore through his left leg. He could never walk right again and was relegated to desk duty until he retired two years later.

O'Reilly had sworn that day to never sit on his instincts again. Training was all well and good, but policing was about reality. He understood what they were trying to teach him, but it didn't reflect what they faced on the streets every day. If he saw someone suspicious trying to run, he had to presume guilt. If he thought someone was pulling a weapon, his first duty was to protect the civilians around him, his partner, and himself.

Diaz shook his head, leaning against the wall. "Jesus," he muttered.

"Listen." O'Reilly modulated his voice, trying for reason. "I know we want to be careful. We don't want to overreact. But we still have to do our jobs. I'm not talking about throwing the kid in jail. I'm just saying, what's the harm in looking into it a bit? You all know what happened with the guy last week who tried to get on the airplane with that trigger hidden in his vape thingy."

"Yeah, but they caught his bag at security," Diaz said.

"Exactly! And the strip mall shooting by that Pakistani teen last month? He was part of an honest-to-god terrorist cell. Fifteen years old! Those cops questioned him and missed it. You want that to be us? You want this on your head if it goes wrong? Either of you?" He looked back and forth between the two of them. "We're talking about an airport here—do I need to remind you? There might also be some federal jurisdiction, FAA or TSA. I know I don't want any of that on my record. *Or* my conscience."

The lieutenant pulled at his earlobe and sighed. "All right, book him on the trespassing and whatever we've got, and let him go on standard bail. Arraignment will probably be a couple of weeks out. See if the detectives find anything else by then."

17

Saturday
4:30 p.m.

IT HADN'T BEEN difficult for Ajay to leave robotics early. Nobody paid him much attention unless there was a programming bug for him to solve, and today everything had worked smoothly.

The best thing about their new home, Ajay thought, was its proximity to the ocean (5.2 miles) and the airport (3.4 miles). There were so many more interesting places he could reach on his bicycle, whereas their old neighborhood was just rows of houses all the same size, in a limited palette of colors and shapes. Occasionally a fire hydrant near the curb or a postal box on the corner was a landmark for him to find his way. That sameness was nice, reassuring, something he could count on. But there wasn't much for him to explore.

In the new neighborhood, not only could he ride his bicycle to school, but he mapped out a path from there to the local airport, which handled mainly regional flights within the state. He'd checked the schedule, and there was a window of approximately seventeen minutes, starting at 4:43 p.m., during which the airspace would be completely clear. No takeoffs, no landings. They were in the annual cycle of daylight saving time, originally instituted to help midwestern farmers lengthen their workday, so it would be light until almost seven, but his parents didn't like him riding his bike that late, so he'd need to be back at school by six, when Robotics Club ended.

Twelve minutes to ride to the airport, twenty minutes to conduct his experiment, twelve minutes back. Plenty of time. He had planned it all out. Drummond was so large, he took the water bottle and granola bar out of his backpack and left them right behind the flagpole until he returned. After Drummond was safely wrapped in his sweatshirt and nestled in the backpack, he climbed onto his bike and pedaled away.

The air blew through his hair, which flopped onto his forehead and into his eyes. His mother had been telling him it was time for a haircut, but last time he had gone to the barber, the buzzing sound of the clippers had bothered him. It felt as if a swarm of hornets, like the ones he'd read about in West Africa, were encircling him. When he shook his head, the barber grew frustrated and finally used the *snip-snip-snip* of his scissors, but it was too late. Loud sounds like that were always bad, and Ajay could hear that buzzing for hours afterward. When he looked in the mirror, he could tell it was a bad haircut, and he didn't see what the point was of enduring all that noise, just for a bad haircut. So, he had refused to go back all summer, but his mother was insisting he go soon.

The map he'd hand-drawn on a piece of scrap paper from the lab was taped to his handlebars. The sun was beginning to fall on the horizon as he rode, and his T-shirt was flapping in the wind. It was his favorite T-shirt, old and frayed at the hem and neckline, but nothing about it bothered him—not the labels or the seams. When he wore it, it felt like he was just in his own skin. But it was getting cool outside, and soon the T-shirt wouldn't be enough.

Right on schedule, he arrived at the airport, riding his bike up to the back fence where people could stand and watch the activity overhead. As expected, there were no planes landing or taking off. He leaned his bike against the fence and opened his backpack, carefully unwrapping Drummond and placing him on the ground. Ajay slid his arms into the sweatshirt, zipped it up, and put on the hood to keep the wind from blowing down the back of his neck. After switching on the controller, he strapped the camera to Drummond. He was excited about capturing the images he'd been so curious about and hadn't found anywhere else. All those patterns of runways and taxiways, creating a geometric labyrinth from the sky.

Now, finally. He stood back and released Drummond into the air to float up like a helium balloon. Up . . . up . . .

Was someone talking to him? Shouting at him? He didn't want to take his eyes off Drummond, but the voice was approaching, louder and louder, hurting his ears. Ajay looked up and saw a man in a dark uniform walking toward him with a strange, stilted gait, holding something at his hip, calling out something he couldn't hear. The voice was muffled by the roar of an airplane overhead, and he looked up, realizing the window was closing . . . He backed away from the man, clutching his controller, moving toward his bike. A terrible buzzing noise grew louder, and Ajay realized, with alarm, that he'd lost control of Drummond. His invention, the one he'd crafted with his own hands, was spiraling now, speeding toward the ground. Would it . . . ?

What was the man shouting? He couldn't understand. It was all so loud. He pulled the drawstring of his hood tight over his ears to muffle the noise. Would he have to leave Drummond behind? He couldn't. He had to. In desperate horror, he saw Drummond crashing to the ground, splintering into pieces.

He would just go now. He would go. The window was closed. He needed to go. Ajay grabbed his backpack and pulled at the handlebars of his bike, which were stuck in the chain-link fence. He yanked them until they came free and swung one leg over his bike.

As he pushed off on his bicycle, Ajay felt a powerful force from behind him. His chin slammed into the handlebar; the ground accelerated toward him. Everything went black.

When he came to a few minutes later, Ajay's hands were cuffed tightly behind his back, his wrists skinned raw by the metal, and one side of his face was scraped from cheekbone to chin. From the corner of his eye, he could see Drummond on the ground, broken into pieces. But maybe he could still be saved. Ajay's left wrist and shoulder throbbed, and his nose was dripping blood into his mouth. The metallic flavor flooded him with familiarity. *Was it the taste of copper or more like aluminum?*

18

Saturday
11:00 p.m.

"THE COMPLAINT INCLUDES charges of trespassing, resisting arrest, and destruction of evidence," Jonathan Stern continued reading from the papers in his hand. "Bail set at one thousand dollars."

The Shah family stood in stunned silence.

Jonathan looked up. "Look, this is good news. You can bail him out and maybe even be home by midnight." He glanced at his watch.

"I don't understand," Priya said. "How can there be any *charges* at all? This must all be a big mix-up, the fact that he's here at all. He must have just been lost or confused . . ." She shook her head.

Jonathan consulted the paper. "The arraignment is two weeks from now. That's when we'll hear the specific charges. But let's not get ahead of ourselves. Let's pay the bail, get him out of here, then we can talk about the rest. Do you have a personal check?"

Ashok felt his pockets on reflex and shook his head.

"You'll have to use the ATM, then. Cash or check only." Jonathan nodded toward the pair of machines in the corner, their purpose suddenly evident. Ashok walked over there, completed the transaction, and returned with a conspicuous wad of cash in his pocket. Then, he and Jonathan went to stand in yet another line in front of another window dedicated to bail payments.

As Priya watched them go, she added a new worry to her list. One thousand dollars of bail, and what would this attorney cost them?

After the down payment and the moving expenses, their savings had been nearly depleted. Ashok had convinced her to stretch for the Pacific Hills house on the promise that his business was growing, and they could handle an interest-only mortgage. It was worth it, he said, to stretch a bit now and gain a considerable advantage for their kids' high school years.

Priya stared at the clock, after eleven p.m., on the cinder-block wall. She thought of Ajay, sitting alone somewhere in the basement of this building, and a small cry escaped from her throat. She had been trying so hard to keep herself together, especially now that the girls were here, but this sound came from her involuntarily.

Priya looked at her daughters, now sitting on the floor. Maya wiped tears from the corners of her eyes, and Deepa reached over to gently rub her sister's back. Priya walked over and crouched down in front of them. "It's late. You girls should go home," she said. There was no reason to subject her daughters to this awful place. "Don't worry. We'll bring him home soon."

Deepa shook her head firmly. "I'm staying. I need to see him."

Maya nodded silently, her eyes reddened. "Me too."

Priya sighed and touched Maya's shoulder. "Okay. I'm sure he'll want to see you too."

Finally, Ashok and Jonathan returned.

"What's happening?" Priya asked, standing up.

"They're processing him for release," Stern said. "We'll go to another area and wait. Shouldn't be too much longer."

But after moving to the release area, they waited another thirty-three minutes until the doors finally opened and an officer led Ajay out by the elbow.

Priya held her breath when she saw him. His nose and lips were crusted with blood, and one cheek was covered with a large bandage. He was walking slowly, unevenly, as if each step caused him pain. She rushed toward him, and the officer stepped to the side while she took Ajay gingerly into her arms. Ashok and the girls waited behind her; they knew he didn't like to be crowded. She would have held him in that embrace forever, but she felt tears welling up inside her, so she moved aside for Ashok.

Her eyes landed upon the police officer, and in an instant, her sorrow transformed into rage. "What did you do to him?" she spat, in as civil a tone as she could muster.

"Ma'am, I'm Officer Diaz." The man stepped forward. "We spoke on the phone earlier." He held out his card. "I believe you have the date and time of the arraignment. Any questions, you can call me."

"What did you *do*?" Priya could barely contain her fury. She felt Ashok gently pull her back by the arm.

"Come on," he said quietly. "Let's just go."

"Don't you see his face?" Priya hissed. "Say *something*."

Ashok turned to Jonathan Stern. "What the hell?" he said in an angry whisper. "How can they do this to him? Doesn't he have rights? Aren't there rules?"

Stern motioned for Ashok to face the other way and continued speaking in a quiet tone. Priya saw Stern gesturing with his hands to try to settle her husband. At last, Ashok was expressing some of the desperate anger she had been feeling all night.

Deepa was now holding Ajay tight. "I'm sorry, I'm so sorry," she was repeating into his shoulder. Ajay was already taller than both of his sisters, but still managed to look like a little boy in Deepa's arms. Maya embraced him next, and Ajay seemed to hug her back.

Priya walked over to the children and lightly touched Ajay's cheek. He winced. "I think we should go to urgent care, just to get you checked out," she said.

"No!" Ajay pulled his arm away, startling them all. "I don't want to. I just want to go home." His voice was loud enough to attract the attention of the few other people standing around. His eyes looked terrified.

"Okay, okay," Priya said, in her most soothing tone. She knew not to touch him when he was like this, to fight her instinct to gather him up in her arms. "Okay, we'll go home. We'll go home."

Ajay exhaled with relief. "Can we take Drummond home? Maybe I can put him back together."

Priya was confused for a moment, until Maya reminded her: "His drone."

Jonathan Stern took two large strides over to them. "Did you say *drone?*"

"Yes, he programs it to fly certain paths and take photos," Maya said.

Stern tilted his head back to face the ceiling for a moment, then put his thumb and index finger astride the bridge of his nose. "It is illegal to fly a drone near an airport without prior authorization." A series of quick expressions traveled across his face. "This just got a lot more complicated." He exhaled loudly. "Well, nothing more we can do tonight. Go home, get some rest. I'll come by in the morning to discuss next steps."

AFTER WATCHING THE boy and his family leave, Officer Diaz retreated through the double doors. He scratched at the back of his scalp as he walked down the winding corridors, the images of the boy's injured face and his mother's expression burned in his mind. Then he stopped and closed his eyes, regretting he hadn't been able to convince O'Reilly earlier. Before he could think too much about it or lose his nerve, Diaz took his phone out of his pocket and scrolled, searching for the number. He hesitated for a moment, then tapped the screen to make the call.

19

Saturday
Midnight

AFTER THEY LEFT the jail, Ajay would barely meet Priya's eyes. At home, she cleaned and re-bandaged the scrapes on his face and helped him change into pajamas, then sat with him on his bed. She tried to help him take some deep breaths, but he complained that his chest hurt. Priya hated feeling powerless to comfort him, so she waited in his room until he finally began to breathe heavily, sometime in the early hours in the morning. The rest of the house was quiet by then, but Priya found herself unable to sleep. Her body had internalized a heightened sense of threat that would not allow her rest. She hadn't had one of these bouts of late-night sleeplessness in years, but the feeling was immediately familiar; the same insomnia had haunted her until shortly after her marriage to Ashok.

It was eighteen years ago they had climbed off that plane, stiff and weary from the journey that had begun over a day earlier and included an overnight layover. After suffering through a long snaking line, and the immigration officer's inquisition in an unfamiliar flavor of English, Ashok hauled their four oversize suitcases—the maximum size and number allowed by the airline—off the carousel. He struggled to secure a luggage cart until a kind woman showed him how to insert money into the device, then gave him a few American bills to do so. Despite their exhaustion and the unwieldy load, when Priya and Ashok finally passed through the last set of airport doors, they were both infused with the excitement of having arrived in the greatest country in the world. Even the air in Los Angeles was clean and fresh compared to Mumbai, holding the promise of a new and independent beginning.

Accustomed to going everywhere in India by train, they had naturally planned to travel that way from LAX to Irvine, not knowing that the train station was on the other side of the sprawling Los Angeles metropolis. The most economical way to get there was by bus, so Ashok struggled to push their overloaded cart through the airport's winding paths while Priya carried their hand luggage and searched for the right bus.

The bus driver mumbled something under his breath when loading their enormous bags into the cargo hold. Finally, after they sank into their seats, Priya leaned against Ashok's shoulder, grasping the bag with their passports and money in her lap. She didn't look around at the other passengers; she was conscious of the stink of sweat emanating from their bodies. They both fell asleep during the hour-plus ride through LA at the height of rush hour, only startling awake with the driver's intercom announcement. Another laden trek through the train station, another awkward stowing of enormous bags as people looked on, another hour-long trip in another vehicle. At every step along the way—from the airplane to LAX, the city bus, the train, and finally to Irvine—Priya became aware of the dwindling number of brown faces around them. She was accustomed, in India, to seeing people of varying complexions, speaking different languages, wearing the outward symbols of many religions, but never had she felt so conspicuous simply for her brown skin.

Ashok's stipend covered graduate student housing, which turned out to be a tiny, drab apartment with a musty odor. Priya was struck by a swell of melancholy the moment they opened the front door. In the coming weeks, she set upon the place with determination to make it a worthy home to begin their married life. She laid colorful batik cloths over all the surfaces, lit sticks of incense, and displayed the three framed photos they had brought: Priya with her parents; Ashok with his parents and brother; and Priya placing a garland over Ashok's neck on their wedding day. When she stood back and tried to assess the place objectively, she knew she had not changed it much. The brown carpet was still covered with stains, and the freezer emitted an unpleasant smell every time she opened its door. Yet she felt a buzz of excitement that they were at the start of something great, something that lay just ahead. And in this little makeshift home, on the lumpy futon she shared with her husband, Priya was finally able to sleep peacefully for a full night, for as long back as she could remember.

Now Priya lay awake in a new house, struck with a longing for that simpler time, when they were both filled with enough optimism and energy to face whatever life in this country posed. They had been diligently working toward, well . . . all of this. This family. This business. This home, neighborhood, school district. Priya had never doubted that it would all be worth it, until the depth of this night that had shaken her beliefs.

PART II

Day by Day

Week 1

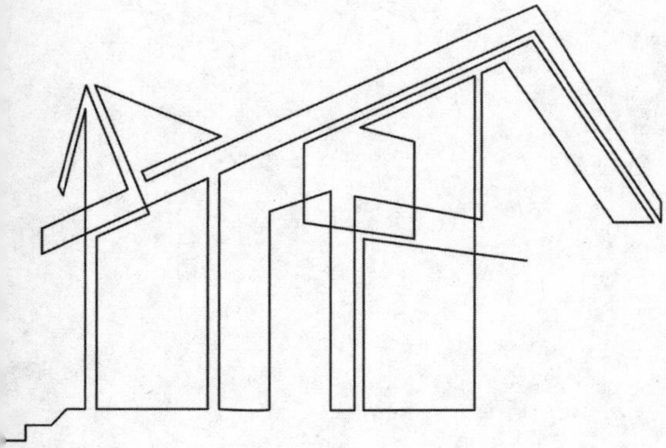

20

Sunday

THE NEXT MORNING promptly at nine o'clock, Jonathan Stern arrived at the Shahs' home. Vikram was already there. Ashok answered the door while Priya carried a tray of tea and biscuits into the living room. The mood was tense as everyone exchanged cursory words and handshakes.

"How is Ajay this morning?" Jonathan asked after they'd settled onto the couches. "Have you spoken with him?"

Ashok looked over at Priya, whose face wore the signs of an exhausting night.

"He's still sleeping," she said. "I tried talking to him last night, but he wouldn't say anything. I didn't want to push him too much, he was already so . . ." She shook her head. "Maybe he'll be better when he wakes up, after some rest."

"Yes," Ashok added, eager for it to be true. "He should be better today."

"As you all know, the arraignment is two weeks from tomorrow," Jonathan said, unlatching his briefcase. "That's when we'll hear the formal charges and Ajay will enter his plea. Right now, it looks like trespassing, resisting arrest, and destroying evidence, which are all misdemeanor charges. I'm going to do everything I can to get those charges reduced or even dropped. We can also request a case transfer to the juvenile system, which usually shows more leniency, especially for first-time offenders. There are a lot of avenues we can try to minimize the impact of this."

The word *offenders* pierced through Ashok's mind. He noticed Vikram nodding vigorously as the lawyer spoke. Did he agree with this assessment, of their son as an *offender*?

"That is the best-case scenario. But"—Jonathan reached for a file folder from his briefcase, and Ashok realized that all of this had been preamble—"I want you to be prepared for the full range of what could happen. A drone near the airport . . . it could get very serious, potentially even result in federal charges. They have a lot of leeway when it comes to—"

Ashok couldn't listen to this anymore. "He's a twelve-year-old kid," he interjected, "an *innocent* kid. He was just playing with his drone. It was an honest mistake."

"They'll argue," Stern said, "that there are signs posted near the airport stating that drones are prohibited without authorization. And even if there weren't signs . . . by law, the drone operator is responsible for keeping up with current regulations."

"But it wasn't anywhere near the airplanes," Ashok said. "His drone can't even go up that high."

"And they'll argue it's illegal to have a drone near an airport, even if you're just holding it in your hands. Even if you don't fly it," Stern said.

"They'll argue? *They?*" Vikram struck his knees with his palms. "You're doing a pretty good job arguing it yourself! You're supposed to be on our side, Jon."

"Look." Jonathan carefully studied both Ashok and Priya. "I just want to make sure you fully understand the situation. Anything related to national security . . . it's a whole different ball game. With what happened at that mosque last year and the strip mall incident . . . ever since 9/11, the rules are just different."

Vikram shook his head. "Believe me, we know. We were all living in this country after 9/11. We saw *exactly* how things changed for those of us with dark skin."

"Ajay just doesn't understand . . . the airport, the implications," Ashok explained. "And he . . . doesn't always deal with people easily."

"Yes, I understand he . . ." Jonathan glanced over at Vikram. "Ajay has . . . some trouble communicating?"

Ashok shifted uncomfortably in his seat. What had Vikram said to this man, and what did he believe? He could feel Priya's eyes on him and knew he should respond before she did. "He is highly intelligent," Ashok said, trying not to sound defensive. "But . . . sometimes he has difficulty with social interactions."

Jonathan nodded, jotting down a note. "That's important, to explain his interactions with law enforcement. Has he ever been diagnosed as being on the spectrum?"

"What? No. He's just a little reserved—there's nothing *wrong* with him," Ashok said, mildly offended.

"This is bullshit." Vikram stood up and began pacing behind the couch. "I could make this go away with one call back home," he said, flinging his hand into the air. "They treat us no better than damn Dalits over here."

Ashok was momentarily disoriented by Vikram's reference, out of context in this discussion and in this country. He'd never heard his friend mention caste—it was not something that came up in their lives here. Perhaps Vikram's angry outburst was just a reflexive show of indignance on behalf of Ashok's family. He was comforted by his friend's support, even if it was in anger.

Jonathan leaned forward. "Listen, I'll see you through the arraignment. But if this case involves more serious criminal charges, you're going to need a different attorney. As Vikram knows, I specialize in employment law, discrimination cases."

"This *is* discrimination," Priya said. "What else could it be? They're calling our son some kind of . . . of . . . *terrorist*."

Vikram stopped pacing and pointed at Stern. "Jon, there's a big civil case in this for you afterward. We're going to sue the pants off that police department for brutality, for discrimination . . ."

Priya looked over at Ashok with shock. *What?* They hadn't discussed anything of the kind. The doorbell rang, providing Priya with a welcome excuse to leave the room for a moment. She took a deep breath before opening the door and was relieved to see Archie, her hair wound into a thick braid, holding a foil-covered dish in each hand. "Mom's dhokla, her go-to crisis food. And brownies from the twins." She stepped into the house, leaned over to kiss Priya's cheek, and pushed off her shoes, all while still holding the dishes. "Deepa!" she said, spotting her coming down the stairs. "My sweet girl, go put these on trays and bring them out." Her hands freed, Archie embraced her friend in a proper hug. "You always have to eat, right?"

Priya felt a swell of emotion, was tempted to allow herself to release into the warmth of her friend's strong arms, but she could not right now. She clenched her jaw, led Archie into the living room, and introduced her to the lawyer. Archie poured herself a cup of tea and took an inconspicuous seat on an ottoman in the corner.

As Jonathan Stern explained the next steps in the process, Priya stole a glance at Archie's face. Since the first day they had met at the elevators of the graduate student housing apartment, their friendship had seen them through the birth of their children, buying homes, worrying over elderly parents, marital tensions, and work troubles. She trusted Archie unequivocally, respected her opinion as someone who possessed a deep inner stability and wisdom. If there was a reason to worry, it would show in her friend's expression now. But Archie seemed only to be listening intently.

"I know a guy at the DA's office," Stern was saying. "I'll see if I can find out anything before the arraignment. The more we know, the better. But the first step is for me to talk to Ajay, to get a detailed account of what happened from his side, so we can build the case for his not-guilty plea. It's best if I speak with him soon, while things are fresh in his mind. You can both be present, of course."

"Can it wait until tomorrow?" Priya asked.

"I'm in settlement conference all day Monday," Jonathan said, his eyes darting over to meet Vikram's. "But I can come back Tuesday, if that's better? Maybe today he should just rest up. In the meantime, if the police call or come by, do not answer any questions without me present. Give them my number." He placed a few business cards on the table. "And don't let them into the house unless they show you a search warrant."

"Maybe we should let them search!" Priya exclaimed. "He's innocent, we're all innocent. We have nothing to hide. What are they going to find? LEGOs and comic books? Maybe that would clear all this up."

"Listen, I know this is scary," Jonathan said. "But now that you're in this process, you have to play it right. Trust me, you have to know the rules of the game. Be careful. Don't talk to anyone else, outside this room."

"Right, wrong—doesn't matter now," Vikram said. "The whole system is shit."

"The best thing you can do right now," Stern continued, "is carry on with your lives. Gather support from your community and friends. You want to show you have strong community ties, you're good neighbors. Start lining up people who will vouch for you. Community leaders, upstanding citizens, high-profile people you may know."

"Meaning wealthy, white Americans. Such bullshit," Vikram muttered again.

"Mom?" came a quiet voice from the foot of the stairs. They all turned to see Ajay standing there, his cheek darkened by deep purple bruises and scabs under his nose. "It hurts to breathe." He touched his lower chest cautiously. His eyes looked weary.

Priya stood and hurried over to Ajay, then swiveled around to face the others. "Do you see?" she said to the lawyer. "Do you see what they did to him?" Before turning back to her son, Priya caught a stricken look on Archie's face. "That's it. I'm taking him to the hospital to get him checked out."

Archie stood up and slung her purse across her body. "I'll drive you."

21

Sunday

PRIYA HAD KNOWN Archana longer than anyone else in this country. One day, soon after she and Ashok had moved into that drab graduate student apartment, the elevator doors opened on the ground floor, where Priya was waiting, and a tall young Indian woman stepped out. Priya and Archana struck up a conversation right there in the lobby until Priya invited her upstairs for chai, and they were still talking when Ashok came home two hours later. Archana and Shrikesh had been in Irvine for two years by then. Ricky, as her husband found it easier to call himself in the US, was getting his PhD in an obscure subspecialty of nanoelectronics.

The Dhillons were Punjabi—from an entirely other region of India, where the language, food, and music were all different from Priya's and Ashok's Gujarati heritage. But these distinctions seemed negligible; later, they would tease each other about the varying terms they used—*nimbu* vs. *limbu* for lime. But in those early days, the couple was a lifeline. The Dhillons had a car, so they would all drive together to the nearest Indian grocery store in Artesia on Sundays. Archana showed Priya how to forage at Goodwill for the sweaters and jackets she would need in this new climate. Ricky gave Ashok driving lessons on the right side of the road, in preparation for the day they might afford their own car. Neighbors confused the two women all the time, despite Archie's long wavy hair and fair freckled skin, and Priya's darker complexion and straight hair. The women would come and go from each other's apartments every day, swapping ingredients and utensils, cooking double quantities of dishes they could share with each other. Priya cooked up batches of savory Gujarati snacks they consumed with their daily chai: spongy dhoklas, crispy handvos, and spicy patras. Archana introduced her to large pots of saucy Punjabi chicken curry and keema made healthier with ground turkey, which all added a dash of novelty to their dinner table.

They amassed dozens of pirated Bollywood DVDs from the Indian store and consumed them voraciously every afternoon. Archie couldn't believe that Priya had memorized the plotline and soundtrack from every popular film of the preceding decade. "How is it that a supremely pragmatic person like you, with an *accounting degree* no less, can get carried away with such melodrama?" Archie teased Priya. "This is your one guilty pleasure?"

Although their friendship was young, Priya felt compelled to tell Archie what she had never told anyone else: those films had saved her, helping her stay awake many late nights in her Mumbai flat.

When she was fourteen, her uncle had come into her room and run his hands over her developing body, touching himself as he lay next to her. Instinctually, Priya devised ways to stave off his visits: studying in the living room, staying up late watching films, finally going to sleep in layers of clothing and sweating all night. Ultimately, it was why she'd been so eager to marry Ashok and move away. She was still a virgin when she met him; he had still been her first kiss. And yet, she had felt tainted and imperfect as a bride. Priya had never confronted her uncle, never told her parents or anyone else. She never went back to India while he was alive, not even when he died, sending Ashok in her stead. Perhaps, Priya realized, she'd been waiting for a friend like Archie all her life to reveal this.

Archana, with her degree in psychology, was unfazed by the admission. "It's more common than you know. Half the women I saw during my counseling internship experienced something like this. You know what it tells me about you?" She grabbed Priya's hand. "You're strong as steel. Look how you handled it, where you've arrived. You can endure anything now."

The two women became so inseparable, their husbands began fusing their names together and playfully calling the pair Priyarcha.

With time, Priya learned to look past the apartment's filthy carpets and hold her breath when retrieving something from the freezer. She trained herself to smile at the bus driver when she boarded and look shopkeepers in the eye, even though she still felt out of place nearly everywhere. The two couples clung to each other for comfort and familiarity, for the sense of belonging and family they had left behind. The world outside their doors may have felt foreign, even hostile at times, but at least they were not alone in this new land. That would have been unbearable.

ONE HOUR AFTER they had arrived at the emergency room, a nurse finally called Ajay into an examination room. When the doctor, a youngish blond woman, asked Ajay to take off his shirt, he hesitated.

"Come on, darling. Just for a moment," Priya said, helping him raise his arms as he winced at the movement. When she saw the deep red streaks across his bare back, she drew in a sharp breath.

The doctor calmly placed her stethoscope on Ajay's back. She gave Priya a quick glance. "Please wait outside while I examine him."

"Oh, it's okay. He wants me here," Priya said, mistaking the doctor's comment as intended to protect Ajay's modesty.

"The nurse will come get you in the waiting room when I'm done." It was not a request. Priya tried to give her son a small smile as she left.

SOME TWENTY MINUTES later, when she was brought back into the examination room, Priya found Ajay still seated on the examination table, now dressed and staring at his hands, while the doctor sat on a stool across from him.

"You have a very brave young man here. Ajay tells me he sustained his injuries in an altercation with the police yesterday. Is that correct?" the doctor asked.

Priya nodded mutely. Is that why she'd been asked to leave? Did the doctor suspect something else? Suspect *her*?

"In addition to the contusions and lacerations on his face, he has significant bruising on his back and chest, suggestive of fairly serious blows. Do you know exactly what happened to him yesterday?"

Priya shook her head. *Why couldn't she speak?*

"I'd like to send him for an X-ray to confirm, but I suspect his ribs are bruised, possibly fractured."

Priya nodded as she tried to make sense of this. "What . . . kind of blow?" she asked tentatively. *Did she want to know?* She had to know.

"A strong kick or being thrown to the ground with some force." The doctor seemed to be watching her for a reaction. "Do you have a police report?"

Priya closed her eyes as she took this in. She couldn't look at her boy. If she saw his face now, she would lose her composure.

"Mrs. Shah?"

"Uh, yes," Priya said. "We have . . . our lawyer has the police report. He can get a copy for you." She fumbled in her purse for Jonathan Stern's card and thrust it toward the doctor. "I'm not sure if . . . I don't know what it says in there, exactly. We're still trying to figure it all out. He was . . . um . . . riding his bicycle somewhere he shouldn't have been." Priya reached for the most innocent explanation for what had happened. If only this were true, perhaps it could all be over soon. She noticed something shift in the doctor's face, her expression soften.

"I see." The doctor nodded, looking at the card. "I'm sorry, but I have to ask when kids come in with these kinds of injuries. We're required to, by law."

Priya just nodded back solemnly, as if she understood. As if any of what was transpiring, the implications and accusations, made any sense at all.

"You will have a report from this visit too," the doctor was saying.

"I'll document all his injuries. We've taken photos, and we'll include a copy of the X-ray. I'll have the nurse give you a copy of the file before you leave." She explained that the treatment for bruised ribs was rest and restricted activity, ice for the swelling. "If you find he has difficulty breathing properly, we can give him medicine for the pain. The biggest risk is pneumonia or other respiratory problems, so keep a close eye on him."

A small noise came from Priya's throat, which she tried to cover with a cough. She nodded firmly at the doctor. "I will."

"The nurse will come to take him for the X-ray," the doctor said. "And you can go with him." She gave Priya a tentative smile on her way out.

AFTER ARCHIE DROVE them home from the hospital, she sat in the kitchen as Priya recounted what the doctor had said, what the examination had revealed.

"He's been through a trauma, Priya," Archie said in a gentle voice. "The confrontation with the police, waiting in the jail for hours . . . that would have an impact on any kid, more so for someone like Ajay." *Someone like Ajay.* A couple of years ago, Archie had encouraged them to have Ajay evaluated by a child psychiatrist. *There are therapies that can help him,* she'd explained. *It's not the end of the world.*

But Ashok was resistant. There was a culture of overdiagnosis in this country, he said, of treating everything with medications and therapy. Children needed to be resilient, to be given high expectations, to work hard for their ambitions. Back in India, they knew plenty of people who were introverted, bookish, eccentric. Ashok's brother was a quiet math genius, and it had landed him at IIT. Every slight personality difference didn't have to be a problem. Ajay was doing well at school and well-behaved at home. What was the problem?

Priya understood Ashok's point, even if she trusted Archie's opinion. She, too, preferred to understand her son as an individual with unique traits, not through labels. And there was another underlying reason neither of them had to vocalize. There was no acknowledgment in their culture of flaws or imperfections, and there was certainly no leeway in their life of striving to accommodate them.

"Once this is all over," Archie said now, "it might be a good idea to have someone work with him on trauma-focused therapy." She placed a hand on Priya's forearm.

Priya covered her face with her hands and began to cry, big shuddering sobs—not only for the thought of another ordeal for her child, another burden for their family—but also for these words of faith from her friend, who could see to a safe time in the future that Priya could not. Archie's strength and optimism were pillars she had come to depend upon.

YEARS EARLIER, WHEN the planes had struck the Twin Towers, the two couples sat glued to the Dhillons' television set, fielding calls from worried relatives back home. They insisted they were safe in California, though they remained secreted in their apartments as reports of attacks on turbaned men appeared on the news. They refused their families' pleas to come home, even as, all around them, work visas were not renewed and academic funding evaporated.

With no savings, Priya and Ashok lived as frugally as possible but, even so, found themselves having to dip into the student loans that Ashok had been offered, just to make ends meet. They never planned to take on debt—it was an inauspicious way to begin their new lives—but they couldn't rely on their families back home for financial support. Ashok's parents, in fact, had been hinting at their own needs, as his father had developed arthritis in his hands and found it harder to do manual work at the sari emporium.

There was no way around two, maybe three, more years of spending at this pace, and the prospect of that ballooning debt sickened them. Priya needed to find paid work. After several tense discussions, in which she reassured Ashok that this was not a reflection of his value as her husband, nor of her lack of belief in him, he agreed. As the trailing spouse on Ashok's graduate student visa, Priya first had to apply for proper authorization to work in the US, which took several months, longer than usual in the wake of 9/11. In the meantime, she collected job postings aligned with her accounting degree, dreaming of how the income might enable them to occasionally go to a restaurant or call their parents in India more often. Yet, when her work permit was granted, none of those employers were willing to hire her for the kind of accounting position all her classmates back home now held. Desperate, she signed up with a temp agency and agreed to take anything. She worked a series of low-level jobs, mostly data entry or warehouse picking. No one wanted to train a temp for the cash registers or have her answer phones if her accent made her more difficult to understand.

One day, Priya was sent on an assignment to a real estate firm, where she told the manager she could do bookkeeping as well, if needed. He gave her some work and, impressed with her skills, hired her for a decent salaried position. A bookkeeper job was still below her capabilities, but she was grateful for the regular work and liked being able to exceed expectations. After a year, just as Ashok was finishing his degree and their immigration status would again be in flux, the firm agreed to complete the paperwork necessary to grant Priya a proper work visa.

While this should have led to a better season, what followed was a tense time in their marriage as Ashok hunted for a job. After working all day, Priya came home to Ashok's dirty dishes in the sink, the detritus of whatever food he'd consumed littering the counter. She made dinner every night; each weekend she carried their clothes basket down to the basement laundry machines. Many days, Ashok sat with his laptop in a disheveled bed all day, and still she went to the effort of making the bed before they went to sleep at night.

On occasion, Priya thumbed through the few volumes of poetry—the only books Ashok had brought with them from India—which now sat untouched near his bedside, gathering dust. She bit back tears when she came to the dog-eared page of a poem he had once recited to her with such aplomb. The enormous effort it took to start life over in a new country was exacting its toll not only on each one of them, but also on their marriage.

She would listen to Ashok complain about not getting any interviews, or getting interviews but not the job, and most often respond with sympathetic murmurs. But one day, a couple of months into the job search, she came home to find him in a particularly foul mood after speaking with a classmate.

"Do you know everybody from my program has already found work? They're all"—Ashok waved a hand in the air—"getting together for happy hour on Friday, and I'm still begging for favors. I feel like a second-class citizen, just like in India."

Priya sat next to him on the couch and touched his knee. "Maybe we can go out for dinner this weekend? I get my paycheck on Friday." She was trying to bring a smile to his face, but Ashok slammed his laptop closed before storming off to the bedroom.

Priya followed him, stooping to pick up a pair of discarded socks in the hallway. "What? Why are you so angry?"

Ashok spun toward her. "You think I need reminders you're the only one earning money here? You think you need to rub my face in it, I don't know already?"

The next day, Priya broke down and tearfully described all of this to Archana, who comforted her as they sat on the couch.

"He just needs to find a job, then everything will change," Archana said. "These men are so tied up in their work. Ricky comes home in such a crap mood when one tiny thing goes wrong in the lab. He's unbearable." She rolled her eyes and smiled. "Just hold on. Keep doing your work, keep supporting him." Perhaps it was Archana's training as a counselor or her innate confidence, but Priya believed her friend when she said, "It'll all get better. You'll see."

Priya was so harried with her daily routine that she was already a couple of weeks late by the time she realized it. When she checked her pill pack, she saw that she had missed a few sporadic days the previous month. The results on her pregnancy test were clear, eliciting both elation and fear. She was scared to tell Ashok, to add one more complication to their lives, which already felt out of balance. But to Priya's surprise, Ashok was delighted. He grabbed her and swung her around, then quickly leaned down to speak directly into her belly, apologizing for squeezing the baby.

The pregnancy seemed to switch on a motor inside her husband, and he found the ad agency IT manager job the very next week. In the two weeks before his new job began, Ashok packed up all their belongings and found a cozy one-bedroom apartment on Magnolia Lane, just a few miles away. It was small but sunny, with a long windowsill in the living room perfect for growing plants. Unable to afford much furniture, they purchased only a mattress for the bedroom and borrowed a folding card table from Archie and Ricky. The rest of the space was empty but filled with their excitement. The only tincture of sadness came when they moved out of grad student housing, saying a weepy farewell to Archie and Ricky. But the very next day, the two couples worked together to get everything unpacked at Magnolia Lane. That evening, they sat on blankets in the empty living room to eat pizza and toast with plastic cups of sparkling apple juice, to old friends and new beginnings.

IN THE KITCHEN of her Pacific Hills home, Priya wiped under her eyes. "Maybe we should've listened to you back then, Arch. Maybe if—"

"You can't live your life with maybes. We just do the best we can." Archie gently took one of Priya's hands again and grasped it firmly between hers. "Listen to me. You *will* get through this." Archie smiled at her in a way that Priya desperately wanted to believe.

22

Sunday

DEEPA KNOCKED ON her sister's bedroom door. "Hey, can I come in?" She listened for an answer, then even though she didn't get one, opened the door. Maya was sitting at her desk under the window, her back to Deepa.

"What?" Maya said, without turning around.

"Can I . . . come in?" Deepa had been the one desperate to have her own room, but sometimes she missed their shared quarters, all those little nothing interactions that made up their day, like watching Maya make her bed just so, with her stuffed elephant propped up on the pillows. When they'd shared a room, Deepa wasn't embarrassed to leave Panda out, but now she tucked him out of sight each morning.

Maya spun her chair around to face Deepa, who sat on the edge of the bed. The weight of the previous night hung over her. When their family had squabbles and tensions, they were minor, innocuous things that stayed within the four walls of their home. Those hours at the police station now seemed surreal, as if they belonged to another family or on television. Deepa couldn't shake the image of the uniformed police officer leading Ajay toward them, her brother's damaged face. She had never seen her parents look so upset, not even when they'd learned their own relatives back in India had died.

"So that thing I went to yesterday . . . the border protest?" Deepa said. "That was the reason I couldn't take you to the mall yesterday when you asked me before. I know you wanted to get Ashley's birthday gift?" Her voice rose to the higher pitch it occupied when she was nervous.

Maya pulled her feet up to sit cross-legged on her desk chair. "Hey, I guess I'm the only kid in the family who didn't get arrested yesterday. Maybe I should get a prize."

Deepa swallowed. "I was . . . *detained*, not arrested. But anyway, it was a mistake for me to go. Or at least, I should've told Mom and Dad I was planning to go—"

"They never would have let you," Maya interrupted. "You know that. That's why you didn't tell them."

Deepa exhaled. "Well, in any case, I should have been there to pick you both up, like I'd promised."

"He was already gone, Deepa. That lawyer guy said the police picked him up at the airport at five. You weren't even supposed to get him from school until six."

"Well, then I could have looked for him earlier. Maybe I would have found him . . ."

"At the *airport*?" Maya exclaimed. "Why would you have gone looking for him at the airport? Don't be stupid. How would anyone know he went to fly his stupid drone there?"

"I don't know, you seem to know him pretty well," Deepa said.

"So, now you're blaming me?" Maya said with a harsh laugh.

"No, that's not what I meant. Trust me, I've been up half the night blaming myself." Deepa tried smiling at her sister. "You just know things he likes, like the concrete cube house."

Maya looked down at her lap and began to pull at a loose thread of the fuzzy socks she always wore at home. She had an entire drawer full of them.

"Well, anyway," Deepa continued, "I'm going to tell Mom and Dad about the protest and the"—she looked at the ceiling—"detainment." Did it sound any better than *arrest*? "Last night didn't seem like the right time. But I will tell them."

"Well, that's just selfish," Maya said.

Deepa looked at her, puzzled. "What?"

"You want to tell them just to get it off your chest. But what about them? They're worried about Ajay right now, and you're going to lay that on them too? So you can make yourself feel better?" Maya pulled a green thread right out of her sock and flicked it onto the floor. "You always want everyone to know what's *right*, Deepa. But you don't think about how being right affects other people. It's over, you're fine. Just move on."

Maya's phone buzzed on her desk, and she grabbed at it.

"Aren't you supposed to turn that off during homework?" Deepa asked gently.

"I'm expecting a message." Maya shot her a dirty look. "What, will I be *arrested* for having it on?"

Deepa got up from the bed. "I can take you to the mall whenever you want this week, to get that gift before the party next weekend." It was a bid to regain some normalcy, and if she was being honest, penance for her behavior yesterday. But Maya wasn't listening anymore, already tapping away at her phone screen.

As she left Maya's room, Deepa found herself longing for the lightweight banter about beauty trends and clothing styles that were her sister's usual concerns. Maya seemed different, preoccupied. Was it what had happened with Ajay? Or was she finally mad at Deepa about last night? Deepa returned to her room, feeling unnerved. Perhaps it was her guilt. Or perhaps Maya was right, and she was just being selfish.

23

Sunday

PRIYA PULLED ASHOK behind the closed door of their bedroom.

"His back and chest are covered with these terrible red streaks, like he was beaten," she said in a hushed tone. "You should've seen how the doctor looked at me, with these accusing eyes." She furrowed her brow. "Like she thought *I* could have done that to my own boy."

"Oh no, do we have to worry about that now?" Ashok asked, panicked. "Is she going to call the police for child abuse or something?"

Priya shook her head. "No. I gave her the lawyer's card so she could get the police report."

Ashok looked at her pointedly. "What, Priya? You think the police will just admit to doing that to him? You can't be so naive. What if this escalates?" He reached for his phone. "I'd better call Jonathan."

Priya caught his wrist. "Why? What's he going to tell you? Ashok—did you even hear what I said? Ajay has marks all over his body and bruised ribs! He's been traumatized, physically and emotionally. That's what we have to focus on right now. That's *our* job, as parents. You can't delegate this."

Ashok drew back from her. "I'm not *delegating*. I'm looking ahead with open eyes so we can avoid more problems."

"Were you looking ahead with open eyes when you refused to get Ajay tested years ago?" Priya snapped. "The lawyer himself asked if he'd ever been diagnosed. That would be pretty helpful with this obstacle right now, don't you think?"

Ashok cocked his head. "Priya, we made that decision together. *We* decided that he didn't need to be evaluated so young, that he needed some time to grow—"

"No," Priya interrupted, pointing a finger at him. "*You* pressured me and I gave in, instead of trusting my instincts. I'm their mother, I *know* what they need."

Ashok blinked a few times as he looked at her. "Where is all this coming from? Are we still talking about Ajay?"

Priya shook her head before turning to leave. "I'm not doing it again, Ashok. I'm not giving in when I know better."

FIFTEEN YEARS EARLIER, as a new mother, Priya had felt a blissful sense of purpose despite the blur of sleep deprivation and nursing around the clock. Ashok was settled into his job at the agency, Priya was on maternity leave from the real estate firm, and they delighted in celebrating each new milestone their baby reached. Deepa meant *light*, and she certainly led their way out of the dark period in their marriage preceding her arrival.

When it was time for Priya to return to work, she found a home-based day care recommended by another young mother on Magnolia Lane. Deepa liked going to Ms. Gabriella's for the first few months, but once she learned to walk, her world opened up and she wanted to exert her will everywhere. Deepa began to wail each morning when Priya walked her up the driveway to Gabriella's house. Priya tried coaxing her, being stern, even bribing her with a box of animal crackers. Still, Deepa protested. She clung to Priya's leg, threw her little body on the front lawn, and kicked her legs. Sometimes she continued crying and screaming so hard after Priya left, she even threw up on Gabriella's floor.

After a few incidents of vomiting, Gabriella called her apologetically. "I'm so sorry, Mrs. Shah, but I can't. I just can't. The vomit, everything, it's too much. It's only me, and I can't handle it with the other kids."

"Yes. No, of course. I understand," Priya said, as tears silently dripped down her face. She understood that Gabriella, a kindly grandmother who had raised four children and run a small day care out of her home for nearly a decade, couldn't handle these outbursts from Deepa. Some days, it was too much even for Priya. She wondered if this headstrong child was payback for any difficulty she'd caused her own parents as a child, a kind of generational karma her mother had invoked occasionally when she was exasperated.

Priya understood, but she was also at a loss. Without day care, she couldn't manage her bookkeeping job at the real estate office. Her manager agreed to her leaving by five o'clock every day so she could pick up Deepa, but she couldn't very well bring a toddler to the office. Priya's income was modest, but they still relied on it to help pay their rent. And they needed medical insurance if Ashok was going to launch his own business. All the other childcare options they'd found in the area were unaffordable.

After Deepa was asleep, she and Ashok discussed the situation. They went in circles, trying to find solutions and dismissing them in turn. Priya could quit her job, but no matter how they penciled it out, they couldn't get by on Ashok's income alone. Perhaps Priya could stretch the groceries a little further, they could remove the international long-distance plan from their phone line, but that wouldn't compensate for the loss of Priya's salary. She felt guilty, as they weighed these things, for having purchased two houseplants last week on impulse. The nursery was having a sale, and she thought some greenery would brighten up their apartment during the rainy season. They weren't even practical plants, like curry leaves or tulsi, which she could have used in cooking; they were simply decorative and seemed like a foolish indulgence now.

Ashok could ask the ad agency for a raise, but he'd done that just six months earlier and been given a small increase. He could begin moonlighting on the weekends with a few clients for extra income. Yet none of these alternatives would solve their underlying problem. They'd been in this country for three years now, working assiduously and living frugally, but seemed only to be treading water. They'd been resolute in not taking on any debt above Ashok's student loans, but they hadn't been able to accumulate any savings, either. They had put away some money to purchase plane tickets for a visit to India, but when the car needed new tires, that fund had been wiped out.

They were grateful to have jobs, a decent apartment, and a healthy little girl. But life in America had been more difficult and less rewarding than they'd envisioned back in India. Those American salaries were impressive when translated into rupees and applied against the Indian cost of living. But in America, in American dollars, everything cost more, and those salaries didn't go as far. Without money or a support system to make their daily life workable, every day in this country felt like walking a tightrope. It was hard to imagine ever being able to afford a small condo of their own, or even to support another child.

After considering all the possibilities, they managed to cobble together a temporary solution. Archana had just given birth to twin boys, and her mother had come from India to help care for the infants. Priya dropped off Deepa at her home three days a week; in exchange, Priya took care of the twins for a couple of evenings and on Sundays, so both Archie and her mother got a break. At the real estate office, she traded off one of her weekdays to work Saturdays, when Ashok was home. The agents, who often worked weekends, had been asking her to do this for some time. Ashok got permission from the ad agency to work one weekday from home, during which he was responsible for Deepa. With this intricate scheme, Priya managed to squeeze out five days a week to maintain her job, as did Ashok. In their remaining days, Ashok took on freelance projects for cash, while Priya watched the three children and shuttled them around. It was exhausting, and only worked if everything went precisely as planned.

This setup bought them a few months, but when it was time for Archie's mother to return to India, they still hadn't found another solution. There was only one possibility left, one that Priya had been pushing to the corners of her mind since Ashok had first raised it. It was common practice for children in India to be cared for by extended family members for periods of time. Ashok's brother had lived with an uncle in Mumbai while he attended a special high school for math, and Priya's mother had cared for her toddler niece for several months while her sister was on bedrest. Grandparents, aunts, and uncles served as surrogate parents, cousins as makeshift siblings. Homes and families expanded to accommodate relatives who came and went. It was all part of the familial culture and very comfortable, at least in theory.

"We have to think about it, Priya," Ashok said as they lay exhausted in bed, facing each other. "She'll be in good hands, you know that. Your mother will love having her. And it's only for a little while, until we get on our feet. We can save some money, buy a bigger place. And when she comes back, she'll be ready for preschool." Ashok brushed back a strand of hair at her temple. "You know we can't go on like this." He took her hand and kissed the back of it.

Priya stayed silent, reflecting on the truth beneath his words but unwilling to face it. She could only even consider this because her uncle was gone, and she knew her mother would be more loving than any sitter or day care here, even if they could afford it. But, although Deepa was a challenging child and made life more difficult for all of them, Priya couldn't bear the thought of not being with her every day. Her entire life now revolved around this child: preparing tiny chunks of banana and soft-cooked yams for her to taste for the first time, pouring cups of warm water over her downy head each evening in the bathtub. She had weaned Deepa in preparation for day care, but the girl still climbed into her lap before bed expecting to suckle. Their lives and bodies were so tightly intertwined, it was impossible to think of unraveling the strands.

In the end, the only alternative they could see was to send Deepa back to Mumbai to be cared for by Priya's mother for a while. She could fly to India for free with Archana's mother, who had become quite attached to her, doling out grandmotherly affection and praise.

Standing at the LAX airport gate, Priya explained to Deepa what a great adventure lay ahead for her, how much her family in India was longing to meet her. She kept her guilt and sadness to herself, at least until she watched the airplane rise silently into the air. Then she stood at the window while tears streamed down her face.

After Deepa was gone, Priya began to move through life with a numbness, learning to buffer herself against dozens of reminders: stowing away rubber ducks and milk bottles, avoiding the playground. For a while, she was ashamed to admit, it was even difficult to be around Archie and Ricky, their life dominated by the twins' needs and clutter. And every Sunday, Priya braced herself for the melancholy that would descend after their weekly phone call to India. While she was proud to hear Deepa chattering in her expanding vocabulary about all her new adventures, Priya was bereft for hours afterward, imagining everything she was missing in her young daughter's life.

The only way for Priya to cope was to push those feelings aside and focus on their reason for being in this country: to work hard, save money, and create a foundation for their family. By the time Deepa returned to them fourteen months later, she was toilet-trained and knew some of her letters and numbers. She clung to her grandmother as they disembarked the plane and, in her other hand, clutched a threadbare stuffed panda Priya had given her when she had left.

Every night for the next week, Deepa insisted that her grandmother put her to sleep. While Priya couldn't take issue with her daughter's burgeoning independence, nor with her strong connection to her grandmother, these things stung. By then, Priya was pregnant with Maya, depleting both her time and energy. Soon, there were more family demands to juggle, increasing again two years later when Ajay was born.

Ashok reassured her that they had done the right thing, the best possible thing for Deepa, but Priya would always wonder if this early chapter hadn't scarred their daughter in some deep, invisible way.

24

Monday

ON MONDAY MORNING, Priya woke up hours before the kids, nursing cup after cup of tea in the kitchen as she tried to keep busy with mindless tasks. Ashok had already left for the office; staying busy at work was always his coping mechanism. They had agreed Priya would stay home with Ajay, who was in no condition to return to school yet.

As the time drew nearer for the girls to wake up, Priya found herself making an elaborate breakfast they wouldn't usually have time for on a weekday.

At last Deepa wandered in, still in her pajamas. "Mom," she said, surveying the kitchen counter strewn with the remains of fruit peels and eggshells. "Mom, I'm worried about Ajay. He's awake, but he's just lying in bed staring at the wall."

Priya swallowed hard against the reality impinging on this morning. "Okay, I'll go check on him in a little while. I made fresh juice," she said, pouring it into three glasses. "And there's a frittata in the oven, should be out in a few minutes."

"Mom! Don't you get it? He doesn't know how to process what's happening." Deepa threw her hands up in front of her in a wild gesture. "That's it—I'm staying home too. At least I can try to help Ajay feel better today."

Despite the sting of Deepa's words, Priya felt a wave of gratitude at this suggestion. Was it selfish of her, to want all her children close?

She felt as if she couldn't make the simplest decision right now. Should she encourage her daughters to carry on as usual, as the lawyer had suggested? It might be irrational, but it felt risky to let them leave the house, to go out into the unpredictability of the world. The idea of them all cocooning at home appealed to her.

"Okay, you can both stay home, just for today. Go, tell Ajay and Maya," Priya said, reaching for her phone. "I'll call the schools."

PRIYA WAS CLEANING up the kitchen after breakfast when the doorbell rang. Archie had mentioned she would stop by today, and Priya warmed with the anticipation of seeing her. But when she opened the door, she saw two strangers standing on her porch. Her heart lurched.

"Mrs. Shah?" The woman who spoke had her hair tightly pulled back from her face, giving her a stark appearance. "I'm Detective Hayes, this is Detective Cooper. We'd like to ask your son some questions about the incident on Saturday night. Is Ajay home?" Detective Hayes's eyes moved past Priya's shoulder, as if she was trying to look up the stairwell behind her.

Instinctively, Priya pulled the door toward her, restricting their view. "No."

"He's not home? Maybe we can talk to you, then?"

"Yes. No. I mean, no, you can't talk to either of us. You have to call our lawyer. He has to be here." Priya hated the way she sounded, unsure of herself. She pushed her shoulders back and spoke a bit louder. "I can give you his number, if you'd like."

"Yeah, we'll take that." The male detective spoke for the first time.

"Hold on just a minute." Priya stepped back and closed the door, recalling what the lawyer had said about not letting anyone in the house. She retrieved his business card and looked at it for a moment, hesitating. She felt like someone who was trying to hide something, someone guilty. When she opened the door, the male detective was already walking back down the driveway toward an unfamiliar gray sedan parked at the curb. The female detective was waiting on the porch; Priya handed her the card.

"Thank you, Mrs. Shah." Detective Hayes held up the card between two fingers. "We'll be in touch."

Priya locked the door and went to the living room window. The two detectives did not get into the sedan, but turned left and walked down the sidewalk, out of her sight.

Priya rushed back to the kitchen and called Ashok. "Two detectives came to the house. *Two*," she blurted out, as if that number meant something. "They wanted to ask questions. They asked about Ajay, they wanted to come in, I think. But I didn't let them."

"Wait, slow down," Ashok said. "What happened?"

After repeating all the salient facts, Priya realized there were not many. It was just what the lawyer had told them to expect. So why was her heart pounding so heavily in her chest?

"Did you tell Jonathan?" Ashok's voice was calm.

"No. Should I?"

"Yes, call and let him know what happened, so he'll be expecting their call. It's all right, honey. Just calm down," Ashok said. "How does Ajay seem today? You know you'll have to prepare him for the interview tomorrow."

Priya exhaled. Ashok was right, of course. She'd thought letting Ajay rest this morning was the best strategy, but the urgency of the situation was intruding upon them. After calling Jonathan's office and leaving a message, she went upstairs to check on her son.

She found him awake but still in bed. He was lying on his side, with a book propped up in front of him: Percy Jackson, one of his favorites.

Priya sat down on the edge of the bed and brushed Ajay's overgrown hair from his forehead. "Maybe I should trim this myself, hm? With some little scissors? We don't have to go to the barber." She tried to picture how he would look younger, more innocent after a haircut.

Ajay shrugged without taking his eyes off the book.

"Come on down," she said. "Did the girls tell you? We're all going to have a fun day at home."

When Priya returned downstairs, there was a text message on her phone from one of their neighbors, the architect across the street who'd brought over home-baked cookies right after their moving truck had left.

Priya—just checking to see if everything is OK over there? Police came by and had lots of questions about your son. Hope everyone is safe? Pls let me know.

Priya closed her eyes and tried taking a few long, deep breaths, working hard to resist the impulse to call the neighbor. She was desperate to know what questions the police were asking, but she was also embarrassed. How many doors had those detectives knocked on? They were so new here and knew so few people. She forwarded the message to Ashok to keep him apprised, and also hoping to diffuse the stress she felt engulfing her. When she peeked out the living room window again, she was relieved to see the gray sedan was gone.

IN THE AFTERNOON, Priya successfully managed to distract all three children, if not herself, with a movie on the family room TV and heaping bowls of popcorn. She suggested a new Bollywood film, but the kids balked.

"I want something fun. *Captain Marvel*?" Ajay suggested, and the girls agreed. He nestled into the couch between his sisters, gangly legs on the ottoman. When a loud battle scene suddenly erupted on-screen, Ajay jumped and covered his ears. Deepa lowered the volume while Maya spread a blanket over the two of them and rested her head on his shoulder.

Priya was still on edge from the detectives' visit, picturing them traveling up and down the block, asking their new neighbors about who knows what. It didn't help that Jonathan Stern hadn't returned her call yet, six hours after she'd phoned. She would sit down with

Ajay after the movie to discuss the next day's interview. But until then, she just wanted to hold her children close.

Priya went to the kitchen to prepare dinner, reassured to hear the kids' banter from the next room. As she sliced a block of paneer into small cubes, she kept glancing at her phone, anxious to hear back from the lawyer. Finally, as five o'clock came and went, she grew exasperated and called again, leaving another curt message.

"WHAT KIND OF lawyer is this?" Priya said to Ashok after he got home, sitting on the bed while he changed out of his work clothes. "I called him *twice* today after those detectives came. Why hasn't he called back? This is a crisis! Isn't he supposed to help us in our crisis?"

Ashok placed a hand on her forearm. "Remember," he said gently, "he said he was in a meeting all day today? We might just need to—"

At that moment, Priya's phone rang. She answered it on speaker and placed the phone between them.

"Jonathan Stern here. Sorry, folks. I didn't get your messages until just now. I was in a settlement conference all day."

"No problem. How was it?" Ashok asked, and Priya glared at him for indulging the man.

"Terrible, actually. But that's my problem," Jonathan said. "So, those detectives who came by—you didn't talk to them, did you?"

"No," Priya said. "I just gave them your card."

"Good, good." He sounded pleased. "Yes, they called my office, and we set a time for them to question Ajay tomorrow, one p.m. at your house. We could do it down at the precinct too, but I thought you'd prefer your home?"

"Okay, good." Ashok let out a long breath. "And yes, home would be better."

They heard a car door shut in the background. "I'll come over in the morning and prep him thoroughly," Jonathan said. "We'll do a full interview, then we'll practice his answers, role-play a bit. You should prepare him for a long day."

After they disconnected the call, Priya shook her head. "I'm not sure we should even *have* a lawyer. I could have explained everything to the detectives in a way they'd understand and put an end to all this. Instead, this is getting bigger. And now we have to put him through a whole grueling thing tomorrow. We're acting like Ajay did something wrong, like he's guilty."

"Honey." Ashok covered her hand with his. "Nobody's saying he's guilty. We both know he's not capable of these things, but we can't just be naive about this. We have to handle it the right way to protect him."

Priya just shook her head, dissatisfied but unable to counter his point. Her phone rang again; it was a local number she didn't recognize.

"Don't answer," Ashok said, but she had already declined the call and silenced her phone. When a voicemail notification popped up a moment later, she played it.

"Hi, Priya! It's Miranda Baker, Ashley's mother. Just wanted to say hello and see how the school year's going for Maya? Ashley says she's already a star on the field hockey team. I'm so glad the girls have become good friends. We just love Maya and she's welcome here anytime. Really, we'd love to have your whole family over for dinner. Maybe next weekend, if you're free? Anyway, I was wondering if Maya would be interested in a field hockey camp over winter break—"

Priya hung up. It seemed absurd to go on with the details of life as it was before. "I'm exhausted," she said, lying back on the bed. "Today was a bloody circus. I don't know how to pretend everything's normal, that everything's going to be all right, when—" Her words were choked off by emotion.

Ashok moved closer and began kneading her shoulders. "I'm sorry you had to deal with all that alone. I didn't know everyone was going to stay home today. But you handled everything just right." His words, an implicit acknowledgment of her grievance the night before, formed a bridge forward.

"And tomorrow will be even worse, with the lawyer and police here." Ashok looked at Priya. "I think the girls should go back to school. You remember, Jonathan said the police might try to come search the house. This could go on for days or weeks. There's no need for them to be exposed to all this, and it won't help Ajay."

Priya immediately felt her sense of protectiveness rise, wanting to keep them all home with her, to replicate that moment of serenity on the couch today. But she knew Ashok was probably right, and she was too spent to argue otherwise. She hoisted herself up from the bed. "I'll tell Deepa to drive Maya to school in the morning."

"And make sure they don't talk to anyone at school!" Ashok called out as she left.

25

Tuesday

"JUST DROP ME at the mall," Maya said to Deepa as soon as she got into the car the next morning. "I'm not going to school today."

Deepa laughed. "What are you talking about?"

"Drop me at the mall, please," Maya said. "You said you'd take me to the mall whenever I wanted this week, and I want to go today."

Deepa stared at her sister, who appeared to be serious.

Maya stared back. "I have money for lunch; I have my homework with me. And I need to find a good birthday gift for Ashley. It's going to take a while. You can just pick me up on your way home from school."

"Maya," Deepa said. "I know it's hard, but you heard Mom. We're supposed to go back to school today."

"Oh, you're really going to be the rule enforcer with me now? Really, Deeps? At least I'm not sneaking all the way down to Mexico. How do you think Mom would feel about that?"

Deepa turned the key in the ignition. She didn't have much of an argument against that point, nor did she have any remaining moral authority over Maya. She and her sister were now bound together by their secrets and guilt, and there didn't seem to be a simple way to extricate this tangle.

MAYA STEPPED INTO Ooh-la-la Boutique, glancing over to the cash desk in the back of the store. Seeing that it was unoccupied, she made her way to the table that held an array of beautiful jewelry: delicate necklaces with small gemstone pendants, dangly earrings that caught the light, cuff bracelets in hammered metal. She ran her fingers lightly over the assortment before landing on a piece she knew would be perfect for Ashley: a rose gold chain with a matching flower pendant, a small pearl at its center. Maya lifted it from the display bar and laid it in a small clump on the table near her left side. When she leaned forward to look at the other necklaces with her right hand, she discreetly swept up the first with her left hand and closed her fist around it. She stepped back from the table, feeling a sudden perspiration under her arms.

A woman emerged from the back room. "Good morning. Help you find anything?" she said.

Maya smiled brightly. "You have a lot of beautiful stuff. I'll definitely come back to find my mother's birthday gift next month."

As she stepped out of the boutique, her fingers wrapped around the chain in her pocket, Maya felt the rush of excitement that always came with triumph. She couldn't wait to see Ashley's face when she opened her gift on Saturday, surrounded by her family.

AFTER THE LAST bell rang at Cesar Chavez High School that afternoon, Deepa sat in the courtyard with Paco.

"Have you told your parents yet about Saturday?" he asked.

Deepa shook her head, feeling the emotion well up inside her. "I just feel so . . . I know *technically* it wasn't my fault. But I can't help this feeling that I . . . like, I *willed* this situation onto my family, you know, the way I am with my parents all the time." She shrugged. "It was so scary, first us getting detained by the police, then going into that horrible jail building, and seeing my little brother with his face all messed up."

"Same shit that's been happening forever," Paco said.

"Yeah, only my parents have never seen it that way," Deepa said.

"They always thought they were exempt from this kind of thing, the 'good' immigrants. Work hard, play by the rules, and eventually you'll get ahead . . ."

"Doesn't matter." Paco shook his head. "Not if you live in the barrio or have dark skin. Not that *you* guys live in the barrio." He leaned his shoulder against hers, trying to garner a smile. The tension between them on Saturday had mostly dissipated, for which Deepa was grateful. She couldn't handle missing Paco right now on top of everything else.

"Yeah, live in a good neighborhood, have a good job," Deepa said. "They thought all that would protect them, I think. Whenever they saw police brutality on the news, they just assumed those people must have done something, broken some rule. Maybe now they'll finally get it. Because their own son's skin color, height, clothing, whatever—landed him in the same place. None of that stuff my parents believe in protected him in the end."

"How's Ajay?" Paco said. "He going to be okay?"

"I hope so," Deepa said. "The lawyer's pushing to get the charges reduced or dropped. But honestly, I think he's already pretty messed up by the whole thing." She felt tears prickle behind her eyes, flowing in to supplant her anger. Deepa found she couldn't speak as her throat tightened, and Paco, who had always been able to read her, wrapped his arm around her shoulders. She leaned against him and allowed herself only a few tears.

After a moment, she wiped her eyes and tried to speak against her tight throat. "His face is all scraped up, and Mom said he has some bruised ribs, which I guess means he was hit pretty hard. And that's just the external stuff. You know how Ajay is. He can spend hours building LEGO models or working on his computer. But now when he's holed up in his room, he's not doing any of those things. Mom says he's had trouble sleeping since the jail, and when he came down for dinner last night, his eyes just look kind of empty."

Paco exhaled and tightened his grip around her shoulders. "You know, when my dad died, Esme had trouble sleeping. I would sit with her in bed, read her stories, sing to her, scratch her back. Sometimes I would fall asleep before her, and she would wake me up to keep reading." He chuckled. "Finally, after a few nights of this, she told me that she was afraid to close her eyes because she thought our father might come back and no one would be there to let him in the house." Paco cleared his throat. "Broke my heart, that sweet little girl. She didn't understand yet that he was really gone."

Deepa looked up at him. "What did you do?"

"I took her outside on the balcony and told her to look for the brightest star in the sky. 'That's Apá,' I told her after she found it. 'He's not here anymore, and he can't come back, but he's out there every day and every night. Even when you can't see him, even when the sun is shining, he's there, looking over you.'"

"And?" Deepa asked.

"She passed out that night, didn't wake up for twelve hours." Paco smiled. "She still has trouble sleeping sometimes, even now. But I just remind her about the stars, and it usually settles her down."

They were quiet for a few minutes together. Across the courtyard, two guys started shooting a basketball at the netless hoop.

"He's at a tender age, your brother," Paco said. "Losing his innocence. Seeing the ugliness in the world. But he'll get through it. You all will."

Deepa nodded, trying to swallow down the stone in her throat.

26

Tuesday

BACK AT THE Shahs' home, Ajay had already been through a grueling day. It took Jonathan Stern a long time to get the full picture of what had happened on Saturday. Then he began preparing Ajay for the kinds of questions the detectives might ask, encouraging him to emphasize certain answers: he had consulted flight schedules to determine when the airspace would be empty, his drone could not fly above 1,000 feet, the police officers had confused and upset him, and he didn't understand what they were asking of him. He didn't intend to crash the drone (and on this front, Ajay was very convincing, as he was already quite upset about Drummond), and he wasn't trying to run from the officer—he was just scared.

Ajay's mother had made him wear the stiff shirt he'd worn for school pictures. It was uncomfortable, the way the cuffs rubbed against his wrists. At least he was able to choose the chair he liked best (the one with the curved armrests) and eat his favorite lunch (warm-not-hot tomato soup with grilled cheese). But he really didn't like the way all five grown-ups in the room were watching him now, so he didn't look back.

First, Mr. Stern had asked him questions all morning, and now the lady with the tight bun was asking him again, mostly the same questions. At least she was nice, nicer than the man who sat next to her writing in his notebook the whole time, even when Ajay wasn't saying anything.

His mother had promised that if he answered all their questions, maybe he'd be able to get Drummond back afterward. So Ajay was concentrating hard: describing how Drummond worked and the images he was trying to capture above the airport, how some of the runways were parallel and others intersected. He told them how the man in the uniform yelled at him, but he couldn't understand; how he knew he should leave when the window closed and the planes started flying overhead. He answered all their questions, and finally, at the end, he asked about Drummond.

Evidence. Custody. Hearing.

When Ajay heard those words, he looked at his mother. It had taken him months to build Drummond the way he wanted. They couldn't mean he had to do that all again, could they? That made no sense. Didn't his mother understand? She came over and sat next to him, put her arm around his shoulders and whispered other words.

Not yet. Not now. Later. Don't worry.

He couldn't hear anymore. He couldn't stand all those people looking at him. He couldn't bear the irritation on his wrists. He yanked at his shirt cuffs, he covered his ears, trying to block it all out. Finally, his mother said he could go. But before going upstairs, he ducked into the kitchen and took the rest of the grilled cheese dippers up to his room. As soon as he could change into his softest hoodie and open his Percy Jackson, everything would be all right.

"WE'D LIKE TO take a look around if we can," Detective Hayes said, looking at Priya. "Ajay's room, and he mentioned a workshop?"

Priya was furious. These people had driven her son to a breaking point with their questions, and now they wanted to search the room where he had retreated? And what workshop were they referring to—the robotics lab at school? She was trying to collect herself to respond when Jonathan Stern interjected.

"Do you have a search warrant, Detective?"

"We can come back with one tomorrow," Detective Cooper said. "Just thought we would spare us all the trouble of a return visit."

"My clients would be happy to comply with a warrant." Jonathan smiled as if he were remarking on the pleasant weather. "But I think we've all had enough for one day." He stood up, and after a moment, the detectives followed suit. Priya felt a flash of gratitude for Jonathan then, for sparing them whatever this was for one more day.

"Thank you," Ashok said in a cheery voice as he opened the front door for the detectives. "Have a good day." He held up his palm in a friendly wave as they left.

After the door closed, Priya looked at him, appalled.

"What?" Ashok said.

"You want to invite them for dinner too?" Priya retorted. "Why are you pandering to these . . . *monsters* who are torturing our son?"

"No harm in being polite, showing them who we really are," Ashok said.

Priya shook her head. "Ashok, they don't care who we are." She found it maddening at times, the way her husband was willing to curry favor with everyone, regardless of their authenticity or integrity. She knew his willingness to deal was one of the qualities that made him successful in business, but sometimes she wished he would just take a stand, regardless of the consequences.

THAT EVENING, THE Shah family dined on a vegetable lasagna Archie had dropped off in a freezer bag on her way home from work. "It's just as easy to make two of these," she had insisted, "once you're doing all the layering and whatnot. And the twins think everything's a competition, so I had them race against each other to assemble these last night."

As Priya dug a fork into her piece, steam and the rich fragrance of tomato sauce rose to meet her. She felt so grateful for this pleasure of a home-cooked meal after the arduous day. She felt her energy slowly restored with each bite, though she could see around the table that not everyone was enjoying their food. Ajay had collected a pile of cubed zucchini on the side of his plate, while Deepa had served herself such a small piece that her dish seemed barren. Priya didn't have the energy to encourage either of them to eat more.

"Sorry, Mom," Ajay said. "I guess I ate too many cheese dippers. They're a lot better than this." He offered Priya a boyish smile, which warmed her inside.

"Oh, Maya, Ashley's mother called me. I haven't had a chance to call her back."

"What?" Maya looked up from her lasagna. "Why?"

"She asked if you wanted to do some kind of field hockey camp over winter break? She sounded very nice and welcoming. She suggested getting our families together—"

"Mom," Maya moaned. "I'm in high school. Can't you just let me have my own friends?"

"Well, I don't have time to worry about social engagements right now, Maya, don't worry," Priya snapped. "Deepa, you can drive Maya to and from school the rest of the week? I'd like to stay home with Ajay."

"Sure," Deepa said.

"And make sure your rooms are tidy before you leave for school tomorrow," Priya added as everyone was dispersing from the table. If those detectives came back with a search warrant, she at least wanted to put forth the best impression of their family.

27

Wednesday

"DETECTIVES, WHAT CAN I do for you?" the judge said as he swept into his chambers, robes flowing behind him.

Serena Hayes rose out of her chair immediately while Joe Cooper stood slowly, pushing off the armrests. "How's the game, Judge?" Cooper said. "Been hitting the court much?"

"Not lately, Joe. Shoulder's been giving me some trouble." The judge touched his right shoulder and moved it in a circular motion under his robes. "How about you? Been down to Baja recently?"

"Caught a four-foot yellowtail near Ensenada last month." Joe Cooper scrolled on his phone to find the photo and proudly showed it to him.

As the two men conversed, Serena noticed a framed photo sitting on the bookshelf, the judge dressed in tennis whites, holding a gold trophy. She cleared her throat and spoke. "Judge, we're requesting a search warrant for a private residence in Pacific Hills. The suspect was arrested Saturday night on charges of trespassing at John Wayne Airport and flying a drone in restricted airspace." She held the papers out to the judge.

He donned his reading glasses as he took them. "Isn't this the FAA's domain?"

"We've notified them, Judge," Joe Cooper said. "They may do their own investigation and bring civil charges."

The judge spent a few moments scanning the affidavit. "Electronic devices and materials used to make explosive devices—that's what you're looking for? So, this would be for a new charge, beyond the trespassing?"

"If we find evidence of terrorist activity or any national security threat, we'll loop in the FBI, of course," Joe Cooper said.

"Probable cause?" the judge asked.

"The drone could have been intended for use as a weapon. Suspect destroyed evidence by crashing the drone when approached by officers," Serena said. "Then he resisted arrest, he was evasive. He told officers he built the drone himself in his workshop, but he didn't have a good answer as to why he was violating FAA regulations. We interviewed the suspect yesterday. He seemed to know an awful lot of technical stuff about drones and flight patterns but claimed he didn't know about airspace restrictions."

"Don't drones have built-in geofencing, to prevent this kind of thing?" the judge asked.

"Only if they're purchased commercially," Serena said. "If you build something yourself, from parts, you can get around that. We've sent the recovered parts to the state lab to see if they find traces of explosives or anything else."

"And did he say why he was there, at the airport?" The judge peered at her over his glasses.

Serena moved her head from side to side. "To get cool images, he said."

"Cool images," the judge repeated. "Any criminal history? Any associations with known terrorist groups?" He flipped through the rest of the warrant application.

"We haven't got access to his digital footprint yet." Joe Cooper cleared his throat. "That's why we want to see if there's a computer. He doesn't have a phone."

The judge stared at him. "Who doesn't have a phone these days?"

Joe Cooper cleared his throat. "He's twelve, Your Honor."

"Jesus." The judge put the papers down on his desk and took off his glasses.

"Given recent events," Joe Cooper said, "that cell that went undetected at the mosque and the teenager who committed the shooting at the mall—"

"Any connection to those?" the judge asked.

Joe Cooper shook his head. "Not that we know of yet. Just being careful."

The judge steepled his fingers and leaned back in his chair, squeezed his eyes shut for a few long moments. Serena Hayes looked over at her partner, who just shrugged.

"There's not much here, Detectives." The judge picked up the papers and looked at them again. "This is barely probable cause. A few evasive comments and a broken drone. He's a kid, for god's sake. He could just be scared witless."

"We don't feel like we can take that chance, Your Honor." Joe Cooper leaned forward in his chair. "He's been arrested on three charges. The arraignment's in twelve days. We just want to cover our bases. A simple search of the house and the kid's workshop, that's it. If there's nothing there, we move on."

The judge leaned forward, grabbed a pen from his desk, struck out a couple of lines, and signed his name to the papers. "I'm restricting your search to the kid's room and workshop only. Tread carefully, Joe."

TWO POLICE CRUISERS followed the detectives' gray sedan on the twelve-mile stretch of highway, then along several city blocks of commercial district, through a modest neighborhood, and up through the winding roads toward Pacific Hills. The vehicles did not announce themselves with sirens or lights. Still, the caravan was conspicuous as it passed increasingly large houses and lawns. The gray sedan pulled up to the curb in front of the house, and the two black-and-whites parked behind it, partially blocking the Shahs' driveway and part of the neighbors' as well. Six people stepped out of the cars and moved in a swarm toward the Shahs' front door, Joe Cooper in front, search warrant in hand.

Next door, the retired banker was retrieving his copies of the *Financial Times* and *Wall Street Journal* from the driveway. Across the street, the architect's husband was getting into his car to drive to work. Other neighbors were walking dogs, jogging down the street. After a few messages circulated, more neighbors began peering out their windows or stepping out of their front doors, some gathering on the sidewalk, curious.

INSIDE THE HOUSE, Ashok was on his laptop at the dining table, attempting to catch up on work that had been neglected over the past few days: client contracts to look over, a few new prospects to follow up on, and some bookkeeping items that demanded attention. He couldn't very well expect Priya to keep up with payroll and accounts receivable invoices right now. It was more important that she be with Ajay as she was now, helping him clean up his room. Priya had a knack for getting their son to do things that Ashok had never really developed.

Ajay's room was filled with dozens of LEGO kits, shelves of fantasy novels and electronics magazines, a few encyclopedic volumes on topics like astronomy or turbine engines that had fascinated him at one time or another. When Ajay was enthralled with a new subject, he loved explaining what he'd learned to the whole family, with the result that they all possessed an esoteric knowledge bank that came in handy during trivia games or cocktail parties. Who, for example, knew that nearly the two hundred highest mountains in the world were all on the Asian continent?

Ashok found the sheer amount of stuff in his son's room mind-boggling to navigate. A rapid double ring of the doorbell followed by a loud knock startled Ashok, and he rose to answer it. The two detectives, along with several uniformed officers, formed an intimidating presence on their porch. Detective Cooper held out a warrant, and Ashok gave it a cursory read before letting them enter, wondering if any neighbors had already seen.

*

UPSTAIRS, PRIYA WAS sitting on the floor of Ajay's bedroom as she had learned to do, asking him about each object before tidying them into boxes and baskets. Her son was particular about how things were organized, a lesson she'd learned when she'd first done a seasonal purge of clothes that no longer fit, and it had troubled him. Priya had then begun going through this process together with Ajay, and it was an opportunity to gain a window into his mind as he told her what was important, why he was holding on to an object, or how he grouped things together.

Today, though, Priya was taking some liberties with the organization. All the bits and pieces from Ajay's various drone kits, for example, she gathered into a shoebox and put on the shelf with his LEGOs. When she found a stack of paper that turned out to be printed flight schedules, she rolled it up discreetly and slid it into the recycling bag, along with the other loose papers. She wasn't destroying or hiding anything. There was no need, because Ajay had done nothing wrong. But Priya had seen how people often misunderstood her son, thinking he was rude or sullen when, in fact, he was kind and gentle. It was only that his mind worked in a different way. Those police officers who found him at the airport had believed him to be criminal and had treated him accordingly. Yesterday's detectives were harsh with their endless questioning. She knew her boy's heart, and she just wanted others to see his goodness too.

When the doorbell rang, she looked up at Ajay, who was preoccupied with the Rubik's Cube they'd come across. He had solved two sides already. She took a quick glance around and found the room presentable: clothes hung, bed made, everything else stacked neatly on the shelves. Priya could hear the voices of the detectives coming from downstairs, intermingled with Ashok's. She knew she couldn't allow Ajay to see them searching his room.

"Come on, we're all done here." Priya stood up, grabbing the trash bags. "Let's go."

"Where?" Ajay asked without looking up from the cube.

"Library?" she offered, then, spontaneously, "And lunch, your choice."

"For real?" Ajay looked up at her. He hadn't been outside the house in three days.

"Yes, but quickly. Let's go!"

Priya took Ajay's hand firmly in hers as they descended the staircase. She felt him pull back as they approached the foyer. The two detectives from the day before stood there, and behind them were several other uniformed officers—how many people had they brought? Priya pulled at Ajay's hand, but he didn't move. His eyes were locked on those policemen.

"I'm going to have to ask you and your family to wait out here, sir," one of the detectives said brusquely to Ashok.

"We were just leaving." Priya pulled at Ajay again, and finally he followed her toward the door to the garage.

ONCE THEY WERE safely ensconced in the car, Priya turned to Ajay, who was shaking his head. "Mom, what are they going to do to me?"

"Nothing, honey. Nothing." But Priya knew no amount of reasoning would counter his fears, triggered by seeing those same uniforms from Saturday. All she could do now was redirect him with the promise of an excursion. "Shall we go to the theater after lunch? What's that new Marvel movie that just came out?"

As the garage door opened, the parked police cruiser came into view, around which Priya had to maneuver. Craning her neck from side to side as she reversed, she noticed neighbors gathered in driveways and on sidewalks, watching with curiosity but averting their eyes as they watched her drive away.

28

Thursday

DEEPA WAS WAITING outside Paco's building when he came down the stairs. As he opened the car door, she held out a large Starbucks cup. "Venti drip, double milk, and sugar." She smiled. Paco refused to order a fancy espresso drink, even when she insisted on buying. *Six bucks is just offensive,* he'd say. *You know my mom could feed the whole family for that much?*

"Thanks," he said, taking the cup as he stowed his backpack between his knees.

"I think my parents are losing it," Deepa said as she began to drive. "The police came to search our house yesterday, and my mom was running around cleaning up like the queen of England was paying a visit. She tore apart Ajay's entire room—his room! That's like his sanctuary—he keeps everything exactly how he likes it. It brings him a sense of peace, you know? So, Mom takes four thousand LEGO pieces and dumps them into plastic bins, and that's the kind of thing that really sets Ajay off, you know?"

She looked over to Paco, who nodded.

"Sometimes, I think she doesn't get him at all. She just wants him to be *normal*, like us. Well, probably just like Maya, actually." Deepa shook her head. "I cannot wait to go away to college. I'm only applying to schools on the East Coast. I'm getting as far away from my family as possible." She grinned at him. "Want to come? Autumn leaves, fresh snow . . . Manhattan just a train ride away." She glanced over at Paco, who was staring ahead at the road. "What?"

"Sounds great, but the East Coast isn't really an option for me," he said. "A four-year university probably isn't even an option, unless it comes with a full ride. My option is to live at home and attend local community college, *maybe* a state university in commuting distance. But I'll still have to work part-time to help my family and cover my expenses. My life circumstances don't magically change with high school graduation, you know." He took a drink of his coffee.

Deepa looked over at him as she pulled into the school parking lot. "But I . . . I thought you were looking into scholarships and writing programs at—"

"No, *you* said we were looking at those, Deepa. I just didn't correct you. It doesn't feel great for me to have to articulate each and every dream I have to bury while I'm watching other people chase theirs."

Deepa pulled into a parking spot and turned to him. "Paco, I'm sorry . . . I didn't . . . I didn't mean to—"

"Forget it," he said as he exited the car, leaving his mostly full coffee cup behind.

NOT LONG AFTER the girls left for school on Thursday morning, the doorbell rang, a previously pleasant sound that now set Priya immediately on edge. She breathed deeply before she looked through the peephole, expecting to see the detectives and preparing a response in her mind. But instead, it was a young woman she saw on the other side of the door. A neighbor? She looked harmless, so Priya opened the door.

The woman was dressed in an army green cargo jacket and jeans. She wore Adidas sneakers and held her phone in one hand, a small notepad in the other.

"Hello?" Priya said.

"Mrs. Shah? Penny Savage, with the *OC Register*. I'm interested in your son's interaction with the police Saturday night? I want to tell you right off the bat that we never print the names of minors, and this can all be off the record, if you prefer. But it's an unusual case, as I'm sure you know, not only because of your son's age."

Priya stood silent, unable to sort through what the woman was saying, much less offer any response.

"I know you've just recently moved into this neighborhood," the reporter continued. "Two months ago, right? Do you have a mosque or other community here?"

What? Priya felt everything sway a bit in front of her eyes.

"Some of your neighbors have described your son as a"—the reporter consulted her notes here—"computer genius, very adept with robotics. Could he—"

"Sorry," Priya mumbled before moving to close the door. But as she did, she heard the reporter call out one more question, with urgency:

"Mrs. Shah, do you believe your son was racially profiled by the police?"

"SLOW DOWN. EXPLAIN exactly what happened with this reporter?" Jonathan Stern's voice sounded tense through the phone.

After Priya described the situation, Stern was quiet for a few moments. Priya and Ashok looked at each other, wondering what this silence meant.

"Look," Stern finally said. "I'm not sure how they got hold of this. But when there's media involved, the police tend to double down to justify their choices. They don't like to lose face. For now, let's try to keep this as neutral as possible, keep it out of the public eye. Don't feed the media, don't talk to the press at all. Go on with your lives as best you can."

"What kind of help is that? He basically told us to do nothing," Priya said after they got off the phone, then added, "This is how he earns his fees? And how much is this lawyer even going to cost, do we know?"

"Don't worry about that," Ashok said.

"What do you mean, don't worry?" Priya snapped. "Don't patronize me."

After a moment, Ashok said, "Vikram's taking care of it. He said he would cover Jonathan's bills. Apparently his firm does a lot of work for Vikram anyway, so he practically has him on full retainer. He said it wasn't a big deal."

"He said that?" Priya asked. "Are you sure?"

"Yes," Ashok replied. "Well, he said it on Sunday when we were all here together after meeting with Jonathan. I haven't spoken to him since."

"Should you check in with him?" Priya said.

Ashok nodded. "I've tried. He hasn't called me back. Must be busy."

"I know you trust him . . . " Priya said, "but is this really a good idea?" She felt a surge of conflicting emotions. On one hand, it was very generous of Vikram, and it certainly relieved a major concern. On the other, she felt uneasy accepting such an offer. It would be one thing coming from Archie and Ricky, who were practically family—but they hadn't known the Sharmas as long or as well.

"I'll call him this weekend, okay?" Ashok said. "Don't worry, it'll all be fine."

A thought rose in Priya's mind to which she hadn't given any mental space before. It bothered her that Veena Sharma had not called or come by all week. She had sent a text message that first night after they'd left the dinner party in a rush, asking if there was anything they could do to help. And of course, Vikram had been with them on Sunday. But Priya was struck by how much emotional support she felt from Archie's physical presence in their home—being in her embrace, tasting her home-cooked food. Priya knew that support and friends came in different forms, so it might not be fair, but she couldn't help but feel bothered by Veena's absence.

29

Friday

IT WAS SUCH a small article—only three inches of a half column buried in the local section of the *Orange County Register*—they hoped no one would read it. It reported the arrest of a juvenile charged with trespassing on government property and destroying evidence, and mentioned possible national security violations. It described the suspect as being from a South Asian immigrant family. And there was a quote, inexplicably, from the imam of the local Islamic Center.

> Our community continues to be unfairly targeted. We are condemned for our beliefs, our religion, our dress, our skin color. Have we learned nothing from the case of the FBI sending informants into our place of worship? Stop persecuting this young man and give him the benefit of the doubt that any other white-skinned American son would expect.

Ashok swore under his breath as he put down the newspaper. Why was this guy being quoted? He didn't know them! They weren't Muslim and had not set foot in this, or any other, mosque. Perhaps Priya's instinct had been correct: they should have just spoken to that reporter when she showed up on their doorstep. At least they could have set the record straight.

While nothing published in the article was inaccurate, the story still felt untrue. Ashok was grateful that, as a minor, Ajay's name had not been printed, but several other notable facts were also omitted. There was no mention of the fact that the Shah family had lived in the United States for nearly twenty years. That all three of their children had been born here. That they were a law-abiding, tax-paying family who had followed every single rule since arriving in the country with a proper visa and legal invitation to come. And no mention of the fact that the defendant was a twelve-year-old American boy whose only real offense was being carried away by his quirky interests and too innocent about the world around him.

WHEN PRIYA READ the article, she was struck not by the words in the piece itself but its undercurrents. The unnamed juvenile offender was from Pacific Hills. *Imagine! A terrorist in their swanky suburban midst.* It might be comical if it didn't sound so ominous. A neighbor had been referenced in the article, saying the family had very recently moved into the neighborhood but had kept to themselves; no one had really gotten to know them yet. Priya wondered if this could be the architect or someone else in their new neighborhood she'd once hoped to meet at a block party or backyard barbecue, not through misrepresentations in the press.

This morning, when she'd stepped outside to retrieve the newspaper from the driveway, the next-door neighbor was getting into his car. Priya said good morning and waved, but he didn't respond. It was nothing, she'd reassured herself, he must not have heard her. But now she wondered if it was something more.

Priya felt more tears coming, impossible to stop these days. Pain mixed with anger, sadness, and that fierce protective instinct she felt for her children. Her powerlessness to protect Ajay hung over her like a dark cloud, following her everywhere. She hadn't felt this overwhelmed since Deepa was a baby. Back then, it had felt like the ultimate failure of her fundamental role, a feeling she thought she had long moved past. They were citizens now, they had steady work and a house, they were financially stable and had a support network. And yet.

When she collected herself, Priya sent a message to Archie.

Can you talk?

The response came within seconds, as if Archie had been waiting for her.

On my way. Btw, don't worry about dinner tonight. Bringing enough chicken tikka for a cricket team.

In fact, don't worry about dinner until further notice.

Priya burst into tears again, then went to splash water on her face.

"AT LEAST THEY didn't print our names," Ashok said that night as they lay together in bed. "What if this gets out?"

"It might," Priya said. "I had to talk to Ajay's school today. I've been saying he's staying home for a family emergency, but the principal called today. She said she was concerned about him, about our family. I had to tell her something."

Ashok tilted his head back and gazed at the ceiling. "What did you say?"

"As little as possible. That he rode his bike home from robotics practice Saturday and ended up in a restricted part of the airport where the police found him," Priya said. "She was nice about it, said we could pick up his homework each day if we want. But honestly, I think she was more worried about their liability, since he left school grounds without an adult and no one knew."

"What?" Ashok let out a bark. "She's worried about *us* suing the school?"

"Yes, right?" Priya laughed. "Just what we need. More legal battles."

"Maybe we should send him back to school next week?" Ashok asked.

Priya shook her head. "We have to minimize his stress so he can be his best at the arraignment. It's only another week."

A prolonged silence followed as the implications of this fact settled on them both.

Ashok's expression suddenly grew grim. "God, how the hell did we end up here?"

THOUGH THE LOCAL newspaper had a dwindling print subscriber base, and though no names were named, the neighborhood gossip network was as strong as ever, and the link to this online article circulated with brash efficiency. It did not take long for the rumor mill to be spinning with news and speculation about the new family that had moved in down the street and their strange, possibly suspicious son.

30

Saturday

BY THE TIME the weekend arrived, Priya felt like she had lived through a year but had barely slept all week. On Saturday morning, Archie unloaded bags in the Shahs' kitchen as Priya sat at the counter, watching through bleary eyes.

"I have some unidentified citrus from Lalitaji's garden," Archie explained, placing a handful of small greenish-yellow fruits into a bowl on the counter. "Could be key limes or tiny underripe lemons. I don't know, maybe kumquats?" She lifted a large covered glass dish onto the counter. "Aloo gobi from the Panchals, and paratha. She makes the best. We can freeze some if you want."

"You don't have to do all this, Arch," Priya said, even as she felt more grateful than she could express.

"And why not?" Archie said with a raised eyebrow and that smile of hers that hinted at mischief. "Your friends want to help. This is how we show love. We feed you and plump you up."

Priya smiled nervously. "What . . . what did you tell them?" She thought of the evasive next-door neighbor, whoever had spoken to the newspaper reporter, and all those people watching across the street as the detectives searched the house. Had the disfavor also spread back to their old neighborhood in Irvine?

Archie placed her hands on the counter, looking at Priya. "I told them the *truth*." She spoke the words clearly. "Ajay—the sweet, innocent boy we all know—was in the wrong place at the wrong time, and now your family is caught up in a big legal and media drama." She looked at Priya and pursed her mouth. "Well, maybe I used some stronger language." She winked and cleared space in the fridge for the casserole dish, then poured milk and water into a small saucepan on the stove to make chai.

Ashok joined them in the kitchen, running a hand through his hair. "Okay, he's working on a LEGO project. That replica of the spaceship from *Star Trek* should keep him occupied for a few hours, hopefully keep his brain from going to complete mush. I don't know how much longer we can keep him home from school. Even if he doesn't want to go, it might be better for him." Ashok always believed in getting back up after a defeat, and he didn't see any reason this shouldn't apply to his son now.

Archie's phone buzzed with a message. She glanced at it. "Wait. Turn on the TV. Channel five."

They went into the family room, and Ashok fumbled with the television remote. When he found the right channel, it was broadcasting the local news, showing a group of people gathered in front of a stately building. They were holding signs and chanting. A middle-aged Black woman wearing a T-shirt that said Justice 4 All was standing with a reporter.

"We just want this family to know that we stand with them in their pursuit of justice. We, too, demand transparency and accountability from the police and the DA," the woman said.

The reporter turned to the camera. "The march will go from the county courthouse steps, as you can see here, through the main square, and end up at the Orange County Sheriff's Department headquarters, a few blocks away.

"The march was organized by Justice 4 All, the same group that led protests in Los Angeles after the police shooting of an unarmed teenaged boy named Theo Young. Theo's mother has become a powerful spokesperson against police brutality and racial profiling. The name of the Orange County adolescent at the center of this recent case is not being released as he is a minor, but the marchers here said they wanted to express their support for the family and demand justice for all."

The screen turned to footage of the protesters marching down the center of the street, behind a pickup truck displaying a large Justice 4 All banner. They were holding signs that read:

STOP Racial Profiling

Brown Skin ≠ Terrorist

Protect ALL Our Children!

The local news shifted to coverage of a new exotic animal petting zoo, and Ashok switched off the TV. There was silence in the room as everyone was struck by the same thought: If that protest was about Ajay, how did they find out?

In fact, someone in the Justice 4 All organization had caught wind of this case from the *Orange County Register* article, attuned to the suggestion of police brutality and racial profiling in a heretofore protected upscale suburb. In addition to fitting with the organization's cause, this case could be good for publicity—a way to broaden the appeal of the group beyond the urban setting, beyond victims who were Black. A way for people to understand how widespread and insidious the problem was. Thus, the march had been mobilized and the media had been notified about this "Show of Solidarity," as the protesters called their gathering.

"I don't know, this might be good," Archie said. "Maybe you could use this support, create some positive energy."

Ashok shook his head. "I don't like the attention. I don't like being associated with all this publicity, aligned with a political cause. This is a private matter for our family—we should keep it that way."

"Ashok, you're aligned already," Archie said. "Hell, you *are* the cause now."

"No," snapped Ashok. "We have to handle this differently. Vikram says people get out of situations like this all the time. He knows kids who've had DUIs wiped off their record, *much* worse things. Ajay didn't harm a soul."

Archie chuckled. "I know those people too, and you know what? They're all wealthy, connected, and *white*. Or at least two out of three. Unfortunately, that's not our situation here. You can't play this white, Ashok, no matter what Vikram tells you."

"I'm not"—Ashok grasped for words—"trying to *play white*. But I also don't think it's fair to just lump everyone else together and say we should all believe the same things." He flung his hand toward the blank TV screen. "It's like we're being . . . *used* for someone else's cause!"

He bristled at the idea of this march happening in their name. He recalled the bandhs back in India, general strikes in which entire neighborhoods came to a standstill. Schools and shops were forced to close, the train system shut down. Everyone was expected to stay home at the behest of a political group's declaration. And for what purpose? Everyone was inconvenienced, people were caught up in skirmishes or even violence, but nothing ever changed.

Archie raised a single arched eyebrow. "Okay, okay. Come on." She linked her arm through Priya's. "Let's go have chai. You both look exhausted."

As they returned to the kitchen, Priya didn't know what to think. Suddenly, there were so many people involved in their business: the lawyer, the detectives, the reporter, now the protesters. Priya didn't care about any of them, and when she really allowed herself to think about it, she didn't really care what the neighbors thought, either. What she wanted—*all* she wanted—was for Ajay to be free of this situation, to recover from his physical injuries and get on with his life, with all the promise that it held just one week ago. She wanted him to have his future back. As she watched Archie add tea leaves and masala to the saucepan, then sprinkle in a touch of brown sugar, Priya thought of the way her friend had referred to the situation as *ours* so naturally. She didn't know what to think about all the other people claiming pieces of her family, but at least here in her home, she could be surrounded by people she loved and trusted. It was this promise to which she tried to cling.

31

Saturday

AT THE BAKER compound, two bunches of rose-gold balloons with confetti inside were tied to the foreboding driveway gate, which now slowly began to slide open. At the top of the driveway, a car backed out of the garage. Maya clutched the gift bag stuffed with lavender tissue in her lap. Her hand was on the door handle, but she was crouching down in her seat, seemingly waiting for something. The car, a BMW, was now directly in front of them, and Deepa could see the driver was a boy about her age.

"Is that Ashley's brother? He drives a Beemer?" Deepa quipped. "Wow, life must be good for—what's his name—Chip? Chandler?" She watched as the sleek navy-blue sedan pulled out onto the road and sped away.

"Chase." Maya slipped off her cardigan to reveal a low-cut sundress and left the sweater in her seat.

Deepa stared at her. "Are you wearing *eye shadow*? Isn't that a bit much for a birthday party?" She waved her hand at Maya's outfit.

"Thanks, *Mom*. I got it." Just as Maya opened the car door to step out, Deepa's phone buzzed three times in succession. She glanced at the screen and was relieved to see a spray of messages from Paco, who had been silent since their tiff a couple of days ago. She clicked on the link in his last message.

"Oh my god," she said, scanning the news report of the march. "Maya, wait." She put her hand on her sister's wrist. "Look at this!"

They both searched for more news on their phones, reading out loud to each other the few details they could find. Deepa put down her phone and leaned her head against the seat. "That march *definitely* has to be about Ajay."

"Great," Maya said. "High school's not hard enough without my brother on the evening news."

"God, Maya, can you stop thinking about yourself for just a minute?" Deepa scoffed.

"Me?" Maya retorted. "What about Ajay? You think this will be *good* for him, if everyone in our neighborhood, everyone in his school, knows about this? Who are *you* thinking about, Deepa?" Maya stepped out of the car and slammed the door behind her.

Deepa felt a buzz of excitement travel up her spine as she drove away. People *saw* and were paying attention. They could see the injustice of what had happened to Ajay and they cared. Tears of relief sprang to her eyes, and she didn't realize quite how isolated she'd felt until now.

IN THE BACKYARD of the Bakers' estate, the party planner was directing the staff to set each table with a rose cloth and a sheer gold overlay, a floral arrangement, and glitter confetti. Clusters of sheer balloons were aloft in the yard, despite the helium shortage in the local market. Miranda Baker surveyed the scene and found, happily, that it surpassed even what she had envisioned for Ashley's birthday party. As her only girl and the youngest of three children, Ashley was the beneficiary of all of Miranda's feminine energy. But Miranda had been determined not to raise her daughter with the same strictures her mother had placed on her. She did not force Ashley into ballet lessons, insist she wear fashionable outfits or have a polished appearance. Miranda rather loved that Ashley had taken to the rough sport of field hockey and that her legs were perennially scabbed. It did drive her a bit mad when Ashley bit her nails to stubby lengths, but her daughter could still look lovely in a dress and carry herself with grace when she made the effort. Ashley was growing up in a different time, with more opportunities, and Miranda wouldn't take a single one away from her. She wanted to give her daughter, like all her children, everything she could. In her position, who wouldn't do the same?

She saw Ashley walking across the lawn now with Maya, reminding her that Priya had yet to return her call about the field hockey camp.

"Hi, girls! Well, what do you think?" Miranda held out her arm. "Doesn't it look fabulous?" She gestured to the yard. "It looks fabulous!" she called to the party planner, who was scooping ice into enormous barrels of agua fresca. "Chase should be back soon with more ice!" *What was it with parties?* Miranda thought. *There was never enough ice.* She was about to suggest that Ashley show Maya where the gift table was, but when she turned back, the girls were gone. Then, the mariachi band arrived and needed to know where to set up.

INSIDE THE BAKER house, Spence was flipping through the newspaper. He'd learned over the years to stay out of the way during party preparations.

"Everything's in good shape outside. What's going on here?" Miranda asked as she entered the house.

"Just catching up on the week's news. Have you heard about this situation?" Spence flipped the newspaper over. "We've got protesters coming down from LA?"

"No, what for?" Miranda took a bottle of Perrier out of the beverage fridge under the counter.

"Apparently, they're worked up about some juvenile who got arrested for trespassing on government property. I guess because the kid's a minority there's a big stink about his getting arrested. They're saying it's discrimination. The whole editorial page is filled with arguments about how the police are racist and their budget should be cut."

"Oh, I *did* hear about that," Miranda said, sipping from the bottle. "From one of the school parents. There's actually a rumor the family lives in Pacific Hills, over near the park."

Spence looked up at her.

"I know, can you believe it?" Miranda shrugged.

Spence's phone rang. He glanced at the screen and stood up. "Better take this call. This lawyer charges ten bucks a minute, probably double on weekends." He crumpled the newspaper into the recycling bin as he left the room.

32

Saturday

DEEPA WAS BRIMMING with excitement when she burst through the door. "Did you hear about the march downtown today? That was for us, for Ajay."

"Deepa, not now," her father said sternly. "Dinner's ready."

"It can only help if other people take up our cause." Deepa dropped her keys and wallet on the counter. "And Justice 4 All is a really high-profile group. They have—"

"Deepa, I said *not now.*" His voice rose in volume. "We can talk about it later." He stared at her until she sat down at the kitchen table.

Dinner was aloo gobi and chicken tikka, paratha, and salad—a feast, yet Deepa could not enjoy it. Feeling chastised and angry, she remained silent for the rest of the meal. She listened to her parents make small talk about tasks that needed to be done around the house and at the office. Ajay answered their questions about the LEGO model he'd spent all day building in the fewest possible words. Maya raved about Ashley's birthday party: the elegant decorations, the live musicians, the elaborate party favors everyone took home. Deepa wanted to scream—how could they all be focused on such trivial things? She waited until the meal was over, lingering in the kitchen after Ajay and Maya retreated to their rooms, to broach the topic again with her parents. "If you guys could just look at the bigger picture, you'd see that Ajay isn't alone. What happened to him is part of a larger pattern.

Black and brown kids all over the country are being mistreated by the police."

"It is not the same, Deepa," her father said, pouring himself a finger of scotch. "What those people are protesting, and what happened to Ajay—you can't group them together."

"Why not?" Deepa said.

"Because they're talking about people in bad neighborhoods, roaming the streets after dark. Places where there's a lot of crime, kids belong to gangs. And this—"

"This is a tall brown kid," Deepa interrupted. "Wearing a hoodie, acting in a way the cops think is suspicious. He just happens to be your kid. *That's* why it's different?"

She watched as her father closed his eyes and took a long sip of his scotch.

"Deepa." Her mother's voice was full of warning.

"Those protesters are useless, just stirring up trouble," her father muttered.

"Well . . . then, I guess I'm useless too," Deepa blurted out. "*I'm* one of those protesters." She was momentarily struck by the expression on her parents' faces, an unexpected flash of fear traveling through her body.

"You . . . were there today?" her mother asked softly.

"No, but I went down to Tijuana last Saturday to protest the detention of immigrants at the border." Deepa felt an exhilaration as she said it. "Because that's something I *believe* in, like those people today—"

"Last Saturday?" her mother said. "What do you mean? *When* Saturday?"

Deepa took two steps toward her mother. "Mom, I was going to tell you, but with everything else . . ." She explained about the crowd acting up and the police detaining everyone, watching her mother's facial expression morph from incredulousness to shock, anger, and finally go blank. Deepa felt her pulse thudding in her neck. "So I was late getting back to pick up Maya and Ajay, but you know . . . he left school even before I was supposed to be there."

"So he would have been standing there, outside the school, waiting for you?" her mother said. "And you didn't even think to call and tell us you were going to be late?"

"I couldn't, Mom," Deepa said. "The police took my phone. By the time I got it back, there was a message from Maya saying she'd gotten a ride home, so I just assumed you picked them both up. The first time I saw you was at the jail, and by then—"

"Stop." Her mother held up her palm. "Just stop. Maya and Ajay are children, but *you* are supposed to know better. I *cannot* believe you." She shook her head, exasperated. "Don't you think we have enough to worry about right now? From now on, you are not going anywhere but to school and back. No friends. No work. Those car keys and your phone stay right here when you're home." Her mother jabbed at the kitchen counter. "From the moment you walk in the door. Understood?" She didn't wait for an answer before storming out of the kitchen.

"You're off fighting for the rights of strangers, and you don't even know when your own siblings are at risk?" her father said, leaning against the kitchen counter.

"Strangers?" Deepa said. "You know, it shouldn't have to *happen* to you for you to *care* about it!"

Her father was shaking his head. "I'm disappointed, Deepa. We trusted you."

Deepa felt the weight of his disappointment acutely, and in its wake, she knew she had nothing left to lose. "All this stuff didn't matter in the end, did it?" she said. "This big house? The fancy neighborhood? All that mattered was the color of Ajay's skin and whatever assumptions those cops made about it." She watched for his response, but her father just stood there, swirling the scotch over ice in his glass. "God, you are such a hypocrite," she said. "You're happy to be a minority when it suits you. How many contracts have you gotten for being a minority-owned business, huh? Or, even better, since you decided to give Mom a role, a woman in a minority-owned business?" Deepa knew her words would cut, but they were true and she was tired of her parents' double standards.

Her father poured himself more scotch and began turning off the lamps, preparing to head upstairs for the night. This infuriated Deepa, and she felt rage boiling inside her as she followed him around. "What about all those 'barter' transactions you do, huh? I'm sure as an upstanding citizen, you pay taxes on all those, or do you cheat there too?"

When her father spun around to face her, his hand was raised, poised to strike. As it hung there, suspended in the air, Deepa stumbled backward. Her parents had never laid a hand on her. She felt her eyes well with tears, as if he had already slapped her. Her vision blurred.

Her father slowly lowered his hand, but fury was blazing in his eyes as he spoke through clenched teeth. "Don't you ever speak to me like that, understand? You have been given your whole life on a silver platter because of the sacrifices your mother and I have made. We left our families, left our country. I haven't seen my parents in four years. I have given up everything that doesn't have to do with creating a good life for you children.

"If I ever spoke to my father that way in my whole life, I would have been thrown onto the street. We broke our backs working to make a good life for you, and all you want to do is spit on it. Opportunities other people would kill for—in India, even in *Irvine*.

"If you had any sense of where you came from and how lucky you are, you would be grateful. You would take those opportunities and make us proud. Instead of *this*." He turned and marched up the staircase. Before he reached the top, Deepa sank to her knees on the bottom step, tears streaming down her face.

PART III

Day by Day

Week 2

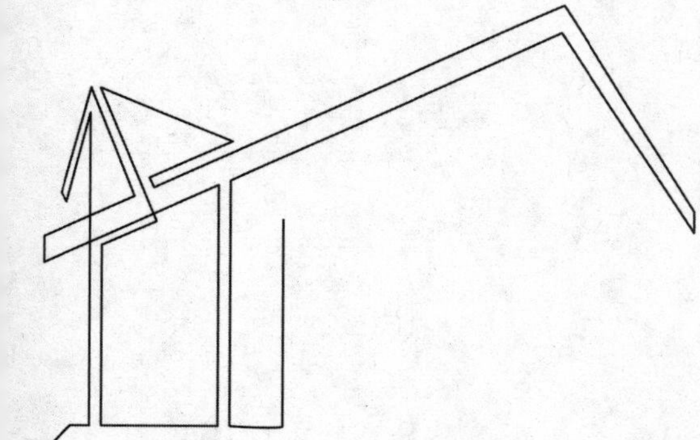

33

Sunday

STANDING UNDER THE hot stream of the shower, Ashok was preoccupied with the editorial in the morning paper, expressing outrage at the clear bigotry of the Orange County Sheriff's Department for their targeting and unfair prosecution of Muslim Americans. It was an uncontrollable wave of misinformation that couldn't be stopped now that it had started. And yet, one particular line stayed with him: *This recent arrest of a young brown boy is simply the latest example in a long pattern of police discrimination.* It niggled at him, tapping into something unleashed by Deepa's rant the night before.

As he dressed, Ashok could hear a commotion from outside. He peered through the bedroom window and felt his heart plummet. Half-dressed, with dripping hair and a towel around his neck, he ran down the stairs and into the kitchen. "Priya! Did you see outside?"

Priya peered through the curtains lining the front window. Two large vehicles were parked outside on the street, bearing the names of television channels, satellite dishes mounted on their roofs. A well-coiffed woman stood at the foot of their driveway holding a microphone, flanked by a cameraman.

"Oh my god," Priya said. "Is this because of those protesters yesterday? That article? But how did they find us? How did they know?" She sank into a chair. "Oh god, this just keeps getting worse."

"I can't believe this." Ashok rubbed his forehead. "Can't believe it!

Don't talk to them. I don't want *anyone* talking to them. Everybody come and go through the garage only, okay? Don't step foot outside. Tell the kids too."

Ashok ran back upstairs to the bedroom, where he could look through the window discreetly. *They couldn't see him up here, could they?* He spotted a man with a camera and wondered if it had the kind of telescopic lens used to catch celebrities at great distances. He gently lowered the blinds on the window and sat down on the bed in the darkened room. His mind raced through the possibilities. The newspapers would print sensational stories about a young terrorist trying to down an airplane. Their names would get out. His clients would see the news and believe it. Why wouldn't they? Even though he'd served them reliably for years, and even though his son was only a naive boy in the wrong place. They didn't know him, Priya, and Ajay as people; they hadn't known his parents because they lived in the same building in Mumbai for over fifty years; they hadn't seen his family intimately through a pattern of daily habits and actions. They knew him only as a remote service provider, a vendor whose name appeared on invoices, and they would abandon him as quickly as their outdated computers.

Ashok's business would dry up overnight as clients canceled contracts and refused to pay their outstanding bills. He would have to lay off his six employees, including Will, whose wife was expecting their first baby. He would lose tens of thousands of dollars to break the lease on the warehouse and the inventory he'd purchased. He would not be able to provide for his family. That one period of prolonged unemployment he'd had, before Deepa was born, had affected him so deeply that he'd been outrunning it ever since.

And the mortgage—oh, the mortgage—which had been a stretch in the first place, and for which they had barely qualified. Priya had been uncomfortable with that mortgage, but it was the only way they could afford to move into Pacific Hills. And now, this house, in this neighborhood they had worked so hard to reach, could all vanish in an instant. Ashok stood up again and peered around the edge of the blinds, hoping the vans and cameras and reporters might somehow have disappeared, that this worsening nightmare would just come to an end.

The door to the bedroom opened and Priya entered. It was clear from her face that she'd been crying. "Archie's cooking bhindi and dal for us for dinner. She said Ricky can bring the twins over later if we want. Might be nice for the kids to have some company."

Ashok nodded, afraid that if he spoke out loud, the stream of fears he harbored inside would escape. But Priya's eyes, too, held such sadness and fear; he reached for her, and they embraced each other tightly. When they parted, they sat on the edge of the bed together.

"They're right outside our *home*," Priya said, exasperated. "How can we protect him? How do we keep him safe with those people right outside our door?"

Ashok scratched at his still-damp hair. "How can this be happening? Everything we've built, our name will be tarnished." He thought of his father's admonitions to protect their good name.

Priya nodded. "I already got a message from a neighbor, asking what's going on. An older man down the block who was very irritated that someone parked a big van under his olive tree and broke some branches. Are they just allowed to be here, without our consent?"

Ashok shrugged. "I think as long as they stay off our private property—on the street and sidewalk—they're allowed. Freedom of the press and all that." This was another fact he knew, without being sure how. "I don't think there's anything we can do, but we should ask Jonathan." He dialed the lawyer's number and held the phone between them as he explained the situation.

"Okay," Jonathan said with a heavy sigh. "We'll have to prepare a statement."

"I thought we were supposed to avoid the media?" Priya asked.

"Well, it's out there now, so we should use it. The court of public opinion will be important if this case moves forward. We have the police arresting a kid, attacking a kid, roughing him up. They'll cry national security, terrorism." Stern's voice was animated now.

"We have to paint a different picture for the public. You are the well-assimilated immigrant family. You've worked hard to achieve the American dream. You've built a family business, you pay your taxes, you live in a nice neighborhood. You've got high-achieving kids, solid American values. We need to show the public you are the model minority and you're well integrated into American society."

"How . . . how do we do that?" Priya asked. "Show all those things, I mean?"

"Well, the first thing is to make it clear you're not Muslim," Stern said. "I'm sorry to say, but Americans associate Muslims with terrorism and you're not Muslim. So, let's show them that. Make a very visible family visit to the Hindu temple together. The whole family together—get dressed up, the whole bit. Go out the front door for the cameras. We'll prepare a statement you can share. Smile and look like a nice, unthreatening family.

"Oh," he added. "And go find an American flag to hang outside your house."

34

Sunday

"EVERYONE NEEDS TO be ready to go at four o'clock, okay?" Ashok said to the family at lunch. "Dressed up and ready. We'll walk out the front door together."

"I still don't understand why we all have to do this," Maya grumbled. "To put on a show for the cameras? I thought we were supposed to lie low." She was appalled at this charade, and at the idea of her family being outed, photographed in Indian clothes, no less. Her only strand of hope was that very few kids her age paid attention to the news.

"Well, things have changed," Ashok retorted. The media vans had been parked outside their house all day. The Shah children had been strictly prohibited from opening the front door. Ashok had gone outside only to collect the newspaper. When he walked down the driveway, he was pelted with questions that left him shaken.

"Mr. Shah, have the police searched your house?"

"When is the last time your family visited Pakistan?"

"Is your son associated with any political groups?"

Ashok smiled tersely for the reporters but didn't answer their questions, not even the factually incorrect one about Pakistan, a place they had never visited. When he reentered the house, he stood with his back against the door until he'd recovered. He repeated his warning to the children not to open the front door under any condition.

No one was going anywhere anyway. Deepa's punishment kept her at home, Maya had barely emerged from her room, and Ajay had been confined to the house and backyard all week, his bicycle still in police custody. He was now upstairs, playing video games again. All screen time limits had gone out the window under the circumstances.

"This is not about putting on a show," Priya hissed. "It's to help your brother, okay?"

"Right," Deepa said under her breath, "to show everyone that we're definitely not Muslim, and *that's* the reason Ajay can't possibly be a terrorist."

"Go get dressed, please," Priya snapped, and Maya and Deepa stood up from the table in unison.

IN AJAY'S ROOM, Priya struggled to get her son to wear his kurta set. She had already cut out the tag at the neckline, taped over some of the interior seams that would otherwise irritate his skin, and pinned up the sleeve cuffs to avoid chafing his wrists. Why on earth hadn't someone found a way to stitch these Indian outfits so they weren't so uncomfortable? Priya had been accustomed to it all her life: the stiff and scratchy fabrics, the drawstring waists tied breathtakingly tight to hold up seven yards of tucked heavy fabric. It was just the cost of looking fashionable, and she and her friends accepted the trade-off without question. But for Ajay, who only wore these outfits a few times a year and had no interest in fashion, it was like torture.

"Can't I just stay home?" Ajay asked. "I don't want to go to the temple. Why can't I just stay here and read?" He eyed a new stack of graphic novels Archie had brought over to help pass Ajay's home detention, as she facetiously referred to it. "Or I can do other stuff—weed the garden and water the plants? Please?"

Priya's heart broke a little at his desperation. She rubbed her hands over her face. Why couldn't she just give her son what he wanted? Yes, they were doing this for him, but they were causing him anguish in the process. She wanted to cry. She wanted to climb into Ajay's bed and cradle his tall gangly body against hers. But she had never been able to follow her affectionate instincts with him. Learning how to mother her son had been like tying up her right hand and teaching herself to do everything with the left. Though she'd grown more adept, it still felt unnatural. "Please, baby, for me? Just for a little while. Then we'll come home and have ice cream. You can pick the flavor, and we'll buy it on the way home."

TWENTY MINUTES LATER, and a half hour past the time Ashok had designated, the family was assembled in the front foyer, all dressed in their Indian attire. Priya smoothed Maya's hair back from her face. Ashok complimented a glum-looking Ajay and gave him a high five. Priya peeked out the front window, as if they were all waiting in the wings to make a grand stage entrance. She took a deep breath and reached for Ajay's hand. "Ready?" Ashok glanced around at the others, then opened the front door. As soon as the reporters and cameramen saw them, they clambered out of their vans.

A blond woman rushed forward and thrust a microphone toward them. Priya recognized her as the reporter who had covered the protest march the day before. "Mr. Shah, care to make a statement about the potential charges against your son?"

Priya tightened her grip on Ajay's hand and stood back with the girls while Ashok took a few steps forward toward the microphone. He waited a few moments for the shutter sounds of the cameras to subside, then made the statement they'd rehearsed to sound extemporaneous. "My family and I are on our way to the Hindu temple for our regular visit, where we will pray for this misunderstanding to be cleared up shortly. We wish you all peace." He put his palms together and bowed slightly.

THAT EVENING, AFTER the media vans had left, Priya stood out on the porch helping Ashok hang the flag they'd purchased at the hardware store on the way home. When she saw the architect walking across the street toward them, she said Ashok's name discreetly and he stepped down from the ladder.

The neighbor approached them with a smile, carrying something in her hands. "Hi," she said. "I baked you some blondies." She held out a plate.

Priya looked at the white ceramic dish, piled with caramel brown squares and wrapped in plastic. It appeared to be a plate from the woman's cupboard, not a paper plate or a disposable plastic tub. This struck her as a true gesture of hope, bringing a dish that hinted at future and reciprocal interactions. The faith implicit in this offering, more so even than the home-baked sweets, was so touching that Priya felt tears rise in her eyes. *God, what was wrong with her!*

"I can imagine this is a very stressful time for your family," the architect said with a small smile. "I just wanted you to know your neighbors are thinking of you, even if you haven't had a chance to really meet many of us yet."

"Thank you," Priya managed to whisper, accepting the plate. "That's very kind of you." Then she added, "I did hear from the gentleman down the street about his damaged olive tree."

"Bernie?" the architect asked. "Oh, screw Bernie! He's always cranky. He's out there all day pruning that thing like it's the damn tree of life." Her exasperation was so genuine that Priya couldn't help but laugh; soon they both were, until Priya was wiping tears from the corners of her eyes. It felt as if she hadn't laughed like this in forever, though it had only been a week.

DEEPA DECIDED TO try one more time to message Paco. She'd thanked him yesterday for sending news of the downtown protest, but he hadn't responded. She was dying to talk to him. She was still wrecked from the fight with her father the night before, and now she was a prisoner at home. What Paco had said to her in the car had been playing on a loop in her mind; how he had to bury his dreams for the sake of his family. Even in this time of crisis for her family, they could defend themselves: they could afford a lawyer, and her father could walk outside and speak to the press, even if it was to spin a story she found hypocritical. Finally, she sent a message in desperation.

I'm sorry for not getting it, and for being a crappy friend. I promise to try harder, if you promise to try a mochaccino. It seriously makes EVERYTHING better.

She waited while the three dots indicated that he might be writing back. They disappeared and reappeared. Then her phone rang, and she exhaled a huge sigh of relief.

"Hey," she said.

"Hey, I'm sorry too." Paco's voice was warm. "Sometimes I just snap. It gets to be a lot, you know—keeping my nose clean, living under this cloud all the time." He paused. "And I can't say anything to my family, so I just keep it all bottled up inside."

Deepa realized this was another luxury afforded to her, being able to express her misgivings to her parents without worrying that she would burden or break them.

"Sometimes, I just want someone to hear me, to understand me," Paco said.

"I get that," Deepa said, and there was a long silence while the parameters of their friendship reorganized themselves into a familiar and reliable shape. "I'll try to do better."

"See you tomorrow, usual time?"

"Oh yeah, about that," Deepa said. "I'm kind of *grounded*, so I can't drive you to school for a while."

"What?" Paco said. "I thought your parents didn't buy into that kind of American punishment."

"Yeah, well, I guess I'm breaking into new territory."

"This should be good." Paco laughed. "Can't wait to hear all the details."

35

Monday

"WELL, OFFICER DIAZ, your case has certainly blown up, hasn't it?" Penny Savage said. "Now we've got the Justice 4 All folks down here, drawing attention . . ."

Diaz set down his notepad on the dashboard of the patrol car so he could hold the phone to his ear. "I think your story might have had something to do with that, huh?"

"I appreciate the tip," Penny said. "Gave me a bit of a lead. Now every outlet's camped out at the family house."

"How'd you guys find them?" Diaz had been wondering about this.

"I'm on some neighborhood chat boards," Penny said. "Your detectives weren't exactly discreet—they knocked on a lot of doors and executed a midday search warrant. Gossip in the Hills travels faster than a spark in fire season."

Diaz chuckled. "Remember, he's a minor."

"I know. We're not printing his name," Penny said. "Anything else you can share about the case? DA's office is being pretty tight-lipped. Are you looking at more charges for the arraignment? The detectives were asking folks about explosives and computers. Anything turn up in the search?"

"Not much in the public realm beyond what I already told you," Diaz said. "You saw the booking logs, I assume. You know he got standard bail and his arraignment date."

"How about a quote?" Penny said. "Do you think the kid was treated appropriately when he was arrested? Any undue force?"

Diaz smiled and said nothing. They both knew this was a futile exercise, but she would go through all the paces anyway. There was silence on the line for a few long moments.

"Well, you have my number, Mateo."

"Have a good day, Penny." As Diaz hung up, he saw O'Reilly approach the cruiser with his third cup of coffee that morning. His partner would probably mainline caffeine if they invented a way to do it. Diaz limited himself to one cup a day or he had trouble sleeping, and there were enough aspects of this job that kept him up at night. He waited until O'Reilly pulled onto the street before speaking.

"So, you remember Ajay Shah, the kid we picked up at the airport?"

"Yeah," O'Reilly said. "The shady kid?"

"Well, that's just it," Diaz said. "The detectives haven't turned up any hard evidence. Nothing that indicates nefarious activity or terrorism."

"So?"

"So, maybe we should think twice before tackling a kid like that and hauling him in because you don't like the way he looks."

"What are you trying to say, Diaz?" O'Reilly glared at him. "You calling me a racist? 'Cuz I'm sure as hell not a racist like Thompson, who's always trying to teach punks a lesson with his Taser."

Diaz let several moments pass before choosing his words carefully. "What I'm saying is, you have a lifetime of conditioning, we all do. So maybe you make assumptions about a brown-skinned kid in a hoodie. Maybe those biases come out more under pressure or fear. And same for the people we encounter. Some of them distrust us, and they have good reason to . . . because there *are* cops like Thompson out there, and they go unchecked. Instead of IA and the union rallying around guys like him, we should cut him loose."

O'Reilly snorted. "Good luck with that. That's the whole reason most cops pay union dues. Look, Diaz, what I'm doing is all risk assessment and probabilities. More often than not—"

"I think we can do better than that," Diaz said. "I think we have to try."

WHEN HER PHONE rang later that morning, Priya answered before recognizing that the phone number belonged to Miranda Baker. That woman really was quite persistent, as if field hockey were the single most important thing in the world.

"I'm so sorry, I haven't had a chance to call you back. It's been a busy . . ." Priya started.

"Oh, no worries," Miranda said. "There's still a few weeks before the camp deadline. I really just wanted to thank you and Maya for the gorgeous necklace she gave Ashley for her birthday."

"Oh . . . yes, of course," Priya said. "And happy birthday to Ashley. Maya said it was a lovely party." She couldn't remember if Maya had said anything about the party; the entire evening was overcast by the Justice 4 All protests that day.

"I just love Perlini—so delicate and elegant. It was so thoughtful and *generous* of you. Really, it's too much. These kids, they grow up with the best of everything!"

Priya tried to grasp for understanding as another call appeared on her screen, this one from Pacific Hills High School. "Miranda, I'm so sorry, but the school is calling. Can I call you later?"

THAT AFTERNOON, WHEN Maya and Deepa came home from school, their mother was waiting in the kitchen. She sat there as the girls dropped their backpacks, pushed off their shoes, and began scavenging the kitchen for snacks. After Maya ducked her head into the pantry and came out with a box of cheddar crackers, her mother finally spoke.

"Maya—your school called today, asking for a note excusing your second absence last week. Apparently, you were out on Tuesday as well, not just Monday when I called for you." She sat back in her chair. "Can you explain that?"

Maya glanced up at her sister. Deepa had warned her that she would get caught. But who was Deepa to give her advice? And why was Maya getting in trouble, anyway? Ajay hadn't gotten in trouble for running off from robotics practice and getting arrested. And Deepa had run off to Tijuana without permission! At least Maya was just doing regular teenage things, like cutting school.

"Maya," her mother snapped. "I'm waiting for an answer! Where were you on Tuesday when you were supposed to be at school?"

"The . . . mall," Maya answered quietly.

Her mother's eyebrows arched. "The *mall*?" she said, as if it were the most offensive thing she could imagine. "Oh, and I suppose that's where you got the necklace? Yes, I also got a call from Miranda Baker." She took a sip of her tea. "She said there was no need for you to get Ashley such an extravagant birthday gift, but she certainly appreciated the Perlini necklace. I hadn't heard of that designer, so I was quite surprised to learn their necklaces start at two hundred dollars. I wonder how you could afford that when I never give you more than twenty dollars at a time?"

Maya could not avoid her mother's eyes, which were now glittering with fury. She imagined bolting out of the house, then remembered the cameras outside. She could escape to her room but knew that would be pointless. Her parents didn't believe in the sanctity of privacy when it came to their children. She knew they had rifled through Deepa's room when they suspected some transgression or the other. Suddenly, she saw her sister cross the kitchen and stand in front of their mother.

Deepa immediately grasped what must have happened and knew their parents would never tolerate it. She recalled Paco's words about always looking out for his family, everything he did for his sisters.

"Mom, it was me," Deepa said. "I made Maya go to the mall with me instead of school. I . . . I just wasn't ready to go back to school and face everyone. And I bought her the necklace, with my ice cream shop money, so she wouldn't tell you. It's my fault. I'm sorry."

This was such a contorted explanation, it should have been hard to believe; Deepa never voluntarily went to the mall. She held her breath as her mother's face twisted with confusion, then resolved itself. But of course, this new information aligned with what she already believed about Deepa, what she thought she knew about which daughter was good and which was bad. It was easier than Deepa had expected to convince her mother. Perhaps, sadly, she shouldn't have found this surprising at all.

LATER, THE SISTERS convened alone upstairs in Deepa's room, sitting on her bed.

"Why would you do that?" Maya said. "You're already in trouble for, like . . . *everything*."

Deepa shrugged. "Might as well double down on the punishment. I'm already grounded, no car, no friends, no phone—basically a prisoner. What else can they do to me?" She smiled at her sister. "Plus, you don't want to get shipped off to India for the summer, trust me."

"No kidding," Maya said. "I can't imagine how much that sucked. Though it was nice to have my own room for the summer."

Deepa elbowed her sister. "Well, just keep being the perfect child, you'll be fine."

Maya rolled her eyes. "You know, literally *no one* has parents this strict." She looked guilty. "I owe you, D."

"It's okay." Deepa nudged her sister with her foot. "Just sneak me some peanut butter with my bread and water."

36

Tuesday

"I FEEL TRAPPED here," Priya whispered to Archie on the phone as she peered out the window at the media vans; they'd been there from early morning until after dinner each of the past three days. "I can't even leave the house for a walk. I'm a prisoner in my own home."

"Forget it," Archie said. "Just forget about them and *stop* looking outside. You guys come over here for dinner tonight—you need a change of scenery, and you're probably grating on each other."

"Yeah," Priya murmured. "Deepa deserves her punishment, but it's not so easy having her around all the time. Everyone's nerves are frayed."

THAT EVENING, AT Archie's insistence, the Shahs went over to the Dhillons' home. All five members of the Shah family didn't have much occasion to ride together in one vehicle anymore, but this was the second time in the last couple of days. It might have been reminiscent of simpler times, until the long-limbed adolescents started jockeying for seat space and no one seemed happy with the temperature. Once they were all inside the car, Priya mentioned that the Bakers had also invited them to dinner on Friday night, but received no response from the children, not even Maya. As the car wended through the recognizable streets of their old Irvine neighborhood, each family member had differing reactions.

Maya stared out the car window, pondering how to keep the spheres of her life separate. Her friendship with Ashley was based on a carefully curated image, and her budding relationship with Chase was even more fragile. Since that night, he had smiled at her a couple of times in the school hallways, and they had spoken once during lunch when she had strategically hovered near the cafeteria door he always used. But they hadn't really had a chance to be alone again, and she was eager for that. Maya surreptitiously checked her phone again to see if he'd responded to her message, nervously hoping he'd like it.

Deepa missed their old community and felt newly torn between the life she'd left behind with Paco and the one her parents had chosen. She was still stinging from their fight over the border protest and resentful at being grounded. And she also felt a ripple of guilt every time she considered how things might have gone differently for Ajay if she'd been around that night.

Ajay counted the houses on each block he recognized, finding peace in the rhythm of this old habit. He wondered what Archana Auntie was making for dinner. Although he liked her food, he was also beginning to miss his mom's cooking.

Ashok was preoccupied, his mind darting between various worries about his business, their mortgage, the attorney, those reporters out front, but mostly about Ajay—not being able to read their son's thoughts and feelings was even more troubling right now. He wondered if they had handled things the right way, as parents. He'd believed the indulgences of Western-style parenting led to fragile, self-satisfied children, the dearth of that *grit* everyone was seeking these days. But seeing Ajay continue to fold into himself over the past week, Ashok wondered if this had been the right approach after all.

Priya felt a deep uneasiness about the welfare of each of her children, feeling as if she couldn't take her protective eye off any of them right now. And as they drove through the old community, she was also surprised by the deep nostalgia she felt, realizing how much she missed easily meeting up with neighbors or just seeing a friendly face.

*

WHEN THEY ARRIVED at the Dhillons' house, Ricky was wheeling a bicycle out of the garage onto the driveway. "Ajay, my man!" He waved as they exited the car. "Look what I found hiding behind the lawn mower. Should be just about the right size. Want to hop on? I can adjust it for you." He smiled broadly as Archie came outside to welcome them.

Ajay stood in place, his feet cemented to the driveway.

"How great!" Ashok said, nudging Ajay forward. "What do you say to Uncle?" He turned to Ricky. "He's really been missing his bike. He loves riding—"

"NO!" Ajay barked, startling everyone. "I don't want it."

"Come, come." Archie stepped forward and pulled the two girls by hand. "I have masala mix inside," she said, referring to the favorite snack she always made for them. Ashok watched as Priya and Ajay followed them inside.

Ricky slung an arm over Ashok's shoulder as they turned toward the house. "I'm sorry, man. I thought he might like it. I shouldn't have—"

"No, *I'm* sorry," Ashok said. "It's just . . . He's just . . ." He shook his head because he couldn't say any more. It felt like all he'd been doing lately was apologizing for his son.

"Hey, don't worry, man," Ricky said. "It's a lot, what you're all going through—Ajay, all of you. We're here for you, man. Anything you need."

And Ashok felt it in that moment, the comfort of this old friendship that required no explanation or posturing on his part. Vikram's distance over the past week had filled him with an uneasiness he hadn't registered until now. Ashok gave himself permission to relax into the evening, to feel safe and let go for the first time since all this had started.

After the children went off to the rec room with enough masala mix to surely ruin their appetites for dinner, the adults gathered on the back patio.

"That's just Ajay's linear thinking," Archie explained. "He was riding his bike when the police arrested him, so now he associates those two things: 'I ride my bike, bad things happen.' He'll get over it with time."

"She warned me," Ricky muttered.

"I did," Archie said sweetly, touching his hand.

"Now he can't even have that anymore," Priya said bitterly. "A simple thing he used to love."

The evening was far from one of their regular dinner clubs, planned for months and featuring elaborate buffets. This was just the two families, huddling over a simple meal of comfort food. It was just what they all needed: unfussy and relaxing, the way that only being with old friends can be—they used paper plates and sat down wherever to eat. The kids played Scrabble on the family room floor, resembling their much younger selves with limbs splayed in all directions. There was no more discussion of the week's activities, no acknowledgment, other than an extended hug and an extra glass of wine. Everything had already been relayed and rehashed, and everyone desperately needed a break from it all.

But eventually, the evening had to draw to a close; there was school and work the next day. They hugged goodbye at the door, and the Shahs left with containers full of lentil stew and couscous. Each family member's mood was considerably lighter on the ride home. As they approached the house, the first thing Ashok noticed was the absence of the media vans, and he exhaled with relief. The second thing he noticed was a giant jagged hole in the front window of the house. "Oh god," Priya said under her breath. "What happened?"

Ashok stopped the car at the foot of the driveway. "Everybody wait here. Lock the doors." He walked up to the porch and quietly opened the front door with his key. Without turning on the lights, he looked toward the living room. Glass shards covered the carpet and sofa near the window. Ashok stood still, attuning his ears to the sounds and silence of the house. He retrieved a baseball bat from the front closet, a hopeful remnant of his (ultimately fruitless) efforts to play with

Ajay. Methodically, he made his way through each room of the house with the bat poised over his shoulder, switching on lights as he went, throwing open closet doors and shower curtains. Finally satisfied the house was empty, Ashok returned to the living room to investigate the damage. When he walked behind the couch, he saw a brick lying amidst the shattered glass. He hesitated, then walked back around the couch, out the front door, and down to the driveway, where his family sat, waiting in the car with the doors and windows locked.

"It's okay," he said, opening the rear door for the kids. "It's safe. Just keep your shoes on and stay out of the living room."

When the kids had gone upstairs, Ashok led Priya into the living room. He stepped over the glass shards and reached down to carefully pick up the brick. Around it was wrapped a piece of paper, secured with a rubber band. The note held only three words, scrawled in messy capital letters: GO BACK HOME.

"ARCHIE SAYS WE should stay over there tonight." Priya covered the phone receiver as she relayed this to Ashok, who was on the phone himself. "She's making up the beds for us."

Ashok nodded. "Vikram knows a security company we can call in the morning."

The two held each other's gaze as inconceivable thoughts traveled through their minds. *How had this come to be their life?*

Ashok reached out his hand and squeezed Priya's wrist. "It's going to be okay."

She nodded determinedly, then began to cry.

The children stood at the top of the staircase, out of range of their parents' view but not their frightened voices. Deepa tried to summon her anger, but her parents' fear was palpable, and it moved in around her like a dark cloud. She stood motionless, unable to comfort her younger siblings. Maya trembled as she finally led Ajay, covering his ears, back to his room.

*

AFTER RICKY HAD driven over with some leftover plywood to help board up the broken window, after the three Shah children had packed up their overnight bags and school backpacks, after all five kids had consumed the three pints of ice cream Archie had fetched from the grocery store in her bathrobe, the children were at last settled with air mattresses and sleeping bags, and the adults convened on the back patio, where their voices wouldn't carry. The leftover wine from dinner had been opened, as well as a bottle of Amrut Indian whisky. As if in mutual silent agreement about what the situation demanded, everyone had a hefty pour in hand before anyone spoke. Even then, it was hard to know where to start.

Ricky, usually the quietest of the group, was the first to speak. "Do you ever think about going home?"

"India?" Archie asked.

He nodded. "Sometimes it feels like it would be easier, doesn't it? We have the education and credentials from having succeeded here. Aren't you tempted sometimes, to go back where you know the rules and how to navigate it all?"

"I think you're romanticizing it, honey," Archie said. "Have you forgotten all the reasons we left?"

"But a lot of those reasons are gone now," Ricky said. "We could afford a nice flat; the kids would get a good education. They'd probably want to come back here for university anyway. Or they could go to Europe, I don't know." He sighed and leaned back to gaze up at the sky. "We could live out our days being served chai and playing bridge. We'd have servants to do everything. I wouldn't have to take out the garbage anymore," he said wistfully.

Archie slapped his forearm. "You like taking out the garbage."

"What I like is having a cigarette in peace at the end of the driveway once a week." Ricky laughed.

"I think about moving back here," Priya spoke up. She shrugged toward Ashok, who looked taken aback. "I do. We're comfortable in this neighborhood, our friends are nearby, we don't have suspicious neighbors watching us all the time."

"Come on, it's not like that," Ashok reasoned. "What about that woman across the street? The . . . the architect?" He turned to Archie. "She brought us cookies, twice!"

"It would be less financial pressure. It would just be . . . simpler." Priya rested her head on the back of the chair.

"Hey, it's not too late," Archie quipped. "Two houses for sale on our block."

Priya looked at her. "You know, I've been thinking about what you said, maybe we *should* align ourselves with those protesters. Maybe we . . . we . . . just have to take our support where we can get it. At least get our side heard."

Archie nodded. "I think you'd get a lot of support from people, once they hear what's really happening, once they understand."

Priya looked at Ashok, who was silently tracing the rim of his glass. He took a drink too quickly and cleared his throat. "What do we gain by aligning ourselves with those people? What do we have in common? We live in different neighborhoods, we have different backgrounds, we face different challenges. Their cause is not our cause. Asians in this country are educated, professional, hardworking. I don't *want* our kids protesting in the streets. I don't *want* to get rid of the police." He took another sip. "I just want to be treated fairly."

"That's all anybody wants, Ashok." Archie leaned toward him and smiled. "It's right in the name—*justice for all*?"

"Well, by that reasoning," Ricky said, "even Asian Americans can't all be grouped together. What do I, a tech start-up CEO, have in common with a Vietnamese nail salon worker? Or a Chinese restaurateur? Or even, for that matter, a Sikh farmer who's been in the Central Valley for generations?"

"We can see each other as fellow humans," Archie said. "We can have empathy, find common cause."

Ashok shook his head. "All I know is, these protesters are bringing us unwanted attention." He reached for the Amrut bottle. "And maybe more death threats."

No one spoke for a while. Everyone took a sip or two of their drinks.

The night air was turning uncomfortably cool, but no one wanted to move.

AFTER EVERYONE HAD finally retired for the night, Priya lay awake, unable to sleep. She was so easily slipping back into her old habit of midnight waking. The nighttime meditations that had begun in her youth as a way to escape the predations of her uncle had become a lifetime pattern to which she now relapsed. Though it was her mind that kept her from sleep, she also thought there might be solace found in these hours, when everyone else was at rest—a time to order her thoughts without any interference from the outside world. But was it illusory to think this was a solution to anything? She hadn't been able to bring order to any of the real problems in her life. She had still suffered at her uncle's hands, still carried the shame and pain of those episodes. She hadn't been able to protect Ajay from the police. Hadn't been able to protect Deepa from taking unnecessary risks. Hadn't been able to protect their family from the hatred and threats and prejudice. Hadn't been able to protect her children and family from so many things. In the midst of that swirl of fears came a thought that felt like a betrayal. Perhaps it was magical thinking, but if they had never moved, maybe none of this would ever have happened.

Priya took her phone and stepped quietly out of the guest bedroom, walking in darkness down the hallway to the bathroom. She sat on the cool floor and after some absent scrolling on her phone, she found herself searching for Theo Young's mother. Priya pulled up a video clip of her speaking at a protest in LA, watched and listened to her words. She tried to put herself in this woman's shoes, imagining what it would feel like to get that knock on the door late at night, to have two uniformed strangers ask you to come down to the morgue to identify your fourteen-year-old son. Just thinking about this resurrected the profound fear she'd felt that night at the jail, and the intense protectiveness that had possessed her since. And yet, her experience wasn't remotely comparable to what Theo's mother had endured. Priya read through the comments posted below the video: many expressions of sympathy and support, fewer (but more striking) criticism and slurs. She kept scrolling, kept reading, kept watching, until she couldn't keep her eyes open anymore.

Before returning to bed, Priya looked in on the children's rooms to reassure herself they were safe and saw Maya and Deepa sleeping as they hadn't since they were much younger, with their arms slung over each other's bodies.

37

Wednesday

THE NEXT MORNING, Priya was home when the police came to take a report. Officers took photos of the broken glass and the brick, inspected all exterior doors and windows and made recommendations for improved home security measures. They were courteous and professional, just as Priya would have expected of any police officers, until ten days ago. Now, she felt conflicted. Of course, she understood intellectually the entire police department wasn't a monolith, but how was she to know who to trust anymore?

After the police left, the glass company came to take measurements for the replacement window. As Priya waited for them to finish up, a text message arrived from Archie.

Have you seen this?!

Priya hesitated. She didn't think she could handle any more news about Ajay's case or the protests, but curiosity compelled her to click on the link, which led to an article.

STATE INVESTIGATES CHARGES OF DISCRIMINATION AT BIOFLEX

The California Department of Fair Employment and Housing (DFEH) is conducting an investigation into charges of discriminatory practices at Southern California's fast-growing medical device manufacturer BioFlex.

Several employees at the Irvine-based company have reported suffering unfair discrimination as "lower-caste" Indians from their "upper-caste" supervisors.

"There is a hidden culture of favoritism among the executive leadership team, mainly Brahmins who have the same pedigree," said one BioFlex employee, on condition of anonymity.

The issue came to light after several similar reports were made through anonymous blog posts on a community board. BioFlex employees complained of being passed over for promotions or plum assignments and left out of informal lunches and after-work social gatherings where relationships were often forged.

"I left India to get away from the stigma of being a Dalit, but caste discrimination is alive and well here in the USA, thanks to Vikram Sharma and other BioFlex leaders," said one such online post, widely circulated on social media with the hashtag #CasteUSA.

After settlement talks between BioFlex management and the group of employees reportedly stalled last week, the workers took their complaint to the state agency. The DFEH is responsible for enforcing state laws prohibiting discrimination against employees for race, color, ancestry or national origin, among other protected characteristics.

While the state law has never been utilized for a case of caste discrimination, a spokesperson for the employee group argued that caste is a form of ancestry-based discrimination and therefore is clearly protected.

The caste system in India is believed to be over 3,000 years old and is among the world's oldest forms of surviving social stratification. Hindus, who make up approximately 80% of India's population today, are divided into four main categories, 3,000 castes, and 25,000 subcastes. Outside of this system are the Dalits or "untouchables," as they were once called. For centuries, many aspects of life in India have been guided by this complex caste hierarchy, from housing and education to marriage.

Another online post comes from a BioFlex engineer who reported being "outed" as a Dalit by a Brahmin colleague. The two had been classmates together at the prestigious Indian Institute of Technology. "He told people I didn't make it to IIT through the general merit list, that I was only there through reservations," he said, referring to India's affirmative action program for lower castes. "After that, my performance reviews and bonuses fell."

"We need this case to answer a question," the employee spokesperson said. "Is America truly a country where people can come from around the world to seek their version of the American dream, or a place where ancient biases and discrimination continue to reign?"

BioFlex was founded by Vikram Sharma in Irvine in 1999 and has frequently been on the region's lists of fastest-growing companies and best places to work. The medical device manufacturer is privately held but is estimated to have earnings in excess of $100 million a year.

Mr. Sharma and BioFlex did not respond to requests for an interview, and the company's legal counsel, Jonathan Stern of Stern & Barton LLP, declined to comment. The DFEH also declined to comment on an ongoing investigation.

When Priya reached the end of the article, she went back to the top and read it again. The second time, she sat back in her chair and exhaled slowly. Was Vikram responsible for this? What did it all mean? She returned to Archie's message and tapped out her response.

Do you think it's true?

Then she picked up her phone and called her husband at the office. When Ashok answered, she said, "I think I know why Vikram's been preoccupied."

ASHOK READ THE article for himself, then searched for any other news he could find about Vikram Sharma, BioFlex, or the state investigation. Using the hashtag #CasteUSA, he found the online posts written by disaffected employees. As he read their accounts of supervisors casually referencing the exclusive cricket clubs and gymkhanas their families had belonged to in India, the way certain conversations halted when they entered a room, Ashok recalled that familiar sense of feeling excluded and overlooked, of being invisible or looked down upon for an inherent characteristic.

Ashok kept searching and reading long past the point he should have. Was he looking for some other explanation? Some counterargument to the accusations being leveled against Vikram? Or was it really so easy to slide back into the way he'd felt as a young man in India, as if his hard work and talents were circumscribed by his allocated rung in the hierarchy? There were enough anecdotal reports mentioning Vikram by name that it seemed likely his friend at least knew about this reported culture at BioFlex, but had he perpetuated it?

When Ashok's search began cycling back to the same stories, he pushed his keyboard away and leaned back in his chair. It was difficult to reconcile what he'd just read with the Vikram he'd come to know over the past several years: the man who'd helped him grow his business and encouraged him to move into Pacific Hills. The man who'd welcomed Ashok into his home and family, who'd stepped up for him in the darkest time. Vikram had never probed at the question of caste with Ashok the way some people did, inquiring about his family's origins or their occupations. Ashok truly felt as if they had met on the same plane of America, united by their experience as immigrants and entrepreneurs.

He wanted to call Vikram right then, for reassurance. But his finger hovered over his phone screen. Indeed, caste had never come up between them, not only because Vikram had never asked, but also because Ashok had never offered any information. Some part of him never wanted to, a small fear in the back of his mind about the impact it might have. The article now forced him to reconsider: Would he and Vikram have been friends in India, where the complex strictures of caste, privilege, and socioeconomic class were harder to escape? Or would Vikram even have become friends with Ashok here, had he known the truth?

Back in their village, Ashok's father's opportunities had been clearly constricted by caste. After they moved to Mumbai, that explicit hierarchy might no longer have been present, but its legacy seemed to follow them. His father was relegated to certain jobs due to his limited education and experience as a laborer, but could these elements be extricated from his upbringing in the village? If the opportunities were greater in Mumbai, so, too, were the class differences. Ashok traveled by train as he watched air-conditioned cars drive by; his family rented a tiny apartment in the shadow of soaring new condominium buildings. It was possible to break out: his wildly talented brother had done so, but so many more could not.

Though Ashok had largely left behind those old constraints when he'd come to this country, he'd swapped them for the new challenges of being a visible minority and an obvious foreigner. Here, his brown skin and accent marked him as different: sometimes to his detriment, occasionally as a boon. Ashok had managed to use his education and professional accomplishments as weapons in the uphill battle against the barriers he faced in America. In some ways, being Indian had even helped him in his work. Clients expected him to be smart and knowledgeable, imbuing Ashok with a credibility in the beginning he hadn't quite earned yet. Deepa's harsh accusations regarding the government contracts that had helped his business grow had stayed with him. Was this so different from the reservation system for Dalits that had frustrated him in India?

It began to dawn on him that America had its own version of a caste system—some visible minorities were on the bottom, hampered by discrimination and historical disadvantages, a constant headwind against their efforts. Others—like he, Vikram, and Ricky—were rewarded for their work and talents and could make a pretty good life for themselves. And people like the Bakers had been born into great privilege because of their race and class, a privilege that would flow to their children regardless. It was a harsh realization that Ashok had fled one hierarchy in India only to find another in America, even if it was one in which he had managed to ascend to a higher rung.

Ashok's mind drifted back to that last night before this crisis with Ajay had erupted, the dinner party at the Sharmas' home. He could envision the glorious sunset streaked across the sky, the feelings of comfort, and the warmth of friendly conversation. And then he recalled what Vikram had said over cocktails at the fire pit—that no one willingly gives up their place of privilege for someone new—words that now took on new meaning.

38

Thursday

THE LAW OFFICES of Stern & Barton LLP were in a soaring building fashioned from glass and chrome. "Look at this," Priya said, staring up at the high-rise through the window of their parked car. She wondered aloud how much all of this would normally cost.

"Vikram will come through," Ashok reassured her. "Don't worry." They had discussed it at length the night before, going in circles about what they knew of him and the reports they'd read. It wasn't clear how much was true, how much Vikram knew about or was responsible for. They debated whether they should even accept Vikram's help, under the circumstances, but the arraignment was now only four days away.

"You don't know that," Priya said, shaking her head. "You don't know what's going to happen or if it's going to be fine. So stop saying it. You were the one who trusted Vikram with all this, and look at who he turned out to be. Just as you thought we had to move into Pacific Hills, and you thought that Ajay didn't need any help."

"Well, I'm sorry I can't do anything right." Ashok's eyes glittered. "Never mind the years I've spent working myself to the bone to support our family. I guess that's not worth anything to you."

They sat in silence, both staring straight ahead through the windshield, each wondering if they'd said too much or not enough. The appointment reminder buzzed on Priya's phone, and they both glanced at it. "We should go," she said, and they collected themselves to enter the building.

ON THE TENTH floor, an impeccably dressed young woman showed Priya and Ashok into a glass-enclosed conference room. She offered them coffee or water, but they both declined. The room had a long marble table surrounded by sleek leather swivel chairs. A gleaming chrome espresso machine sat on the credenza.

"Hello, hello," Jonathan Stern said as he entered the room, a large brown accordion folder under his arm. "Sorry to keep you waiting. It's been a crazy week."

"We read about BioFlex in the news yesterday," Ashok said.

Stern nodded. "Yes, I thought so. Listen, I advised Vikram not to talk to anybody about this, not even close friends. So, if you're wondering why he hasn't mentioned it, blame me." He sighed. "Needless to say, the Sharmas won't be able to offer you much public support. They need to lie low right now, and it probably wouldn't help you much anyway." He began taking papers and folders out of his accordion file, spreading them out on the conference table.

Priya took out a notebook and pen. The glass door to the conference room opened, and a tall Asian woman entered the room, carrying a laptop computer.

"Ah, there she is," Stern said. "Meet my partner, Helen Wu. She's going to be working with me on your case. Helen has expertise in national security and law enforcement."

"Good to meet you." Helen smiled as she firmly shook each of their hands. Ashok noticed her voice carried no trace of an accent.

Helen took the chair next to Jonathan and flipped open her laptop. Jonathan placed his palms face down on top of the papers in front of him. "So, I was finally able to have a discussion with the district attorney earlier this week. I explained the situation from our perspective, how Ajay has trouble communicating, perhaps didn't respond appropriately to the police but meant no harm, and so on. I explained we'd be willing to discuss a deal, to consider a suspended sentence or probation." He paused. "I'm hopeful they heard me and they might be willing to meet us partway, but unfortunately it's not going to happen before the arraignment."

"What? Why?" Ashok asked.

Jonathan tilted his head. "They might still be sorting through evidence turned up from the search warrant . . . We just don't know at this point."

"Could it be the media?" Priya asked. "The fact that it's been in the news?"

"Or the protests?" Ashok leaned forward. "We had nothing to do with that."

Jonathan nodded and leaned back in his chair. "Look, I know this is hard, and we were hoping for a resolution before Monday. But all we can do is play the hand we've been dealt. Right now, that means we have to prepare for the arraignment. Obviously, Ajay will enter a not guilty plea. We'll request a transfer to the juvenile system, which shouldn't be an issue as long as they don't bring any more serious charges." He glanced over at Helen. "That's the biggest risk at this point, but Helen is well versed in case law when it comes to terrorism charges and national security issues."

Ashok nodded. "How . . . how long have you been here?" he ventured.

"I've been with the firm five years," Helen said.

"Our youngest partner." Jonathan beamed. "We had to lock her in before she was poached."

"Oh, yes . . . but here, in this country?" Ashok said.

Helen smiled. "Actually, my ancestors came to California one hundred fifty years ago to help build the railroad. I'm the seventh generation of the Wu clan in America."

"Oh, I'm sorry," Ashok said. "I didn't mean—"

Helen held up a hand. "No offense taken."

Jonathan chuckled. "Helen's people have been here longer than any of us, but she still gets asked where she's from. I *never* get that question, even though I'm only one generation out of Poland. My mother was a baby when her parents escaped the Holocaust. I may have white skin, but with a name like Stern, you can't really escape anti-Semitism. Which is all to say, both Helen and I understand where you're coming from. An immigrant-rich country like ours makes for a complex fabric. These are tricky things to navigate in our society, which is something Vikram's learning as well. We are here to help you."

Ashok swallowed hard against the lump rising in his throat and nodded silently.

Jonathan nodded. "We do want you to be prepared for what could happen at the arraignment. You should bring Ajay's passport to surrender, in case they ask for it. Make sure you have enough liquid assets to post a higher bail if necessary. And there is a chance, a small chance, they'll want to take him into custody."

Priya gave Ashok a worried look.

"We do want to have character witnesses lined up for Ajay and for you two, as his parents. A teacher or coach who knows him well, who can speak to his quirkiness or his communication problems, maybe explain some of those unusual hobbies or interests."

"The robotics team coach," Priya said, jotting it down. "And his math teacher."

"Neighbors from Pacific Hills who know you, have seen the family together."

Priya and Ashok exchanged a worried glance. "Maybe the architect?" she offered.

Ashok agreed. Surely, the woman who had brought a smile to his wife's face for the first time in a week would support them.

"Anyone high profile who's fond of your family? Business leaders, politicians, that kind of thing? Hell, even a sports figure if you know one. People get irrational when they see a sports hero." Jonathan looked between them. "It would make a big difference to have someone respected in the community stand up for you."

"Maybe I could ask Miranda Baker?" Priya said.

"Baker Development?" Jonathan asked.

Priya nodded. "Our daughters are good friends; Miranda always tells me how much she loves Maya. She's been very welcoming. She just invited our family over for dinner."

"Well, the Baker name certainly holds a lot of weight in this area," Jonathan said. "Their support would go a long way in bringing people around to your side. And it probably wouldn't hurt with the police department either, for them to know you have someone powerful in your corner." He tapped his pen against his chin as he thought. "We don't want to overplay it. But if you socialize with them, and they're willing to give a comment to the press about what wonderful neighbors and friends you are . . . that could be very useful."

As they left the office, Ashok felt the direness of the situation weigh on him. In the back of the crowded elevator, he silently reached for Priya's hand. She clasped his back firmly. The safety of their children, the well-being of their family—this took precedence above all else. They would be aligned on this, as they always were. Whatever had transpired before, whatever their issues with each other, they could sort them out later.

Back in the car, Priya tapped out a quick message to Miranda, accepting her invitation to dinner on Friday.

THAT EVENING, PRIYA informed the children they would be going to the Bakers' house for dinner the following night. "Make sure you wear something nice," she said. "No ripped jeans."

"Mom, I told you I don't want go over there," Maya said.

"You're going," Ashok said.

"Why?" Maya said. "We never have to socialize with any of Deepa's friends or Ajay's."

Left unspoken around the table was the fact that Ajay didn't have any friends and that Deepa's were of the wrong sort.

"Maya, stop pouting," Priya said. "This is not about you, okay?"

"Fine, then I'll stay home," Maya said.

"You're going." Ashok spoke in a steely voice. "You are *all* going!" He looked pointedly at each of them.

LATER THAT NIGHT, sitting alone at the dining table with his laptop and papers, Ashok's mind kept returning to the meeting in Jonathan's office, to the BioFlex article, to Vikram. It was after ten o'clock, but he suspected his friend would still be awake, so before he could lose his nerve, he picked up the phone and called.

Vikram answered immediately. "How's everything going with Ajay? Jonathan is taking care of you all right? The hearing is on Monday?"

"Uh, yes. Jonathan's been great. We're getting prepared for Monday. But . . ." Ashok hesitated. "How are you? That article . . . ?"

"Ah, it's just a legal headache. And you know what else?" Vikram said. "Another way for them to divide us. The British used caste to divide Indians during colonial rule, and now this government agency is doing the same thing. We have to stick together, no? We're already a minority in this country—we can't afford to let these differences separate us, especially when they're irrelevant here, ten thousand miles away."

"So, there's no truth to it?" Ashok asked, a little taken aback by Vikram's nonchalance.

"Some disgruntled employees, that's all. How could I even tell anybody's caste in the office? I can't help it if my team chooses who to hire and promote; I can't control who they're most comfortable with and who they trust," Vikram said. "Ashok, *you* know this—meritocracy is the founding stone of the tech industry. That's how an individual survives and grows here. Maybe caste is a problem in India, but not here. Am I right?"

Ashok found himself nodding along silently, unsure if he agreed or not but wanting to believe.

39

Friday

DEEPA SAT WITH Paco on the school's worn bleachers for their lunch period. The benches were warped and cold, but it was quieter out here, away from the lunchtime fray in the cafeteria.

"So how long is this penance supposed to last?" Paco asked as he unwrapped his sandwich.

"I don't know." Deepa tore open a bag of crackers, one of the handful of packaged snacks she grabbed for lunch, a sign of her hasty departure from home that morning. "Probably till college?"

Paco smiled. "You have to cut your folks some slack. They're dealing with a lot right now."

"Yeah, I know," Deepa said, a little sheepish. She knew how much Paco missed having his father around and his family intact. "Well, I do get a hall pass tonight. The whole family's going to Maya's friend's house for dinner, although none of us want to go, not even Maya."

"Why?" Paco asked.

Deepa shrugged. "She's been super-sensitive about her friends lately. At first, I thought she was just upset about Ajay, but I don't know . . . I guess we cramp her style? It *is* kind of annoying the way our parents suddenly want to be all chummy with the Bakers."

Paco looked up at her, stopped chewing. "Baker?" he asked.

"Yeah, Ashley Baker. Maya's friend. The family's super-wealthy and connected. The dad's some big developer, I guess. They live in this mansion way up in the Hills. And get this, their son, who must be our age, drives a brand-new BMW. I think he's a bit of a jerk, but Maya . . ." As Deepa took a drink from her water bottle, she paused at his expression. "What?"

"Baker, as in Baker Development?" Paco finally swallowed his bite.

"I think so," Deepa said. "I think they own a big construction company. Why?"

Paco nodded slowly, as if gears were turning in his mind. "Baker Development is the company that's been dragging their feet on our settlement payment, tying things up with lawyers for years now." He looked into Deepa's eyes. "The company responsible for my apá's death."

Deepa stopped chewing as she tried to piece together what Paco was saying. She took a big gulp of water to wash down a sticky mouthful of crackers, but before she could speak, Paco stood and grabbed his backpack. "I've got to go."

DEEPA WAS WRECKED for the rest of the afternoon. She kept turning the situation over in her mind: marrying together that terrible day that Paco's uncle had come to school with the palatial house adorned by grand columns where the Bakers lived. The Bakers—whose business had torn a hole through her best friend's life, whose daughter was her sister's best friend. It was too much to process, impossible to reconcile.

Paco had been right that night of the protest. Deepa didn't have to put anything on the line when she wanted to take a stand, not like he did, and perhaps it was time she changed that. She'd thought Maya's indiscretions at the mall were just regular teenage mischief, but now her suspicions were mounting.

Deepa held off on saying anything when she picked up Maya after school, and all during their drive home. She wanted to be able to see her sister's face when she asked. Once they were parked in the garage, she switched off the ignition and turned to her. "Hey, Maya," Deepa said gently, "that necklace you got for Ashley? How could you possibly afford a three-hundred-dollar piece of jewelry?" She watched carefully for a reaction, but Maya's expression was inscrutable. Maybe this was how her sister got away with so much.

"Cutting school is bad enough, Maya, but shoplifting? You might be able to fool Mom, but do you know how much trouble you could get into? Why would you take that risk for someone who's supposedly your friend? And you practically ducked out of sight when you saw Ashley's brother in the driveway last weekend." Deepa tried to keep her voice calm. "Did something . . . anything happen with him?"

"God! You, Mom, Dad—" Maya opened the car door and grabbed her backpack. "Why do you all have to be in my business? Can't you just let me be and have my friends?"

Deepa followed her sister out of the car. "Listen, Maya, you don't have to protect him. They're not good people, the Bakers."

"How would you know?" Maya snapped back. "Because they have money? That's why you don't like them?" She flung open the door and strode through the house.

"I know they use their money and power to take advantage of people." Deepa followed her up the stairs, two at a time. "And I don't want—"

Maya slammed her bedroom door behind her.

As Deepa stood outside her sister's room, considering whether to knock or just go in, Ajay emerged from his room into the hallway. "Oh, hey, bud," Deepa said, releasing some of the tension from her shoulders. "How was your day?"

Ajay shrugged. "Mediocre."

This was one of the things Deepa appreciated most about her brother, how he didn't feel compelled to sugarcoat anything. Ajay didn't say he was good when he wasn't, or politely decline the last doughnut if he really wanted it. It was refreshing, the way she never had to guess at his true feelings or thoughts. On impulse, she opened her arms to see if her brother would accept a hug, and to her surprise, he took a step toward her. As she wrapped her arms around Ajay's shoulders, she wondered how different the world would be if everyone was as transparent as her brother.

*

DOWNSTAIRS IN THE kitchen, Priya was rearranging various leftovers cooked by other people in the fridge. Ashok was sitting at the kitchen island with what had become his nightly glass of scotch.

"What did he say?" Priya asked her husband, whose drawn face wore a discernible stress.

Ashok stared into the glass and shrugged one shoulder. "Not much. He said it was blown out of proportion. Just some frustrated employees looking for attention."

"Do you believe that?" Priya leaned across the island toward him.

Ashok was silent for several moments before answering. "I'm more inclined to believe the employees," he said. "Why would they ever want to bring attention to the fact that they're lower caste? Why would any of us want to? We left India to get away from that system, so why bring it up? Unless you have to. Unless there's good reason."

She saw her husband struggling with demons from his past, intruding into a world where they didn't belong. Despite her outburst yesterday, she couldn't blame Ashok for garnering Vikram's support, because where would they be without it? "Shouldn't we give him the benefit of the doubt, as our friend? He has been there for us."

Ashok nodded. "Yes, and I told him so. We're here for him if there's anything we can do. I'm just not sure how much we should count on him. I was . . ." He cleared his throat and took a sip of scotch.

"What?" Priya asked, placing a hand over his. She felt the void of Ashok's optimism, so accustomed to his reassurances that everything would turn out all right.

"I was going to tell him, you know, that we're Vaishyas, my family. Just to see how he would react, to see if it changed anything."

"And?" Priya asked gently.

Ashok shook his head. "I couldn't do it. Maybe I don't really want to know, not right now."

They heard footsteps racing down the staircase, and moments later Deepa entered the kitchen. "Uh . . . about the dinner tonight?" she said, out of breath.

"Don't you start too," Ashok said. "This is not up for discussion."

"No, I know. I'm going, we're all going. It's fine," Deepa said. "I just think you should be careful with the Bakers."

Priya cast her eyes over to Ashok, then back to Deepa. "What do you mean?"

Deepa exhaled a big breath. "I just mean, you shouldn't really trust them. They screwed over Paco's family—at least Mr. Baker did, through his company."

"What? How—?" Priya began, but then Ajay entered the kitchen.

"Can I bring my iPad tonight?" he asked. "If I have to go, I at least want to work on my astronomy project. I'm mapping the entire galaxy; it's going to take some time."

"Uh, yes, okay. Come on now, we should all get ready." Priya ushered them out of the kitchen, recognizing how much was at stake for her family tonight. Her encounter with the architect the other night had opened her up a crack, made her realize that not all their wealthy white neighbors were suspicious of them. *You have to take your support where you can,* Archie had said after the protest, and Priya was trying to gather strength from the idea of assembling a force of support behind them.

40

Friday

"WELCOME!" MIRANDA BAKER beamed as she swung open the massive front door. She reached out to embrace Maya. "Hi, honey, Ashley and Chase are out in the pool house. Why don't you take your brother and sister out there?" Priya was glad to see all three kids head off obligingly.

Miranda took Priya's hand warmly in both of hers, then turned and did the same to Ashok. "*So* good to have you all here. I thought we could sit out on the patio. It's such a beautiful night. We can watch the sunset."

"Sounds wonderful." Priya smiled as she and Ashok followed their host through the grand house. Everything here was constructed on a different scale: the ceilings soared, the chandeliers were enormous, the dining table was surrounded by a dozen chairs. Priya felt like one of those miniature figurines in an oversize dollhouse. She and Ashok exchanged a glance as they trailed Miranda down a lengthy corridor with wide wooden beams overhead, highlighted by a string of wrought-iron chandeliers. *How did one change the light bulbs in such a house?* Priya thought.

When they arrived at the back patio, the view was spectacular—270 degrees of ocean and sky without obstruction. From this overlook, the Bakers' home truly seemed to be perched at the crest of Pacific Hills, towering above all other houses. Miranda led them to a pergola at the far end of the back lawn, ideally situated to take in the view, and invited them to sit on a set of couches that seemed too elegant to be outdoors. The table held a bottle of wine, four glasses, and a very artistic cheese board, garnished with a wedge of raw honeycomb and a sprig of olive leaves. Spence Baker approached from yet another side of the sprawling yard and introduced himself with a handshake. They all sat down, facing the magnificent vista as Spence uncorked and poured the wine.

"I have to tell you, we just *love* Maya," Miranda gushed. "She is so kind and polite. And *smart*. You must be so proud of her."

"Oh, well. You're very kind to say that." Priya smiled. "We've been lucky. Maya's always been that way." She took a sip of the wine, enjoying its rich, fruity flavor.

Miranda popped a petite green olive into her mouth. "It's been so nice for Ashley to have someone new this year at Pacific Hills High. You know she's been with these same girls practically since kindergarten, and I think they're a little tired of each other. Maya's so . . . *different*, and that's been great for her."

"And she gives Ashley a run for her money on the field too," Spence said. "Maya can block a lot of her shots." He chuckled. "Goalie's a tough position. A lot of standing around watching the action downfield, and then *boom*!" He slapped his hand on his leg. "You have to be *on* when that ball's coming at you."

When Priya had picked up Maya from field hockey practice, she had been stunned to recognize the figure emerging from all that cagelike protective gear as her daughter. Now, she tried to picture Maya standing in the net on the Bakers' side lawn as Ashley repeatedly shot a small hard ball toward her.

"Does your older daughter play too?" Miranda asked.

Ashok shook his head. "Oh no. Deepa's not really into sports. She's more interested in, uh . . . debate, politics, journalism . . . that kind of thing."

"Yes, she has a lot of opinions." Priya smiled.

"Don't they all?" Spence said. "Our older boys gave me most of this." He brushed his fingers through the salt-and-pepper hair at his temple and everyone laughed.

*

MEANWHILE, IN THE pool house, the Baker and Shah kids were awkwardly trying to agree on a collective activity. Ashley proposed watching a movie: the pool house was equipped with a sixty-inch screen and surround sound that replicated the atmosphere of a theater. With a single touch of the remote, Chase closed the blackout blinds, and it was this move that put Deepa on high alert. She didn't like the way he'd grinned at Maya when they entered the pool house. As the room darkened, she squeezed herself awkwardly on the couch between Chase and Maya, who glared at her. Ajay sat nestled into a beanbag in the corner, his face illuminated by his tablet. After two weeks, his bruises were barely visible. Anyone looking at him now would see a typical adolescent boy, playing his video games.

As Ashley handed out tubs of popcorn and bottles of root beer, Deepa caught a glimpse of why her sister liked being over here so much; it was a different world from the cozy, collective existence their family shared at home. She turned back to the screen to see the opening credits of the movie the others had chosen, some sort of science fiction romance. It featured a conventionally handsome man who awakens from an interplanetary hibernation and decides to wake a beautiful female passenger solely to serve as his companion. The two predictably fall in love, though their relationship is based on a lie. Deepa found herself growing irked by the whole premise: a woman giving up her entire life and future to be with a man who uses and lies to her. Finally, when the gooey-eyed woman proclaimed her fear of living without this man, Deepa could stand it no longer. This huge-budget, special-effects-laden drivel was worse than one of her mother's Bollywood fantasies.

"I'm sorry, but this is ridiculous," she said. "Can't you all see how totally misogynistic this is?"

Chase reached for the remote control and turned up the volume.

"Seriously." Deepa turned to Maya and Ashley. "How can you guys watch this crap? It's pathetic!"

"Aw, I think it's kinda sweet," Ashley said. "They're giving up everything to be together."

"It's not supposed to be realistic, Deepa." Maya spoke in a kindergarten teacher voice. "It's Hollywood."

"Yeah, they're traveling for a hundred years to another planet. Not exactly real life," Chase said without taking his eyes off the screen.

"It's a negative portrayal of women and their agency. That is very real," Deepa shot back.

"Nobody's forcing you to watch." Chase held his popcorn bowl up to his mouth and shook the remaining dregs into it.

But Deepa knew she couldn't leave Maya here alone; she had no choice but to sit back and fume as the movie continued.

UNDER THE PERGOLA, the parents had loosened up from the wine and genial conversation. Miranda Baker signaled the family's personal chef to begin bringing out the food for dinner. Since Miranda wasn't sure of the Shahs' tastes or whether they were vegetarian, she had selected an extensive menu: heirloom tomato and mozzarella salad, ricotta and wild mushroom tart, pumpkin risotto with sage, pan-seared halibut in lemon butter, roasted brussels sprouts with bacon. For dessert later, there would be butterscotch budino with caramel sauce and fresh berry napoleons.

The outdoor dining table had been set in a rustic Italian style, with white and yellow roses mixed with lemons and their leaves, glowing candles, small glass bottles of olive oil, and ceramic dishes of mixed olives. Spence had remarked that this all seemed like a lot for a casual dinner with just one other family, but Miranda had wanted the night to be special, wanted the Shahs to feel truly welcomed for their first visit.

"So, Priya, what do you think about that field hockey camp over winter break?"

"Sounds like a good idea," Priya said. "December, right?"

"Yes, great!" Miranda clapped her hands together. "I'm happy to help you get the footage for Maya's submission reel. We've already arranged to film a couple of games this month."

"Oh, you don't have to do that. I'm sure we can arrange whatever Maya needs."

Miranda beamed. "No, no, I don't mind at all. We're already paying the videographer to get footage. It just makes sense to have him cover Maya too." These kinds of services were obscenely expensive, especially with the top people, and Miranda didn't want anything hindering Maya's ability to participate. How did regular people afford it? she wondered sometimes: thousands of dollars for camps, thousands more for the private coaches and equipment.

"Maya has been such a good friend to Ashley this year, so anything we can do for your family." Miranda beamed. "We're happy to help."

"That's very generous of you." Priya smiled.

An olivewood plank, abundant with charcuterie, sat on the table between them, and Miranda now began pointing out each of the cheeses.

Priya feigned interest as she selected a slice, wanting to appear gracious. The field hockey discussion made her wary of being indebted to the Bakers before she could ask for what they really needed. When she spotted the chef carrying artfully arranged platters out to the long patio, Priya grew nervous. It appeared as if they would all be dining together, with the children. She'd intended to talk to the Bakers about Ajay when he wasn't around. "Actually, there is something we wanted to ask you."

"Yes, of course, anything!" Miranda leaned forward.

Priya looked over to catch Ashok's eye, so they could do this now, together. But he and Spence seemed deeply engaged in conversation.

"Orange County's always been a great place to do business," Spence was saying. "We've got to keep it that way. I swear, these regulatory agencies multiply like rabbits—Contractors State License Board, Coastal Commission, OSHA. The more successful your business is, the more government gets *into* your business. That's your reward. You know how much I have to pay for insurance in this state? Twice as much as in Arizona or Nevada."

Ashok was listening intently to Spence, trying to parse his meaning, but he was also tangentially aware that Priya was now watching him.

"*You* know this, as an entrepreneur, Ashok. We've got to let free markets operate as they're supposed to. That's what this country is built on. That's how we created the greatest economy in the world. That's what attracted *you* here, right?"

"Yes, right," Ashok answered, probably too quickly. He wasn't quite following Spence, but it seemed important to agree with their host, to lay the groundwork for what they were going to ask. He glanced over and met Priya's eyes briefly, to acknowledge her silent appeal.

"I'm all for government playing its role, but it should be a limited role. Defense, abroad and at home. Keep our borders and streets safe. Now we've got people agitating for less police. Have you read the letters in the *OC Register* lately? The police try to keep us safe, and people are up in arms because they don't get it perfect all the time. You can't condemn the whole department for one or two bad apples."

"Yes," Miranda added. "That story about the young man in Pacific Hills? It's shocking."

"Well, actually," Priya said, injecting her voice unnaturally, "that's what we wanted—"

"A jihadi kid in Pacific Hills." Spence chuckled, shaking his head. "What is happening to the neighborhood?" He reached over and slapped Ashok's armrest. "Well, it's not all bad changes. You guys are here now, right?"

Ashok felt that word *jihadi* like a blow to his gut. His body was immobilized, his mind whirring, unable to sort out what to do. Priya glared at him, as if he somehow held the key to unlock this whole fraught situation.

The five adolescents, having been informed by the housekeeper that dinner was ready, were both hungry and eager for a break from the awkward atmosphere of the pool house. They were now walking in a loose herd across the expanse of lawn toward the patio table. Miranda rose out of her seat. "Oh, good, everyone's here. I hope you're hungry!"

*

ONCE EVERYONE WAS seated at the beautifully laid table, they passed platters around between them. The kids were all clustered together at one end of the table; Ashley sat between Chase and Maya, and across the table from them, Deepa sat next to Ajay.

"So, Deepa, how are you liking Pacific Hills High?" Miranda asked.

"Oh, I'm not . . ." Deepa fumbled a bit, instinctively glancing over at her parents. "I actually stayed at Cesar Chavez."

"Oh, why's that?" Miranda asked.

As Deepa saw her father's eyes harden, she swallowed the truth. "It was just easier, as a junior, to finish out high school there. Too late to switch, really." She felt annoyed and relieved in equal measures when her father gave a small nod.

"Oh, that's too bad. It's such a great school, I'm sure Maya's told you all about it." Miranda smiled and turned to Ajay. "And how about you, young man? You're in middle school?"

"Seventh grade," Ajay answered without looking up from his plate. "Eighth for math and science, which are most important anyway."

Laughter rippled around the table.

"Sounds like you might take after your father, in the computer business?" Miranda asked.

Ajay shrugged. "Not really. My dad does information technology. I'm more interested in higher-level applications: robotics and drones. I like using computers to build things."

Spence beamed. "You like to build things? Hey, me too, buddy. I build homes and offices and stores. It's a very important role people like us provide in this world, building things of consequence to help other people."

Ajay shoveled a forkful of risotto into his mouth and chewed. "But how do you screw people over?"

Priya's fork clattered onto her plate.

Spence drew back in surprise and chuckled. "Wow, this kid doesn't mince words—I like that. Well, son, there *are* lot of different ways to run a business, but at Baker Development, we treat everyone with respect and operate with the highest level of integrity. Screwing people over actually hurts your business in the long run."

Deepa dug her nails into her palms to keep from opening her mouth. All she could think of was Paco and his family, their truth and these easy lies.

"But what about my sister's friend?" Ajay continued, still not looking up at Spence. "Didn't your company screw his family over?"

In a flash of horror, Deepa recognized the words she'd spoken earlier to her parents. Ajay must have overheard her in the kitchen.

"Ajay!" Priya snapped, standing. "I'm sorry, he doesn't know what he's talking about. I apologize." She put her hands on Ajay's shoulders. "Come on, let's take a walk."

Spence Baker's genial smile had dissolved. "No, I'd really like to hear what he meant by that," he said, a hard edge in his voice. "That's quite a statement."

As Priya ushered Ajay away from the table, Ashok leaned forward. "Our son is . . . he's a little different, awkward. He speaks without thinking sometimes, without any filter. I'm so sorry. I don't know what got into him, what he's talking about. Obviously, we would never think—"

"What did he mean, his sister's friend?" Spence sat back in his chair, fingers tented on his chest, as if presiding over a board room. He turned to Maya. "Is that your friend he's talking about, Maya?"

Deepa's face flushed with heat. Her palms were sweaty, and her heart raced. "No, it . . . it was me. He was talking about my friend." She felt everyone's eyes on her as she tried to explain in the most factual way possible, sifting out all her anger and indignation. "My friend Paco, his father worked for your company. He was a stucco mason. There was an accident on his job site a couple of years ago and he . . . died. It's been really hard on the whole family, Paco and his two little sisters, their mom. They've had to make a lot of sacrifices while they wait for the settlement to come through, had to leave their home. It's devastated his family.

"But I . . . I apologize for what my brother said, and for the words we used. That wasn't right," Deepa said. "I just think people—all of us—we have to own our actions." She couldn't help glancing at Chase across the table.

"What, you think I have something to apologize for?" Chase said, shoving his chair back from the table. "You don't even know me." He glanced over at Maya with incredulity.

Maya stood up and hurried away from the table.

Chase leaned toward Deepa. "Hey, *she* sent me that pic on her own," he whispered. "I didn't ask for anything."

WITHIN THE SPACE of a few minutes, the nine people once gathered at the patio table had been scattered around the Baker family compound.

Priya was sitting with Ajay on the front doorstep of the house, oscillating between halfheartedly consoling her son and fighting the impulse to berate him for his behavior. She finally settled on berating herself for the failures of parenting or foresight that had gotten them into this mess.

Maya had run all the way across the property and found a spot behind some shrubbery, shrouded from view along with the pool equipment. She rested her head onto her knees and cried big ugly, gulping sobs. The entire world she'd worked to create was crumbling down around her. Why did her family always have to make everything worse?

Spence had excused himself to retreat to his mahogany-paneled home office, where he poured himself some bourbon and rifled through papers on his desk. His departure was a break shot, after which Ashok went in search of Priya, then Deepa left to chase after Maya.

In the end, Miranda Baker was left staring at the detritus of her beautiful Tuscan table, while Chase continued to eat and Ashley cried silently into her napkin.

41

Saturday

WHEN MAYA WOKE up the next morning, she was newly horrified by the memory of what had unfolded at the Bakers' house. Before even getting out of bed, she heard a knock at her door and Deepa's voice.

"Go. Away," Maya yelled to the closed door from her fetal position in bed, but she heard the door open and her sister's footsteps approach.

"Why do you have to ruin *everything*?" Maya infused her voice with as much venom as she could muster.

Deepa sat on the foot of her bed. "Maya, I'm so sorry for last night. I really am. I didn't mean for everything to come out like that."

Maya refused to meet her sister's eyes.

"Maya," Deepa asked, "what did Chase mean about the pic? Did you send him a photo of yourself?"

At this, Maya covered her now-burning face with her hands. "Oh god. What did . . . ?"

"He said something to me after you left the table. I don't think anyone else heard." Deepa's voice was kinder than Maya expected. "So . . . was it something bad?"

Still covering her face, the image emblazoned in her mind, Maya said, "I wasn't naked. It was just . . . a cleavage shot. My face wasn't in it. But obviously, anyone can tell from the skin color . . . *Oh god!* I can't believe this. I thought . . ." She thought what? "I felt like I had to do something to make him see me as something other than his sister's nerdy friend. I . . ." Maya had no further explanation. Hearing these words out loud made her burn with shame. "I'm scared, D."

"You should be," Deepa said. "You gave that guy power over you. But you can take it back. Tell him very clearly to delete the picture."

Maya opened her eyes and scanned the ceiling, as if the way out would be mapped there.

Deepa exhaled and placed a hand on Maya's knee. "You've got to stop with all this stuff, Maya. Look at what you've been doing to fit in with this family, this crowd—stealing things, sending those kinds of pictures . . . It's really messed up. You shouldn't have to do any of that for people who care about you. You shouldn't have to compromise yourself. No one is worth that."

Maya's heart raced as she sat up, clutching a pillow to her chest. "Are you going to tell them?"

Deepa watched her for a moment. "I think it might be better if you just come clean yourself, M."

Maya wondered how her sister could be so confident. It wasn't as if Deepa's constant headbutting with their parents had led to anything but strife and punishment. And how could she lay more on her parents right now, with Ajay's arraignment two days away?

After Deepa left her room, Maya scrunched back down under the bedcovers and rolled over to her side. No one even knew about all the other things she'd pinched over the past year: mascara from the pharmacy, bead bracelets from the beach shop, a vintage tee from the thrift store. Ashley's necklace at that boutique was the boldest she'd ever been—it was $319 and the kind of gift she knew would impress her friend and cement their relationship. Just as she'd hoped the sexy pic she'd taken for Chase would have some impact. Being with Chase in the privacy of her bedroom, where they'd kissed and touched, was one thing. Being with him out in the open would change the way people saw her at school.

Was it messed up? It *was* exhausting, Maya conceded, working so hard to make up for these deficiencies, just to have it all come crashing down, as it did last night. What had it all been for, in the end?

Her phone buzzed with a message, and she grabbed it from her nightstand. Chase. Maya's heart pounded rapidly as she opened it.

Not cool for your sister to shake down my family. How would you like it if I aired your dirty laundry?

Maya closed her eyes, the mass of her secrets keeping her pinned to her bed as she played through various mortifying scenarios in her mind.

LATER THAT NIGHT, on the back patio, Ashok recounted the entire painful dinner party for the Dhillons. "It was a complete disaster," he said, shaking his head. "No other word for it."

"Dumpster fire?" Ricky suggested.

"Shit show?!" Archie grinned.

"You're both taking pleasure in this, aren't you?" Ashok said.

"No, of course not." Archie reached over to slap his knee. "Just trying to ease your mood a little. You could use a little lightness."

"As much as it pains me to say it, Arch, you were right," Ashok said. "I guess we'll never really belong in that world."

"Who needs wealthy, connected friends when you've got us?" Archie winked at him. Next to her, Ricky raised his palm sheepishly, and Archie batted it away. "And how's she doing?" Archie nodded her head toward the kitchen, where Priya was checking on the food.

"You know—pretty well, actually," Ashok said, pleasantly surprised to find it was true. "It's like something's clicked into place for her. She seems more resolved, in some way."

"Yeah," Archie said, cocking her head. "She *insisted* on cooking everything herself tonight. Wouldn't let me bring anything, not even takeout."

Ashok nodded and took a sip of his drink. It was so nice to just be at home, comfortable with old friends and the familiarity of a home-cooked meal: a small illusion of normalcy in the storm of the past two weeks. The living room window had been replaced yesterday, and the reporters were gone for the night. Jonathan Stern had warned them, though, to expect a swarm of media at Ajay's scheduled arraignment on Monday. The spectacle at the Bakers' house had extinguished their last hope of conjuring a miracle; there was now nothing more they could do but show up at the hearing, tell the truth, and hope for the best. Ashok leaned against his chair, trying to relax his shoulders.

Priya joined them on the back deck, carrying a platter of fried paneer.

"Mm," Archie said. "Is there anything in the world better than fried cheese?" She stabbed a toothpick into a paneer cube and dipped it into green chutney before popping it in her mouth. "Every cuisine has their own version, you know? Greeks have their *saganaki*, Mexicans have *queso fundido* . . ."

"Italians have their mozzarella sticks," Ricky added.

Archie scoffed. "I think those are more American than Italian."

"Whatever." Ricky spoke through a mouthful. "Still fried cheese and still delicious. But . . ." He held up a toothpick. "Not as good as these, Priya."

"Any word from Veena or Vikram?" Archie asked.

Priya shook her head. "I never heard back from Veena about tonight, but it was very last minute."

"Can't blame them," Archie said. "That BioFlex story made a couple of national business journals. He can't be happy about that."

"I spoke to him yesterday," Ashok said. "He said the company was growing like crazy, and he trusted his senior execs to hire quickly. It was natural for them to find people from their own communities, their own engineering colleges. People they could connect with, who were lower risk." Ashok shrugged.

"There's something to that," Ricky said. "People call our engineering department the Tam-Brahms." He chuckled, referring to the Tamil Brahmins from South India that populated the group. "My CTO recruited them. He has an easy rapport, they work well together, socialize together."

"But are they keeping other folks out?" Ashok asked.

Ricky cocked his head, considering this. "I don't think it's as much about keeping other people out, more about favoring their own community. But I can see how others might feel excluded. Especially if they have a history of that—if they're particularly sensitive to that sort of thing."

Ashok reflected on this. Was he oversensitive in this regard? Could his personal history cause him to ascribe intentions to actions that weren't ill conceived?

"So, this is just our version of the old boys' club?" Archie laughed. "How is it any different than favoring rich white men from Harvard Business School? It sounds like Vikram showed a lack of awareness, at the least."

"Note to self," Ricky said. "Call HR Monday morning about the Tam-Brahms."

"It's complicated." Priya sighed.

"Do you remember when it wasn't?" Ricky said. "Just the four of us at a folding table with pizza and paper plates? None of . . . this." He waved his glass around, indicating in a single gesture the trappings of the house, the surrounding community of Pacific Hills, their five children gathered upstairs.

"It did seem simpler," Ashok mused. "Even if we didn't know it back then."

"To old friends," Archie said, raising her glass.

"To *real* friends." Priya clinked, and they all took a drink.

"Now." Archie raised an eyebrow. "Explain to me why my darling Deepa is still grounded, simply for exercising her civic rights? Hasn't this house arrest lasted long enough?"

Priya couldn't help but smile. Archie had always harbored a special fondness for Deepa, born of those early years when they'd watched each other's babies. Archie and her mother had loved dressing up Deepa and doing her hair, the only girl alongside their twin boys. It was as if Archie always remembered Deepa this way, as a sweet cherubic baby with none of the baggage that had come in the intervening hormonal, angst-ridden years.

"Yes, one can hardly keep up with all the delinquencies around here." Priya sighed. "That protest was the *original* reason, but then we learned that instead of taking Maya to school last week, she made her spend an entire day at the mall." Priya shook her head. "Can you believe it?"

"No, not really." Archie furrowed her brow, head tilted to one side. "Deepa hates the mall. Isn't she always railing against rampant material consumption and all that?"

Priya blinked rapidly. *What did it matter?* Deepa hardly seemed to be making rational choices anymore.

"Wait, did you say the week *after* Ajay was arrested?" Archie asked. "But Deepa was at Chavez then; she *definitely* was. The boys saw her. I told them to ask her about Ajay every day. They reported back to me each night on how you all were doing."

Priya tried to turn this over in her mind. Deepa had admitted to skipping school that day, to dragging Maya along with her, even buying her silence with that pricey necklace. It seemed her daughter, like the rest of the world, made little sense to her anymore.

42

Sunday

THE NIGHT BEFORE had provided a reprieve of sorts, a chance to relax in the comfort of friends and forget their troubles. But as soon as the light of Sunday morning coaxed open Priya's eyes, she realized what day it was. It might be the last day they had with Ajay.

For the past two weeks, tomorrow's date had been looming in her mind with the hope that the arraignment would allow for the truth to come out, for the misunderstanding to be resolved, for their son to be vindicated. But after their plea to the Bakers had been aborted, after the bad press about Vikram's company, after their lawyer had no good news from the DA's office, after the articles and the rumors, and after that brick shattered their living room window and any remaining faith, Priya's hopeful thinking had evaporated like the rest of their support. She had to face the reality that this might be the last day they had with their son.

She would make it special—make chocolate chip pancakes with whipped cream, fresh berry smoothies, and those roasted potatoes Ajay loved to dip in a mixture of ketchup and chutney. This thought entered Priya's mind and then, for the first time she could remember, she felt a complete lack of energy to do anything about it. She lay on her side, eyes slowly focusing on the numbers marking time on her bedside clock. She should get up before the kids, before Ajay. She should be there to wake him gently, to usher him into this day, of all days.

And yet, Priya felt restrained by some invisible force. She rolled over and saw Ashok lying on his back, one arm folded behind his head, eyes wide open and staring at the ceiling. "How long have you been up?" she murmured, moving closer to feel the warmth of his body against hers.

Ashok closed his eyes briefly. "I'm not sure I actually slept."

Priya felt a cold wave rush into her chest cavity, her dread taking on looming proportions now that it was shared and confirmed. She tightened an arm around her husband and allowed herself one last moment before she would force herself up, whether she felt like it or not.

THE PANCAKES TURNED out flat, the chocolate chips burned on the griddle. The children all woke up and wandered into the kitchen at different times, eating a little or not at all. The day passed unremarkably: Deepa retreating to her bedroom to study for the SAT, Maya taking a homework break to go for a run through the neighborhood. Priya went into each of their rooms that afternoon, helping her daughters choose suitable outfits for the arraignment and setting aside some items to iron.

Ashok tried to busy himself with work, but his mind was incapable of focusing. His thoughts kept flitting back to that night at the jail, seeing Ajay's face and the hollow look in his eyes. Ajay had recovered somewhat since then, and today he was even happily absorbed in YouTube recordings of robotics competitions, preoccupied with his team's upcoming regional meet. Perhaps it was a blessing that their son thought differently, perhaps his mind was protecting him from facing the harsh reality before them.

When he saw glimmers of Ajay's humor and his endearing quirks, Ashok thought that he had been right; his kid didn't need to live with a label. Despite the tensions between him and Priya, despite their differences over how they'd handled their son, Ashok knew they both desperately wanted the best for him. Though it was one thing they were aligned on, it was also out of their power. Ajay's fate was in the hands of a judge who would meet him for the first time tomorrow. A stranger who would evaluate his son based on what—whether he could make eye contact, answer questions directly, show remorse?

"We have to talk to him," Priya said. "We have to prepare him for tomorrow."

Ashok nodded, knowing they could no longer allow Ajay the luxury of being the innocent child he was.

THEY ENTERED HIS room together and sat on either side of the bed. "Ajay, please put the computer away," Ashok said. "We need to speak with you."

Ajay didn't avert his eyes from the screen, but he closed the lid of the laptop and placed his palms on top.

"You remember what Mr. Stern told us, about the hearing tomorrow?" Priya asked.

Ajay nodded slightly, without looking at them.

"We're going to court," Priya continued, "and Mr. Stern is going to explain to the judge what happened with you at the airport, with Drummond and the police officers."

"Mr. Stern will do all the talking," Ashok interjected. "You don't need to say anything, except when the judge asks you how you plead, you say, 'Not guilty'—you remember that? Mr. Stern will tell you when it's time. Otherwise, you just sit quietly."

Ajay slowly looked up now. "Will you be with me?"

"We . . ." Priya hesitated, then said, "We'll be sitting right behind you, all four of us."

"And there will be other people in the courtroom," Ashok said. "It might be crowded. The police officers will probably be there, and the detectives who spoke to you here."

"But other people you know too," Priya added quickly. "Archie Auntie and Ricky Uncle." As she said this, she realized she didn't know who else would actually show up for them tomorrow.

Ajay looked toward the bedroom door, and Priya turned to see Deepa and Maya standing there. She waved them in. The girls sat down on the bed, and Deepa put a hand on Ajay's ankle. "Hi, bud."

"We're not sure what will happen tomorrow," Ashok said. "You could come home with us, and the police will keep investigating. They might want to talk to you again. Or—it's not likely, but possible—that you'll have to go with them, with the police officers, and stay in a facility for a little while."

Ajay's head jerked up then, and he looked at Priya with the same betrayed expression as when he got a vaccination shot at the pediatrician. "We're doing everything possible to stop that from happening." Priya placed her hand over his. "Mr. Stern, everybody's working really hard, okay?" Tears rose in her eyes, and she blinked them back, clenched her jaw. "If that does happen, just know that we love you and we'll do everything we can to bring you home as soon as we can."

A small whimper escaped from Maya, which she tried to obscure by clearing her throat.

"Just remember," Ashok said. "Don't say anything, don't answer any questions. Mr. Stern will do all the talking. Okay?"

Priya nodded along to reinforce this point, after what had happened at the Bakers' house.

"But, Dad?" Ajay said softly. "Then how will they know the truth?"

Priya saw a wounded look flicker across Ashok's face, her husband's fortitude finally splintered by his son's innocence.

FOR DINNER THAT night, Ajay had requested their old favorite pizzeria in Irvine, so Deepa was driving there to pick it up. She'd immediately agreed to go when her mother had asked, any resentment about having her freedoms curtailed for the past week forgotten. Now she switched off the radio and drove in silence, her stomach knotted as she thought about the arraignment the next day. As she clenched the steering wheel, Deepa felt anger bubbling inside her. In desperation, she screamed—tentatively at first, then again at full force.

She screamed and screamed, until her throat was raw and she was sweating. She couldn't tell where to direct her anger. Her parents seemed helpless. The lawyer seemed to be trying his best. The police were a faceless specter. Whoever had thrown that brick through their window was an anonymous coward. Their neighbors had been silent. Their real community all lived back in Irvine: Paco, Archie Auntie, Ricky Uncle. When it came down to it, the Shahs were being held up by their strongest friendships and held together by themselves. Deepa hadn't felt this close to her family in a very long time.

BACK AT HOME, Maya was in the kitchen alone, preparing her brother's favorite peanut butter cookies. She went through each step deliberately, searching for rhythm in the tasks: measuring flour and sugar, cracking eggs, and melting butter. Until today, Maya had assumed everything would be fine with Ajay. She tried to cheer him up and make him happy, but she didn't think anything bad would actually happen to him tomorrow. She expected it would all get worked out: Ajay was a kid, weird but innocent, their parents were on top of it, and they had a good lawyer.

But the look on her father's face in Ajay's bedroom just now made Maya realize this was real and it was serious, so serious her parents could not promise them it would all be okay. For the second time this week, Maya heard fear in their voices, and it frightened her.

UPSTAIRS, PRIYA WAS grateful for her daughter's positivity. *A double batch,* Maya had said, explaining why she needed a full pound of butter. *One dozen for tonight, one for the rest of the week.* Sitting on the edge of the bathtub behind their closed bedroom door with Ashok, Priya wished she could feel some of Maya's optimism right now, or even Deepa's resolve.

"Remember when we had Ajay's birthday party at Luigi's—the huge mess those kids made with all the pizza dough?" Priya said.

"Everyone had flour in their hair. Ajay was so disappointed we weren't actually eating the crusts they rolled. And all the parents were so relieved we weren't." She smiled, recalling how she'd guiltily offered to clean up the table afterward, but Luigi had just poured her another glass of wine, on the house, and told her they loved having bambinos at the restaurant.

Ashok was rifling through the dresser.

"We don't have a neighborhood place like that here," Priya mused. "I miss it, someplace old, where they know us."

"Have you seen my tie?" Ashok said. "It's green with little pinwheels. I want to wear it tomorrow. Did you put it somewhere?"

Priya shook her head. "Why would I move your tie?"

"I don't know, but I keep all my ties right here in this drawer, and it's not here." He shoved the drawer closed and opened another.

"Just wear another tie! What does it matter?"

"That's my lucky tie!" Ashok threw his hands in the air. "I can't believe it's missing. That's a bad omen."

"Lucky tie?" Priya said wryly. "Well, there's still a few boxes from the move in the garage that haven't been unpacked yet. You can check there." Then a thought drifted through her mind, not for the first time, but this time she reached out, caught it, and voiced it. "If we still lived there, if there were people around who knew Ajay, who could vouch for him—do you think this would have happened?"

Ashok stopped, turned to her. "This did *not* happen because we moved to Pacific Hills."

Priya shrugged, then shook her head. "You don't know that."

"Priya, it was bad luck, bad timing. It's a new neighborhood, a *better* neighborhood, a safer neighborhood—he was just confused, he got carried away."

"Luck! Timing! Omens!" Priya cried. "When did you become so superstitious? What happened to the man who believed in making your own luck, changing your fate?" She rubbed at her temple. After a few moments, she spoke softly. "This wasn't some random event, Ashok." She stood and walked toward him, then sat down on the foot of the bed.

Ashok closed the drawer and leaned back against the dresser to face her.

"If it wasn't this, it would be something else—another incident, a different misunderstanding," Priya said. "And it still could be. It could be even worse next time." She extended a hand toward her husband. He took it and sat next to her on the bed.

Priya stroked his hand. "Ajay's differences are . . . hurting him right now. But we could help him get the support he needs and protect him a bit more."

FROM HER BEDROOM, Maya could hear her parents' raised voices down the hall, if not the words they spoke. She sat cross-legged on her bed, her phone clutched in her hands, thumbs hovering over the screen as she deliberated. Navigating to the secret folder where she'd saved the compromising photo, she deleted it once, then again permanently out of the trash. Maya let out a long, slow exhale. She tried writing the message several different ways, then went back and removed all the apologies and emojis.

That photo I sent you was a mistake. Please delete it.

She hit send and waited, but no reply came.

43

Monday

ASHOK AND AJAY were dressed in suits, though they wouldn't make Ajay put on his tie until just before entering the courtroom. For now, the Shah family was waiting in a windowless room on another floor of the courthouse, to keep Ajay as calm as possible before the hearing. Priya was wearing a navy dress with a Rajasthani block print, manufactured in India but purchased from the Gap. Even Deepa and Maya were dressed nicely without having to be asked.

They had arrived over an hour early, but even then, Justice 4 All supporters were gathered in front of the courthouse holding their signs: Moms 4 Justice, Protect ALL Kids. Jonathan Stern and Helen Wu had led them past the scrum of cameras and shouting reporters, all melding into a blurred cacophony.

Ashok had brought his checkbook, having transferred all their available cash into the account, and all five of their passports. Priya had tucked a copy of the hospital report, including photos of Ajay's bruised body, into her purse. Jonathan and Helen were huddled on one side of the room, reviewing papers from a thick accordion file. Archie sent Priya an update from inside the courtroom, telling her the gallery was full and people were now filing into the standing-room section at the back. The hour first ticked on interminably, then all of a sudden, it was time.

*

WHEN PRIYA ENTERED the courtroom, she felt an eerie recollection of walking toward the mandap at her own wedding, the only other time in her life she'd felt every set of eyes in the room trained on her. Like then, her stomach was clenched with tension, and her body was flooded with a mix of emotions: nerves, trepidation, adrenaline. Unlike then, Ashok was now by her side, holding her hand, and Priya did not avert her eyes in the demure gaze expected of Indian brides; she held her head up and met the eyes of each person she passed in the courtroom. She saw the police officer who had escorted Ajay out at the jail, the detectives who had interviewed their son at home, the reporter from the *Orange County Register* who had shown up on her doorstep, a few people in Justice 4 All shirts.

She was heartened to see a sizable crowd of Indian friends from their old neighborhood in Irvine, many of whom she hadn't seen since they'd moved. She passed Veena Sharma, wearing a tight smile, and walked toward Archie and Ricky, who were holding seats for them in the first row. Only after sitting and glancing down the row did she see the architect with her husband. Ajay's math teacher and robotics coach were there to serve as potential character witnesses, and the school principal and counselor were also sitting with them. She nodded toward each of them, managing a small smile of gratitude.

Priya reached for Ashok's hand and clasped it tightly. In front of them, Ajay sat next to the two attorneys. Priya's heart clenched as they were asked to rise for the judge.

After everyone was seated again, the judge spoke. "I understand the prosecution would like to be heard before proceedings begin."

"Yes, Your Honor." A man in a gray suit on the other side of the courtroom stood up. "After completing our investigation over the past two weeks, the State believes the defendant did not commit a prosecutable criminal offense here, and thus we are dropping all charges."

Priya turned to Ashok, confused. Deepa leaned over and whispered, "What does that mean?"

Jonathan Stern put a hand on Ajay's shoulder as he rose out of his chair. "We have no objection, of course. We commend the district attorney's office for coming to the right conclusion and request that bail be returned."

"So granted. Bail will be returned. Defendant is free to go." The judge banged his gavel, and the courtroom erupted with cheers. Ajay turned around and looked searchingly at Priya. "It's over?" he asked.

Priya looked at Jonathan, who was beaming. "It's over," he said.

Priya reached out to embrace Ajay. "It's over." She felt Ashok's arms wrap around them, heard Deepa's cries, and felt the warmth of her daughters' bodies against her back.

BACK IN THE windowless room, Jonathan Stern replayed what had happened in the courtroom. "The trial and the investigation are over. The prosecutor is making the same recommendation to the FAA—that this was an unfortunate but innocent mistake."

"He'll have no criminal record, nothing?" Ashok asked.

Jonathan shook his head. "Nothing. Ajay gets to go back to being a regular kid."

Ajay looked up. "Can I get Drummond back now?"

"Let's stay away from the drones for a while, okay, buddy?" Jonathan placed a hand on his client's shoulder, and there was laughter in the room for the first time.

Priya smiled at Ajay. "We'll find something better, okay?"

Jonathan grabbed his bag and moved toward the door. "We can go out the back of the courthouse to avoid the cameras, if you'd like."

Priya stood up. "No, let's go out the front. I want them to see us."

THREE DAYS EARLIER, the prosecutor, detectives, and arresting officers had gathered to discuss Ajay's case in a nondescript conference room.

"Well, this has certainly grown into a PR nightmare," the prosecutor said, tossing a newspaper down on the table. "Please tell me we have something to justify keeping this kid in custody?"

"We absolutely did when we picked him up," Officer O'Reilly said. "Trespassing, destruction of evidence, evading arrest . . ." He ticked off the offenses on his fingers. "He wouldn't talk, didn't tell us his age. And he's big, he looks older. Suspicion of terrorism—we had to play it safe. Serve and protect." He folded his hands together on his chest, the question satisfied as far as he was concerned.

Officer Diaz shook his head slightly but stayed quiet. He wanted to reserve his horsepower for when he needed it.

The prosecutor turned to the detectives. "What did the search warrant turn up? Did you find anything at the house?"

"Nothing definitive," Detective Hayes said. "He has some compulsive interests that are concerning: robotics, wiring diagrams, flight patterns, aeronautic engines. But he also has a ton of LEGOs and fantasy books. We think he's probably just a science geek and an awkward kid. Neighbors and folks at his new school couldn't say much about him. Seems like a loner, for sure."

"So . . . ?" the prosecutor prodded.

"Also, keep in mind," Diaz interjected now, "the boy seems like he might be on the autism spectrum. Common symptoms are inability to have social interactions, read nonverbal cues, make eye contact . . . also, intense obsession with a couple of narrow topics." He waited a beat. "I think this could explain a lot of the behavior O'Reilly found troubling at the time of arrest, and what the detectives found in their investigation."

Officer O'Reilly shrugged. "Jeez, when'd you become such a medical expert, Greenie?"

Detective Hayes spoke up. "That makes sense. One of his teachers mentioned something like that. We didn't find any evidence of criminal threat—explosives, firearms, history of violent behavior—and the computer didn't show any tracking to known terrorist groups." She cleared her throat. "Also, not that it should matter, but the family's Hindu, not Muslim."

The prosecutor nodded slowly, staring at the newspaper on the table.

"I know it's not my decision," Officer Diaz said, "but I think we should drop all the charges, even the initial ones. We can't prove much, the kid's not a threat, and we have more important work to do." On this last point, everyone in the room could agree.

BACK AT CHAVEZ High, Paco felt his phone buzz persistently in his jacket pocket during first period. It was too early for Deepa to know anything, as the arraignment had just begun, but he asked to be excused and slipped into the bathroom. Seeing his mother's name on the screen caused a flood of adrenaline through his body. A call from his family in the middle of day could mean one of his sisters needed to be picked up from school or something had happened to Amá.

"Gracias a Dios, gracias a Dios," Lucia said breathlessly when he answered the phone. "The lawyer called, a settlement. After three years, finally, our prayers have been answered."

"Wait, Amá, slow down," Paco said. "I can't understand you."

But the words were pouring out of Lucia like a broken spigot, and Paco tried to catch what he could. "Just called . . . from nowhere . . . weren't supposed to hear anything for months."

"Amá, they're offering a settlement?"

"Sí! Sí! That's what I'm saying," Lucia shouted. "Gracias a Dios. I go to the lawyer's office tomorrow. He said they have an offer for us."

Paco sat down on the toilet seat.

"Maybe we can buy our own house." Lucia was crying now. "You don't have to share a room with your sisters. Maybe you go to college, Paco."

Paco was staring at the flyer taped to the back of the bathroom stall, advertising the upcoming winter dance. The words on the page began to swim before him. He shook his head. "But how?" It came out in a whisper.

"Your blessed father, may he rest in peace," Lucia said. "He is looking down on us. He is taking care of us still."

*

LATER THAT EVENING, after the Shah family had finished dinner, Priya and Ashok asked their daughters to stay behind in the kitchen.

Priya dipped a tea bag into her cup as she spoke. "Do you two want to tell us the truth about what happened that day, when you said you were both at the mall?"

Maya glanced over at her sister. Deepa's eyes flickered between her parents.

"I called both your schools today, to report your absence," Priya said. "Chavez confirmed that you *were* at school that day, Deepa. You even took a math test." She turned to Maya. "And *you* definitely weren't. I had Pacific Hills double-check their attendance records."

Maya felt her mouth go dry, then suddenly fill with saliva as if she was going to throw up. She walked over to the kitchen sink and braced herself against its edge. She'd had this persistent nausea for the past two days, since Chase hadn't responded to her message, imagining all the ways he could humiliate her at school. All yesterday, her stomach had been in knots, anticipating what might happen today at Ajay's arraignment. She'd woken up before dawn this morning, wondering if this would be the last time she'd have breakfast with her brother. And now, even though she should be relieved and they should all be celebrating, it felt as if everything else could come crashing down. What would happen tomorrow when she had to return to school and face Ashley and Chase after the scene at their house? What if Chase showed that picture around school? Maya turned on the kitchen faucet and cupped her hand underneath to drink some water.

"Maya?" her mother's voice came from behind her. "Maya!"

Maya turned around to face them and looked into Deepa's shiny eyes. Her throat tightened as she spoke. "Please don't be mad. I have to tell you something."

AFTER SHE TOLD her parents everything—because once she started, she found she couldn't stop—Maya felt the ugly weight of all those truths settle around her like a heavy fog. She saw the disappointment in her father's eyes when he learned that stealing had become sport for her. She watched pain contort her mother's face as her accumulation of lies became clear. After their parents sent them away so they could discuss it all in private, she felt Deepa's silent support as they lay together, side by side, on her bed.

Staring up at her bedroom ceiling, Maya began to feel the tension very slowly draining out of her body. There would be consequences, but she felt unexpectedly lighter having jettisoned the secrets she'd been carrying, knowing that her parents were now sharing their weight. As long as they still loved her, as long as Ajay was home safe with them, maybe the rest of it would all, eventually, be okay too. Overwhelmed by emotion and stress, Maya felt tears begin to fill her eyes and trail down her cheeks.

"It was my fault," Maya confessed, without looking at her sister. "I invited him in because no one was home. I wanted him to like me, to kiss me. Then everything moved so fast . . . I thought it was a good sign, that he liked me. Afterward, in my body, it . . . didn't feel right. But in my mind, I was trying to believe it was good. I really wanted him to like me . . ." She shook her head. "So then, I took that photo . . ."

Deepa had been listening silently. Maya wondered if her sister was disappointed in her, if she thought differently of her now.

"I asked him to delete it," Maya said. "He didn't respond."

"Ask again," Deepa said, sitting up. She reached over and took Maya's phone from the nightstand. "Do it now."

Maya took her phone, tapped out the message, same as before, with the addition of an exclamation point. She waited as three dots appeared, and then his message.

Already did. Not worth keeping.

Maya felt the sting of his response before the relief. Wordlessly, she passed the phone to Deepa.

"Asshole," Deepa muttered. "Good riddance."

"I know I should feel that way, but some part of me still . . ." Maya sighed, clutching a pillow to her chest. "God, I'm so screwed up."

"Welcome to the club," Deepa said.

Maya smacked her sister's shoulder. "At least I don't have a police record."

"Not *yet*." Deepa jabbed her back, and they both began to laugh.

PART IV

Afterward

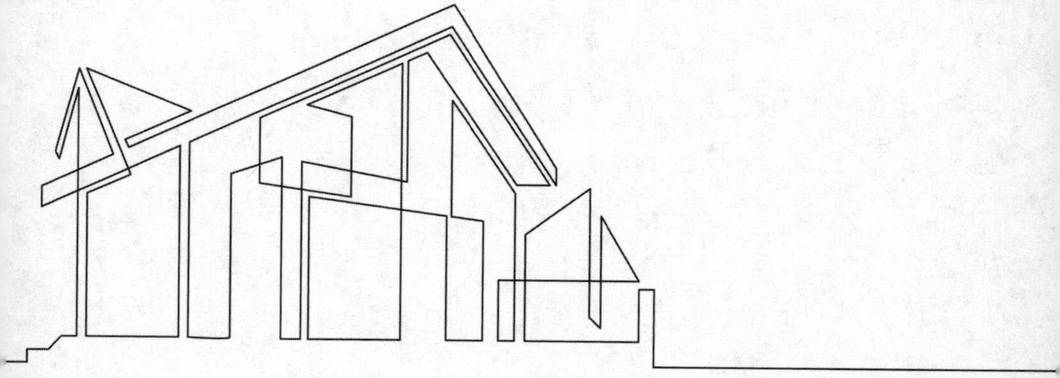

44

One week later

PRIYA WAS SEATED on the patio of a new urban tasting room Archie had found, two sweating glasses of wine on the bistro table between them.

Archie held up her glass for a toast. "You can exhale now."

"It seems like a lifetime since that night at Veena's," Priya said. How much had changed in the past few weeks—not only her understanding of the world, which she now knew had been limited and perhaps naive—but her understanding of her own children. "I really thought we were doing a decent job, as parents." Priya sighed.

"You are," Archie said. "None of us do it perfectly, and you can't control the outside world."

"But I thought I knew my children," Priya said pensively.

"You *do* know them," Archie said. "They're just complicated little creatures, like all of us."

"I never even worried about Maya," Priya said. "I could always count on her to be well-behaved, do well at school . . ." She took a sip. "But it turns out, I missed this thing entirely."

"*Or* she hid it well," Archie interjected. "The smart ones know how to do that."

"All this stuff with the boy, especially," Priya said. "It makes me sick to think what could have happened. I should have seen it. You know . . ." She shrugged at Archie. "Because of what happened to me."

Archie shook her head gently. "How would you have seen it, when

Maya was trying to keep it from you? Do you blame your mother for not seeing it back then, living under the same roof?"

Priya shook her head. "No, of course not. And I didn't want her to—it would have torn my family apart." If she didn't blame her mother, could she still blame herself? Priya understood now that while she had been consumed with Deepa's troublemaking and handling Ajay's challenges, her middle child had been lost in the shuffle. "All this time, Maya's been a sort of chameleon, doing whatever it takes to get by and fit in."

"Which," Archie said, "can be a very helpful quality in life. In a different way, isn't that what you've tried to do the whole time you've been in this country? Adaptation is a survival strategy. You just have to redirect Maya to a better path, but that girl has mad life skills. She's going to fare well in the world."

"Well, I suppose that's something," Priya said, tracing the rim of her wineglass with her index finger. "Unlike Ajay." She stared at her glass. "We've decided to take him for an assessment. Ashok finally agreed."

"Good!" Archie smiled, sitting back in her chair. "I'll send you a few recommendations."

"Just send one," Priya said. "I trust you."

Archie nodded. "You'll see, once he starts working with someone, he'll learn how to interact with the world a bit better. He'll be fine. *Better* than fine."

Priya nodded, tears springing to her eyes. "Sorry." She laughed, reaching for a napkin. "I'm doing it again."

Archie reached over and squeezed her hand. "You never have to be sorry."

Priya dabbed at the corner of her eye. "Ajay's challenges, they've always been *our* problems, as a family. But now . . ." Now that her sweet, unusual boy was growing up and interacting with the outside world, those challenges had become weightier, potentially dangerous. "The world doesn't feel safe for him anymore."

"The truth is," Archie said, raising an eyebrow, "it never was."

Priya nodded slowly. "I suppose Deepa was right about some things."

Archie winked. "Pains you to say it, doesn't it?"

"Perhaps her worldview does have some basis." Priya tried to smile. "She's just so combative about everything—she can't ever just be content with the rules. I always thought her attitude was that of a child who never had to struggle much." She shrugged. "But maybe we messed up. Maybe we should never have sent her back to India."

"When she was a baby, and you had no better choice?" Archie asked.

"Or the second time," Priya said. "Maybe I overreacted—I was so worried about her behavior and those influences on her. We were both working to build the business; we couldn't be around much." She shook her head and took a long sip of her wine.

"Or," Archie said, "maybe that exposure to her extended family, another country, her parents' culture, maybe all of that helped shape the person she is today—her values, her loyalty, her strength."

Priya wobbled her head, neither an assent nor a dispute.

"Trust me, that fire in Deepa is going to save us all." Archie chuckled.

"If it doesn't kill me first." Priya took another sip. Deepa had certainly proven herself to be more caring than Priya had given her credit for, to the point of sacrificing herself for her sister. Perhaps Maya's behavior was the natural endpoint of all the assimilation and success she and Ashok had encouraged in their children, but what was the cost of this American dream? In the end, the protective bubble of Pacific Hills hadn't saved them, nor had proximity to the wealth and privilege of the Bakers; even the Sharmas had proved to be less powerful than they might have thought.

Priya wasn't sure how she and Ashok would help their children navigate their way through this new territory she'd reluctantly discovered. But she knew one way to start.

45

One month later

WITHIN A FEW weeks, the placidity of Pacific Hills had been restored, and the neighborhood returned to its pleasant hum. The air turned crisp, and the leaves that fell from majestic trees were meticulously groomed by teams of Mexican workers. Neighbors waved to one another as they walked their purebred dogs and jogged in their performance gear. The story of the suspicious new family had faded to a mild stain that people were largely eager to forget. Such rumors were injurious to property values, after all.

Even at the Shahs' house, one might think that things were back to normal. The reporters and cameras had long since disappeared, and vehicles came and went from the house as its occupants resumed their regular school and work routines. On the surface, everything may have seemed the same, but inside the house, something had shifted, in greater and lesser ways, for each member of the family.

One pressing question was whether the Shah family would attend the Sharmas' annual Diwali party in a few days. Vikram and Veena had issued invitations with their usual flair, and the Indian community was buzzing with speculation about Vikram's fate with BioFlex, so attendance promised to be robust.

"I would really rather not be around that scene," Ashok said.

"You'd mean you'd rather not be around Vikram?" Priya asked. "Have you even talked to him, since the arraignment? Veena did come out to support us."

Ashok nodded. "I know. And I'll call him. I'm just not ready yet."

"So until then, you want to just ignore the whole situation?" Priya said.

"God, Priya, that is what I've been doing my whole life!" Ashok said. "That's how I've gotten here—built a business, bought this house, moved to Pacific Hills. That's how we *got* here. I put my head down, worked hard, and didn't make a fuss. Until recently, you did that too."

"Yes, exactly," Priya said with precision. "That is how we got here." They stared at each other for a few moments before she spoke again. "Are you ashamed, Ashok, of what happened with Ajay? Is that why you don't want to see people?"

"Of course not," Ashok shot back. "But I don't want to rehash it, either. It's finally over and we can go back to our lives, forget this nightmare ever happened."

"How can you say that?" Priya's voice rose. "How can you pretend we can just go back to the same life? Don't you see how everything's changed? The world is not safe for Ajay anymore. This could happen again, to him or someone else—"

"Someone else is not our concern," Ashok said. "We have enough on our hands." He rubbed his temples. "Look, Priya, we're getting Ajay help. That's all we can do, take care of our own family the best we can. That is enough."

"I don't think it is," Priya said. "I know you think Ajay was just unfortunate—wrong place, wrong time, wrong circumstances—and you're right about that. What happened to him shouldn't have happened. But he also *was* fortunate, because it could have turned out so much worse. Think of what might have happened if he were Black. Or if he were Muslim. Or if he had been rude to or assertive with the police because it wasn't the first time they'd stopped him." A tear trailed down Priya's cheek. "It could have been so much worse, Ashok.

"One thing I've realized in the past month is how much I've been blind to—how the outside world sees Ajay, how Maya has been hiding things from us . . . Even this neighborhood isn't what we thought it would be."

Ashok threw his hands up in the air. "Now you're starting to sound like Deepa."

Priya shrugged and smiled at her husband. She patted the seat next to her.

"So, what are you saying?" Ashok sat down, resigned. "What do you want to do?"

"I'D LIKE YOUR help," Priya said to Deepa. "Could you help me get in touch with Theo Young's mother?"

"The boy in LA . . . who was shot by the police?" Deepa asked.

Priya nodded. "I've been thinking about her a lot these last few weeks. I'd like to meet her, if she's willing."

"I don't know, Mom," Deepa said. "As bad as this whole thing was for Ajay—and I know he's still going to be recovering for a long time—we're still lucky. Lucky that he gets the chance to recover. Lucky we had a good lawyer. Lucky the charges were dropped."

Priya held up a finger. "Not just luck—"

"Yeah, I know," Deepa finished. "Not just luck, hard work. Look, I know you and Dad have worked your tails off. I know you've made a lot of sacrifices and it hasn't been easy. I know you did it all for us. And that's part of *our* good luck—Maya, Ajay, and me—that we've had you as parents."

Priya felt a shiver radiate through her body as she heard these words from her daughter for the first time.

"But for some people, hard work just isn't enough to overcome the cards they've been dealt. If Ajay had been Jasmine's son, it probably would have turned out very differently," Deepa said, her voice softening. "And it did, for her."

Priya nodded. "I'm beginning to see that now."

*

JASMINE YOUNG WAS facing a wide-open weekend, the kind of thing she dreaded these days. Staying busy made her feel better, so she was contemplating a garage cleanout or baking up a storm for the church potluck when she received the phone call. Zeke, the volunteer at Justice 4 All who handled press inquiries, asked if she was willing to go down to Orange County to meet with someone. Jasmine had heard of the case; it was impossible not to mentally mark every other instance of police aggression that made the news and consider the many more she knew didn't.

The next morning, as Zeke drove them down a crowded stretch of interstate out of Los Angeles, he filled her in on what he knew. A young boy, about Theo's age, brutalized by the police and held in custody for hours before his parents were contacted, had been under suspicion for weeks before the sham charges were finally dropped. The boy had been guilty of flying his toy drone near the local airport, an infraction worthy of a warning or a civil penalty, perhaps. It was a family of immigrants, perhaps Muslim, certainly brown-skinned.

As Jasmine listened, she gazed out the window as the scenery transitioned from urban concrete to sparse industrial parks, and finally to rolling green hills. Her mind traveled, as it often did, to all the possibilities that might have changed the outcome for Theo. What had made the difference between her son, lying underground in a graveyard, and this boy in Orange County who was still drawing breath? Theo hadn't committed any crime, not even a minor one. He'd been walking in broad daylight through a neighborhood where someone deemed him suspicious because of his hooded sweatshirt, his baggy pockets, his skin color.

Was it this suburban landscape where the family lived—the miles of distance from the angry pressure-filled city she called home? Was it the gradations of melanin in the two boys' skin, a few shades making the crucial difference? Was it the slower reflexes, moment of hesitancy, or sliver of decency in the mind of the police officer?

Jasmine knew it wasn't productive to think like this, to constantly question the things she couldn't control, or even the choices she had.

None of it would change the ending. So she redirected her mind toward what she could do now: help the woman she would soon meet, and perhaps recruit her to join their cause.

WHEN ZEKE'S CAR pulled up to the Shah family home, Priya was watching through the new living room window, already marred with bird droppings. She pulled the elastic from her hair and tucked the loose strands behind her ears. Opening the front door, she walked down the driveway to greet Jasmine as she stepped onto the sidewalk. The two women considered each other silently for a moment, no playbook for what should come next. Priya outstretched a hand and Jasmine walked toward her, taking that hand and extending her other hand as well. The two women stood arm's distance from each other, both hands clasped, until Priya spoke.

"Thank you for being here."

"I'd rather not, to be honest," Jasmine said. "I wish I wasn't in this position."

Priya nodded, squeezing her hands.

"And I'm sure you feel the same way," Jasmine continued. "But here we are."

"Here we are," Priya echoed. "Please," she said, turning toward the house. "Come inside."

Priya and Jasmine sat alone in the kitchen, a teapot and plate of cookies untouched between them. Their discussion began tentatively but moved swiftly into an intimate realm born of their shared experience. As the two women spoke, exchanged stories and memories, shared tears and frustrations, Zeke made calls from the war room of his car.

Inside, Ashok and Deepa came downstairs to meet Jasmine Young, to hear stories about Theo and how he'd loved Marvel comics and playing baseball, how he'd never been to visit Disneyland, which Jasmine had passed on the drive down. Eventually, Maya and Ajay came downstairs too. Jasmine stood up and looked at the young man who didn't resemble her son in any meaningful way. Still, she moved toward Ajay to hug him, and the rest of the Shah family held their collective breath. But he did not push her away or wriggle from her grasp, though she held him for a long time.

JONATHAN STERN AND Helen Wu arrived at the house after lunch to help brainstorm and draft a statement, though Priya was insistent she wanted it to be in her own words.

By five o'clock, reporters and cameras had gathered outside the house, not just local crews but some major outlets from LA. Five or six carloads of supporters from Justice 4 All had arrived, wearing matching turquoise shirts that bore the J4A logo. Ricky and the twins had assembled a podium from an old music stand at the top of the driveway while Archie helped Priya get dressed upstairs.

Archie handed her friend a tube of lipstick in a muted tone. "Nervous?"

"A little," Priya said. "But after so long, feeling like all these things were just happening to us, we're finally doing something. It might not mean anything, but it feels good."

"It means something," Archie said as she gave her friend a final hug.

THE CAMERAS BEGAN snapping as soon as they opened the front door. Priya headed toward the makeshift podium and rested her notes on it. Ashok stood on her left side, holding Ajay's hand; Deepa and Maya stood behind them. On Priya's right stood Jasmine Young, holding herself erect and keeping her focus on Priya, not the gaggle of cameras. Priya looked beyond the cameras to the sea of turquoise T-shirts, supporters holding signs. Archie, Ricky, and the twins stood under a tree. Neighbors were gathered across the street.

"Several weeks ago," Priya began reading, "our twelve-year-old son was arrested by the Orange County Sheriff's Department. He was physically assaulted by the police and detained in a jail cell for hours before we were contacted, then for several more hours after we arrived.

In the end, he was held for over six hours in an adult facility without access to his parents or an attorney." Priya's voice began to crack with emotion. She took a moment before continuing. "When we finally saw him, he had lacerations all over his face, bruises on his arms and torso, and two bruised ribs. The doctor at the emergency room said his injuries were consistent with a severe blow or being thrown hard to the ground. He, and we all, still have a lot of healing to do." Some shouts of disapproval emitted from the Justice 4 All protesters. Priya looked up from her notes and now recognized, standing directly in front of her, the reporter from the *OC Register*. She turned to Ashok, who moved toward the podium and tilted the microphone toward himself.

"After being here for twenty years, we have built a company that provides an important service and good jobs. Our children do well in school. We are good citizens, community members, neighbors, taxpayers. We are proud Americans." He looked up at the cameras. "Yet, all of that felt like it was swept away in an instant.

"What our son did that day may have been wrong, in some small technical way. But the rest of this was very wrong too—a brick through our window telling us to go home." He paused and looked around at the reporters, their cameras. "Roughing up a child and bruising his ribs. The ongoing psychological toll of police actions on our entire family. We believe the police provide an important public service, and they should also be accountable to the public.

"While we are grateful the charges against our son were dropped, there has been no apology from the police or the DA's office, no accountability or even acknowledgment of the damage done—to our son's physical and mental health, to our family, our home, our reputation." Ashok turned the microphone back to Priya.

"We didn't speak up before," Priya said, "because, frankly, we were ashamed. Ashamed to have something bad happen to us in our new neighborhood, where we haven't lived for very long. Ashamed because I didn't know how to explain that our son is different, that he interacts with people in a way that might be hard to understand." She stared at her paper for a moment, choking back the lump in her throat. "I was ashamed to be mistaken for a Muslim, even though I shouldn't be. Because we saw what happened to our Muslim friends in this country after 9/11, and over the past few years with the rhetoric and hate spouted by our politicians.

"And I was ashamed"—Priya swallowed hard and waited until she could continue—"to be grouped in with the other stories I saw splashed in the papers and on TV. I did not want to be a headline. I am a mother first, and my first duty is to protect my children.

"But as terrible as this experience was for our family, we also know it could have been much, much worse." Priya looked over at Jasmine, who now stepped forward to stand next to her. "So, I came out here today to speak to other mothers, other parents." She looked up now, directly into the cameras. "Do everything you can to keep your children safe. But know that sometimes you can do your best, you can do everything right, and bad things can still happen. That is when we have to support each other. I encourage you to look out for your neighbors and your neighbors' kids. Thank you." Priya extended her hand to Jasmine, who took it. They stood together facing the cameras while shutters clicked furiously, and reporters began shouting questions.

Jonathan Stern stepped in front of them and leaned toward the microphone. "As you've heard, this has been quite an ordeal for the Shah family, so we ask that you respect their privacy. We won't be taking any questions at this time. But we do encourage folks at home to contact their elected representatives and the sheriff's department public affairs unit with comments."

Priya looked past the flashing cameras at the cluster of neighbors gathered across the street. Among that sea of faces, camouflaged in one of the turquoise shirts, she spotted the architect from across the street, beaming a confident smile.

Inside the house, after a final cup of chai and some photos, Jasmine said her goodbyes. She and Priya shared a long hug, promising to talk again soon. After Jasmine drove away with Zeke, Jonathan and Helen departed, and the rest of the J4A activists had left, only the Dhillon and Shah families remained.

*

"WELL, THAT WAS quite a farewell eff-you to the neighborhood." Archie sat heavily into a dining chair and put her feet atop a stack of boxes. "Moving truck comes tomorrow?"

"Nine o'clock," Ashok answered.

"What's left to do?" Archie asked.

"Oh, not much," Priya groaned. "Just pack up the kitchen."

"All right, then," Archie said, hoisting herself out of the chair. "Let's get started."

Ricky reached for his phone. "Luigi's pizza for dinner?"

"I think I saw some paper plates left in the cupboard," Ashok said.

Ricky reached out for the platter of home-baked cookies on the kitchen counter. "Dessert?"

Priya playfully slapped his hand away. "Not for you!" She picked up the platter and walked outside, where the last of the media personnel were packing up. No one seemed interested in photographing her as she crossed the street.

Priya rang the architect's doorbell. When her neighbor opened the door, she smiled and reached out to give Priya a warm hug. "I'm so glad things worked out for Ajay. And I'm sorry you had to go through all that. I can't imagine."

Priya nodded, smiling. "Well, hopefully, you'll never have to." She held out the platter. "I made you some of my infamous chili-chocolate cookies."

"Thank you," the architect said, accepting her platter back. "What makes them infamous?"

"Mm, let's just say you need a strong stomach to enjoy them. Indians like to put chili powder in everything." Priya chuckled.

The architect smiled. "I'm sorry you're moving, and that . . . we didn't get to know each other better."

"Me too," Priya said. "But Irvine's only twenty minutes away. Come visit anytime." She waved as she crossed the street back to her own house, fairly sure she would not see her neighbor again.

The Shahs' Pacific Hills house had sold in nine days at enough profit to cover the sales commission and their moving costs. Their new house (in their old neighborhood) was a few short blocks from the Dhillons'—an easy walking distance so long as you weren't carrying full pots of food. The move had been Priya's idea, but Ashok was easily persuaded. His business had suffered from inattention over the past couple of months, and the financial strain of the mortgage and his overhead had become too stressful. He was already sleeping better now that ends would be easier to meet. Besides, the promise of Pacific Hills had not proven to be all that he thought it would. As an entrepreneur, Ashok knew how to take in new data and make changes; this was how he had built and grown his business, after all. In their quiet moments, he and Priya reassured themselves that this was not giving up—it was going home.

Deepa was thrilled to be back in the community and closer to school, and that her friendship with Paco had been restored. Ajay, who didn't like change very much, had been convinced that he would enjoy being back where the streets were familiar. Even though the bicycle the Dhillons had given him sat untouched in the garage, everyone was hopeful that one day Ajay would be ready to ride it. His therapist assured them that, in time, he could learn to interact with a world that didn't always understand him. Even Maya was appreciative of the fresh start. Though Ashley had remained friendly toward her, the social network at Pacific Hills High had been difficult to navigate even before the rumors circulating after her brother's arraignment and the constant risk of running into Chase. Besides, Chavez wasn't all new to her: she had some friends from her old middle school, and the field hockey team was in desperate need of a star goalie.

Upstairs, Ajay and the twins worked on a new robot that would pitch and sink a small foam basketball. In the kitchen, Deepa and Maya helped the two mothers wrap dishes and glasses in newspaper and nestle them into boxes. Ashok and Ricky taped up cartons in the garage with the door open, keeping an eye out for the delivery van. When the pizza arrived, the men would carry it inside like garlic-scented heroes, and everyone would eat from paper plates, drink from plastic cups, and again share a toast to old friends and new beginnings.

Author's Note

In the summer of 1989, I worked as an intern with the Minneapolis Police Department as part of my college scholarship. The program was designed to open my eyes to different ways of life and help me better understand the world around me. That summer certainly expanded my horizons; with nightly patrol car ride-alongs, I saw everything from crack house raids to undercover prostitution stings, too many domestic violence disputes, and an elderly couple's presumed accidental death revealed as a murder-suicide in the autopsy. I developed appreciation for the dangers police officers face every day, and respect for those who put their lives on the line to improve their communities. Based on those experiences, I later did police ride-alongs in my home city of Toronto to better understand what I had missed while growing up there.

Thirty years later, when the Minneapolis Police Department was in the news, I watched in shock and sorrow, as did many others, as the life of George Floyd was extinguished by an officer of the law. I thought more about what I'd seen that summer as a nineteen-year-old, trying to reconcile the many brave and decent officers I'd met with what I now saw in a horrific eight minute, forty-six second video clip. It was not, of course, the first nor the last time such a tragedy would occur. Incidents of police brutality have always been part of our society, but the rise of smartphones and social media have made them more visible and made us all more aware. In the following months, the discussions I witnessed were fraught and often extreme, with people starkly defending one side or the other, and most eager for a decisive solution. It struck me that these conversations were lacking.

While some incidents (like Floyd's) are easy to adjudicate as wrong, the systems and influences behind those situations are often complicated. How police officers are trained, departmental hierarchy, personal safety risks, the role of subconscious bias, cultivated instinct, and the necessity to respond quickly—these can all influence an officer's response. The way neighborhoods are patrolled, a history of unfair treatment, the desire for safe communities, and mental states altered by illness or drug use are just a few of the elements that might affect how a civilian reacts to a police encounter. While it might be easy to diagnose this particular societal ill, finding the remedy is not quite as simple.

At the same time, in those early months of the pandemic, violence against Asian Americans saw a disturbing rise in frequency and boldness. This seemed particularly notable in the San Francisco Bay Area, where I'd lived for many years and where the Asian community had long enjoyed a strong foothold. A new conversation was starting to emerge in South Asian American circles as well. The minority group often deemed to be "model" in the US was being forced to reconsider its role and comfort level in this country. Should we be seeking common cause with other communities of color? Or protecting ourselves in dangerous times? What did it mean to be an American in this new context, hyphenated or otherwise?

These were the ideas—the social, cultural, and political forces in America today—I wanted to explore in this novel. While this story is set in Southern California, it is not meant to be a representation of any one place. The neighborhood of Pacific Hills is fictional, as are Pacific Hills High and Cesar Chavez High. For the purposes of storytelling, I've intermingled them with real landmarks, like the Mexico–United States border, Disneyland, the airport, and the city of Irvine not to depict this specific geography, but to construct the type of community found many places where neighborhoods live side by side, containing a mosaic of racial and ethnic groups.

Acknowledgments

This story was inspired in part by my internship with the Minneapolis Police Department in the summer of 1989. For that and many other life-changing opportunities, I am grateful beyond measure to the Morehead-Cain Foundation.

The Ragdale Foundation granted me an artist's residency on its beautiful campus in the summer of 2021, an opportunity to accelerate my work on this novel. I'm indebted to the staff who made my stay so comfortable, and to my fellow artists, James Stewart and Ryan Matthews, for all those great dinner conversations.

Many people helped with my research for this novel. David Ball, with his extensive knowledge of constitutional law and work with the ACLU, helped me to craft the circumstances around Ajay's encounter with the police, and to understand the many ways in which our policing and judicial systems can be compromised, such as in the Orange County mosque case, *Riverside v. McLaughlin*, referenced in Chapter 29. Travis Anderson introduced me to retired sheriff Dave Corn, who was a wealth of knowledge regarding arrest, booking, county jail, investigations, warrants, arraignments, jurisdiction, and drones at airports. I appreciate his patience in fielding my endless questions. Daniel Hale, a master drone photographer, schooled me on both the technical details and the artistic perspective to round out my story. I consulted with Suraj Yengde of Harvard University and University of Oxford, a leading researcher on India's caste system, about its legacy and manifestations in India and among the Indian diaspora. I appreciate his time and candidness. While I could not have crafted this novel without the generosity and knowledge of these folks, any errors or omissions are mine alone.

Several people read parts of this manuscript along the way. Roopa McNealis helped explain the nuances of caste as it manifests in Indian and American society and the workplace. Janora McDuffie and Leila Ryan were willing to explore the many layers, complexities, and tensions of race and policing today. Thrity Umrigar graciously offered her journalistic knowledge for the news article in Chapter 37.

The novel is an interactive art form, cocreated by author and readers, so I am indebted to early readers who carved out weeks of their life to read a full manuscript draft. Their honest feedback helped me see gaps and deficiencies and find opportunities for enhancement. I'm grateful to Raquel Gerber, Raksha Borkar, and Dionn Schaffner for offering keen insights on culture, race, class, caste, immigration, language, food, media, parenting, psychology, neurodiversity, and more.

Thank you to Katherine Dunleavy for now having read early drafts of every one of my novels, and also for being my partner in crime that summer in Minneapolis. Who knew we'd be talking about those stories thirty years later?

Celia Strauss, your wisdom about things on and off the page has been one of the great gifts of my life. I appreciate the hours you spent talking about ideas, reading drafts, and sharing your thoughts. Time is precious, and I'm so grateful for yours.

In bringing this story to fruition, I was fortunate to work again with the stellar team at Mariner Books and HarperCollins. Kate Nintzel, I'm grateful for your sharp editorial mind and keen market insights, but mostly for being such a wonderful partner. Eliza Rosenberry, your passion for this story was evident from day one, and I appreciate you bringing all that sparkle to the party. Tavia Kowalchuk, what a treat to have worked with you since the beginning—thank you for your creativity and dedication. Molly Gendell, I appreciate the countless things you did to usher this project to completion. Thanks to Jennifer Hart for her sales prowess. So long as books have covers, I hope mine continue to be designed by Mumtaz Mustafa. And I appreciate the many others in the publicity, marketing, production, art, and sales departments who brought this book to life. Liate Stehlik, thank you for giving me an abiding home.

It was also a pleasure to work with the Doubleday Canada team. I appreciate Bhavna Chauhan for her editorial insights and great enthusiasm, as well as Val Gow, Kaitlin Smith, and the rest of the team at Penguin Random House Canada.

Ayesha Pande, where would I be without you taking a chance on me fifteen years ago? Thank you for that first gamble and for all the excellent advice and support since then. I'm so grateful to have you as a champion and a partner. My appreciation extends to the entire Pande Literary team for doing so much to manage the intricacies of a literary career. Thank you to all my foreign agents and publishers who've brought my novels to readers around the world.

I'm lucky to have a community of fellow writers, especially my San Diego crew: Michelle Gable, Tatjana Soli, Sue Meissner, and Jennifer Coburn; and also the Fiction Writers Co-op, my virtual tribe.

I have a deep love for booksellers everywhere, particularly my hometown Warwicks and my home country Chapters Indigo—not only for championing and handselling my novels, but for being an invaluable part of the community.

Thank you to all the readers who invest of themselves to participate in a story, to open their minds to other people, other ways, other ideas. I appreciate every time you invite me to your lively book clubs, post artistic cover photos, email me with questions, or share reviews online.

I am fortunate to have the most extraordinary friends one could hope for. I don't know where I would be without their intelligence, humor, and compassion—certainly someplace much less interesting and joyful. Thanks to every one of you—for helping me grow, navigate the world, laugh, and celebrate life.

Above all, I am deeply grateful to my family. Thank you for tolerating my flaws, easing my crunch times, finding so many ways to have fun together, and always cheering the loudest. Anand, none of this would be possible without your support. In my wildest imagination, I could not have conceived of a better partner to walk with me through life. Mira and Bela, you bring the greatest joy and meaning to me. I hope you always remember your strength and compassion as you carry us into a better future.

ABOUT

MARINER BOOKS

MARINER BOOKS traces its beginnings to 1832 when William Ticknor cofounded the Old Corner Bookstore in Boston, from which he would run the legendary firm Ticknor and Fields, publisher of Ralph Waldo Emerson, Harriet Beecher Stowe, Nathaniel Hawthorne, and Henry David Thoreau. Following Ticknor's death, Henry Oscar Houghton acquired Ticknor and Fields and, in 1880, formed Houghton Mifflin, which later merged with venerable Harcourt Publishing to form Houghton Mifflin Harcourt. HarperCollins purchased HMH's trade publishing business in 2021 and reestablished their storied lists and editorial team under the name Mariner Books.

Uniting the legacies of Houghton Mifflin, Harcourt Brace, and Ticknor and Fields, Mariner Books continues one of the great traditions in American bookselling. Our imprints have introduced an incomparable roster of enduring classics, including Hawthorne's *The Scarlet Letter*, Thoreau's *Walden*, Willa Cather's *O Pioneers!*, Virginia Woolf's *To the Lighthouse*, W.E.B. Du Bois's *Black Reconstruction*, J.R.R. Tolkien's *The Lord of the Rings*, Carson McCullers's *The Heart Is a Lonely Hunter*, Ann Petry's *The Narrows*, George Orwell's *Animal Farm* and *Nineteen Eighty-Four*, Rachel Carson's *Silent Spring*, Margaret Walker's *Jubilee*, Italo Calvino's *Invisible Cities*, Alice Walker's *The Color Purple*, Margaret Atwood's *The Handmaid's Tale*, Tim O'Brien's *The Things They Carried*, Philip Roth's *The Plot Against America*, Jhumpa Lahiri's *Interpreter of Maladies*, and many others. Today Mariner Books remains proudly committed to the craft of fine publishing established nearly two centuries ago at the Old Corner Bookstore.